Dedication

This book is dedicated to Nana and Papa, the real ones. Also, to my late sister Kathryn Elaine Deal. In the ways that matter the most, you were the best of us. And finally to chicken farmers everywhere who rarely have movies or books written of them.

Table of Contents

Chapter One

Secrets have a life of their own in small towns. They live around the corner, in dark backwoods, or sometime in your own home. The worst secrets are the ones nobody ever talks about, but everyone knows. Not really secrets at all, kept at most from one or two people. The problem with those secrets, are you always wonder if you are the only one who does not know of them. Maybe your steady girl has been loose with the Downer boys. Or your father spent time in jail before you were born. Things like that haunt everyone in small towns. We fear public secrets, not the dark, hidden kind that normal people have. We fear the secrets that people spread on the streets and in Sunday School classes disguised as prayer requests. Those kinds of secrets make people look at you funny and turn to their companions to whisper when you pass them on the street. Those are the dangerous kind.

My hometown grows secrets like kudzu in summer, some of them actually true, most not. It mattered very little one way or the other. We would catch them like colds, get sick over them, and then spread them to the neighbors. It did not matter if they were hurtful things, things that carried no purpose but to cause someone else heartache. It did not matter if they were lies. A secret, even a false one, made the water sweeter, the air fresher, and the peaches tastier for those who possessed them. They made us feel like we had something others wanted. We were in the know, not ignorant or ignored like lesser mortals. Our town supported a corporate addiction to secrets. I don't know if the same is true for all small towns as I've never lived in any other. I don't know if it's the same for cities but I doubt it. They are too big and the people do not know one another well enough to enjoy a good secret like small town folks can.

One particular secret bound the people of our little town as tightly as any blood-pledge ever could. It was a dirty secret, shameful and wicked. The worst part for me was that it was a secret I did not discover until that terrible summer before my junior year in high school. That made me one of the invisible, lesser people for most of my growing up years. Perhaps it was the reason that people passed me on the street and did not even acknowledge I was there-- like I was invisible or just part of the landscape. I thought such behavior was normal until the secret came out. I thought all towns were like that. Now I do not know if it was me, the town, or just the nature of people in general. Nevertheless, only two kinds of people lived where I grew up—the known and the unknown. Very few people crossed between the two classes, fewer still socialized with both. We were a divided community, in many ways more so than during the Great War. Most of the blacks stayed with the invisible unknown, crossing over only briefly when they excelled at a sport, then fading quickly back into anonymity. For poor whites like me, not even sports stardom bridged the gulf. That was my town, Toccoa, Georgia. A place of secrets.

Cherokee Indians gave the area its name. In their nearly forgotten language it means "The Beautiful," and pretty it was, with a history as deep and full of famous names as would surprise most folks. James Brown, the great singer, claimed to have shined shoes outside of the Five and Dime Store on Main Street. Camp Toccoa held the honor of being the training site for the Band of Brothers made famous by the book and movie about the 101st Airborne Division. They still relive those days each year in a reenactment, but the real men who fought in that war to end all wars were getting pretty rare even when I was growing up there and the whole thing seems a bit hollow nowadays.

Paul Anderson was from Toccoa, so I stand in good company. If you were alive in 1956, you might remember him-- a chubby, short youngster from a place no one heard of, much less thought important. He worked out alone, all day in between farm chores. That day in some place called Melbourne, when he told the Olympic judges to put a world record weight on his barbell, everyone laughed at him. They all thought he was "audacious," as the newspaper put it. But that day belonged to Paul. The entire stadium broke out in applause when he threw that weight over his head. He came back to Toccoa with a gold medal hung over his neck. The entire town came out to see him, or so I'm told. You see, I was born that year, 1956, so I do not have much memory of Paul's early days. I only saw him later, lifting cars on his back to raise money for his orphaned boy's home. Later still I saw him in a wheel chair, all swollen, looking sick. His kidneys gave out. But everyone in Toccoa knows about Paul. Pass through these parts, and you will too. Signs on all the roads going into Stephens County say "Home of Paul Anderson, strongest man in the world." I could not say if he is still strongest, but it matters little. They will never take those signs down.

My name is Roy Davis. Roy is a good name. Easy to spell. Easy to say. No one messes it up. I think I'm the only white one in town. Black folks here like the name Roy. There must be fifteen or twenty Roys on Whitman Street where most of the town blacks live. I played ball with two of them.

My grandmother on the Wiley side always gave me the impression our Davis name was well known in North Georgia. I recall nothing exactly in what she said, just the way she implied that we possessed family fame. If that is true, none of it seemed to have rubbed off on her children or their children. We possessed the most well hidden fame of any family I knew and seemed pretty much invisible in the social life of Toccoa We were never invited to grocery store openings or historic plaque dedications, things more prominent residents of the town attended. Jealousy teemed in Toccoa, or so my grandmother said. Why else would they fail to invite us? It made no sense to her, me either when I was young. It made sense later, though. By the time I was ten, I knew we were not invited because hardly anyone worth anything knew who we were. Being snubbed from jealousy is easier to swallow than just being unknown. I guess that's why my grandmother liked to think of herself and her family as the oppressed nobility of Toccoa. Such standing made it tolerable, sitting on the hill stringing beans alone while the rest of the visible world passed by. It's hard to be unknown in a town as small as Toccoa, but somehow the Davis family managed.

I spent most of my early years working my grandfather's chicken farm. We called him Papa, accented on both syllables equally, not the last like French people do. His real name was Duncan, a name even my grandmother seemed to forget. She called him Papa too. I guess I got my height from him. He was only a couple of inches short of my six foot six inch frame, though thinner than the other Davises. Papa was good-natured, smiled and laughed constantly, as if the whole world and all of God's children were put here just to entertain him. It made him fun to be with, though somewhat hard to talk to. I once told him about my favorite rabbit dog getting hit by a car. I wanted to tell someone how I grieved for him, felt guilty for letting him follow me to the store the day the car ran him down. Papa laughed as if grief for a dog was a great joke. It was not for me. Down past the laughing, it was not a joke to him either. The only time I saw him cry was when lightning struck the tree he had chained old Duke to. Even years later his eyes would get all watery every time he spoke of the great birddog.

Nana, the way we referred to my grandmother, had an uppity name--
Estelle. Everyone, even her mother accented the first "e" not the second.
Some people could say her name that way, but she always corrected anyone
not family. She thought accenting the second "e" made her sound more
important, more refined, more like oppressed nobility I suppose. People
ignored her corrections and said her name like her Mama said it.

Nana lived for sickness, seemed fixated on death. She always spoke
of how she would die young. She had great grandchildren on her knee and
still she talked of dying young. I never remember her standing completely
upright, though I saw some old picture of her ramrod straight and smiling.
Mostly she hunched over, grumbled about her health, and swept every floor
her family owned and a few they did not. No matter that it was an unfinished
plank floor to the back porch of a feed store, she swept it. She dipped snuff,
spit in the number ten cans she scattered around the floor, and swept. I
remember the way she smelled, the rich odor of snuff cutting through corn
dust and lilac powder.

Nana knew many secrets, kept none of them to herself. She made
secrets into news, as freely spread as weather reports. No secret was too
personal for her rendering its details to the most uninterested party. She
usually punctuated her statements with a woeful "bless their heart." It made
the secrets seem less like gossip and therefore less un-Christian to repeat.

We discovered one of Nana's secrets that dreadful summer. When it
came to light it brought death to our family and nearly took the town of
Toccoa apart. The story goes all the way back to the Civil War, or the "War
of Northern Aggression," as people in these parts like to call it. The difference
in this secret and most of the others she stowed in that gray head of hers was,
this one was true. It took some mighty serious digging to prove, but true as
true can be it was. It seemed Nana knew to be gospel truth what the rest of the
town hoped was a lie. You see, Nana owned Toccoa, or most of it. Owned it
flat out. Her name did not show up on any deeds, but it was hers. This likely
was the only secret she ever kept, which was made even more odd by the fact
that it was the only secret that she could profit from. When the secret was told,
the town changed forever. The Davis family changed forever. I cannot say I
cared much for what happened. I wish it could go away, put things back like
they used to be. But some things, once dug up, just cannot be put back. Some
secrets become like gods, sending us this way and that whether we want to go
or not. That is exactly what happened to us that summer. We got swept along
in a dirty old secret that nearly got the whole Davis clan killed.

Chapter Two

My father worked my grandfather's chicken farm on and off for the biggest part of my childhood. Mostly he drove trucks. I helped him when I could. We would drive a covered flatbed up to a farm, load the weeks gathering of eggs, and bring them to a great refrigerated trailer where they joined the eggs of other farmers around the area. We packed them in tight, thirty eggs to a flat, twelve flats to a box, stacked ten boxes wide and seven boxes high. When we had filled them up, Daddy drove the tractor-trailer rigs to New Jersey where other men sorted them into sizes and then shipped them to stores and restaurants in New York City. Each side of the trip took him three days. On the way back he picked up whatever he could to carry back to Atlanta. Most of the time it was legal. Sometimes it was only close. He never got caught, so we did not talk about it. When he was home, he joined me, Papa, Nana, a smattering of other grandchildren to work on the farm.

The chickens occupied most of our time, but a few cows, hogs, and even an occasional flock of turkeys came and went on our small piece of Georgia. Since Papa had retired from the Post Office, he could afford to work a farm that barely paid its own bills. This was a good thing since he was not a particularly gifted farmer. We were always losing crops, flocks, and herds of something. We buried enough livestock around his place to fertilize the ground for a generation. Papa always told us to not get too attached to the livestock. He said you would have a hard time eating something you named. We always thought he really felt this way because so many of the animals died under his care.

We came upon the grave while pulling stumps from a low section of the farm that backed up on River Road. The land, mostly a tangle of short pines and saw-briers, sloped gently from the road down to a small creek. The other side rose up a steep bank of thirty feet or so. The top was flat because Papa had graded it himself. On it sat the Number Seven and Number Nine chicken houses. Number Eight did not exist, but was planned in the future. Papa never got around to building that Number Eight house.

We had just sold the last flock of pullets to a laying-hen farmer down in Lavonia so the houses were empty. Papa decided to use the short break before the next group of chickens came in to clear out the bottom section and make room for a couple more cows. He liked raising cows, I believe to this day, only because they allowed him to take them to the Sale Barn near our house on Highway 17. There he could dicker with the auctioneer and slaughterhouse buyers, stand at the side of the center ring, shout, spit, and cuss in public-- all things Nana forbade. Otherwise he seemed to hate cattle of all types. They seemed to harbor a particular prejudice toward him as well, manifest by the number of the old man's bones they had broken.

Daddy looped the chain around the main root of a muscadine vine, hooked it to the tractor and signaled me to pull away. I eased the clutch up, feeling quite important and powerful for a fifteen-year-old boy. The tractor bucked a couple of times, and then slowly eased forward, pulling the snarl of weeds and young trees with it. As the tractor pulled the tangle of vines away, a stone, obviously shaped by the hand of man, slid part way up the bank. I stopped the tractor and it fell away from the roots which had embraced it. Not more than two feet square and rounded at one end, it lay face down in the red clay. I put the tractor in neutral and looked back at it.

My father climbed over the chain, and stood staring down at the stone.

"What is it, Daddy?" I asked.

"I don't know, Son," he said. "Looks like a grave stone."

He stooped down and brushed the dirt away. The exposed side of the stone showed no markings so he turned it over. Though worn and covered with lichen, I could see lettering chiseled into its face.

"Well, I'll be damned," Daddy said. "I'll just be damned. It's a gravestone alright."

"Whose," I asked.

My father kept cursing to himself.

"If it's who the stone says it is, this is your great-great grandfather," he answered.

"Which one?" I asked, hopping off the tractor.

Before he could answer, I read the inscription for myself. Something was wrong here, I thought. Little did I know then just how wrong.

Ebenezer Wiley
1833 - 1866

"But didn't you always tell me Ebenezer died in the battle of Atlanta and was buried somewhere in Gwinnett County," I asked.

Daddy just nodded.

"Then what's this doing here?"

"Can't say, Son," he answered. "Maybe it's just a stone they threw away and never used. But that makes no sense. Why would they have dates on it?"

We both turned to look at the patch of ground where the stone had sat. Scores of fist-sized rocks made a near perfect rectangle, interwoven with weeds and briars. At the other end stood a one-foot stone square with no markings.

"Looks like a real grave to me," I said.

Daddy knelt down and inspected a couple of the stones. They were granite, the type found around Elberton, not here. The same as the gravestone.

"Looks that way to me, too," he said.

Papa appeared at the top of the hill.

"You boys run into trouble down there?" he shouted.

"No trouble," Daddy answered. "But you ought to come down and see what we found."

Papa scrambled down the steep bank, dislodging clods of dirt that rolled down against our boots. He came to stand beside Daddy. When they stood side by side, Daddy's posture and mannerisms echoed his father's perfectly. He was only slightly heavier than Papa, had a little more hair and a few less wrinkles. Daddy's nose curved just like Papa's, a little hawk-like. When they concentrated, their eyebrows converged exactly the same. They stood looking at the grave, images of one another separated only by the changes of time. Papa leaned his face close the headstone and read the name.

"I'll be damned," he said.

It could have been Daddy's voice.

He stood for a minute, looked around as if to determine if anyone was watching, then spoke.

"Let's go home," he pronounced, then he turned abruptly and began climbing back up the hill.

It was not what I expected.

"Is this Ebenezer Wiley's grave?" I asked.

"That's what the headstone says, isn't it?" he replied over his shoulder.

"But we were always told..."

"I know what you were told," he answered, now at the top of the hill looking down at us. "And right now I'm telling you both something else. I don't want either of you speaking of this to anyone. You hear. No one. I'll sort this thing out, me and Nana. I don't want anyone else snooping around here and digging up stuff best left alone. And I'm not just talking about a corpse. Just keep it to yourselves for now."

He turned away and disappeared over the crest of the hill. Daddy and I exchanged curious looks. I climbed back on the tractor, pulled it into first gear, high axle, and headed down the creek. Daddy stepped up on the sideboard. Neither of us spoke, which was not unusual. But I could tell looking at Daddy's sweat-streaked face he wanted to talk. He wanted to say plenty. I did not ask. Papa rarely ordered us around, mostly relying on guilt to get work from us. But when he did, we knew better than to disobey. By the time I had brought the tractor up the lower side of the bank, Papa had left. We rode the tractor all the way to the Office going not much faster than we could walk. We passed the Number Four, Number Two, and Number One chicken houses—all empty, waiting for the next batch of chicks. Red dust kicked up around us as the tractor bounced along. Usually I would stop and search a tree for green apples on the way back. Not today. We would found something big in that bottom section of the farm. I could not tell if it was excitement or concern that set Daddy's jaw like it was, but clearly Papa's response puzzled him, made him worry a bit. Papa has always been a bit hard to read, even a about normal stuff.

The "Office", as we called it, was a cement block building with a tin roof. No one recalls why we called it the Office, since most of the time it was used as a store. A covered porch on the back doubled as a loading dock. Papa intermittently sold produce, eggs, feed, and farm implements from the Office. At one end of the roof, a big white sign, bordered by the Purina checkerboard logo read:

Big A Farm and Garden

Papa's white Chevy pickup sat to the side. We pulled up, turned the tractor off, and went in the side door. Papa was nowhere to be seen, but we knew where he was. We pulled open the metal door to one of the walk-in coolers where he stored eggs waiting for the next truck. He was inside sitting on an upturned bucket. The cooler stayed near fifty degrees all the time. When not filled with eggs, we used it to store other produce, especially watermelons. Papa sat munching on a wedge of a Congo watermelon that had a rind so dark it was almost black. He already sliced off pieces for us, so we joined him.

No one spoke. We sat, enjoyed the coolness of the locker, slurped and crunched the sweet red meat of the watermelon. Papa cut a watermelon every day they were in season. He bought them by the score, stored them in the cooler under the guise of selling them with the rest of the produce, and ate them himself. It was my favorite of his many vices.

When we had eaten enough to necessitate loosening our belts a little, he tossed us both dirty towels to wipe our sticky faces.

"Hot out there today," Papa finally said.

We both nodded. By now our sweat had mostly dried and I was a bit cold.

"I'll plow the field under tomorrow," Papa added. "Maybe even scatter some of the left over fescue seeds. They'll be grass enough for cows by September. Maybe a few doves, too."

We nodded again, acting like grass and melons was all that was on our minds. What we really wanted to know was why our family patron was buried in a hidden grave on the back side of an otherwise forgotten patch of land? I could stand it no longer.

"Did you know that grave was there, Papa?" I asked.

Daddy sat studying the watermelon rinds, his head lowered as if I had embarrassed him.

Papa did not answer at first. Then he laughed to himself and shook his head. He stood and walked to the door. We thought he would leave and ignore the question all together. He would do that sometimes, just walk away if the conversation did not suit him.

"I can't say for sure whose grave it really is," Papa said. "Shouldn't say at all until I find a few things out. No, I didn't know a grave was there. Nobody's ever tried to plant that patch of land. It was no good for hunting either. The perfect place to hide a grave you didn't want found for a long while. I think you've found something real important out there. Something that's likely to dredge up all sorts of things your Nana would just as soon leave alone. Can't say for sure. She's hard to figure some times. Just can't say."

He trailed off, laughing to himself. "Damn hard to figure, that woman. After forty or fifty years you would think I'd know what she wants.

Can't tell what she'll make of it 'till I tell her. Best not speak of it for now. Not to anyone, you hear?"

We both nodded, but Papa did not look at us. He knew we would do like he wanted.

Papa walked out still laughing, leaving the door open like he expected us to follow. Daddy and I picked up our rinds and walked out. By the time we had tossed them in a ditch behind the Office, Papa had pulled his pickup onto Big A Road and headed into town. We watched him leave, trailing clouds of red dust. Yellow jackets buzzed behind us, drawn to the pile of watermelon rinds we had just enlarged. Everything felt dusty and hot, hotter even still now we had gotten used to the cooler.

Chapter Three

"Let's call it a day," Daddy said.

I nodded as I watched Papa round the hill and disappear from sight. Someone was walking beside the road near the top. I saw him wave toward Papa. Likely Papa waved back. It was the way here in Toccoa. People waved like they knew you, even if they did not. Likely our parents passed the habit to us when the county's population was so small you knew everyone you saw on the road.

We walked down the road in the opposite direction from Papa. Normally he would give us a ride home. It was only half a mile or so, so it really did not matter much. Daddy and I walked along a worn path beside the two-lane highway. Great four-inch grasshoppers flew from under our feet as we passed. In the back of my mind I made plans to catch a few of them and use them as bait at a nearby pond. People drove by, waved, and we waved back. In the distance, we could hear the bellowing of cattle and screaming of horses from the Sale Barn. The sun still sat high on the western sky, the air thick and still. We kept to the shady side of the road. More people passed and waved.

Our house sat fifty yards down the road and across the highway from the cultural center of Toccoa. The Sale Barn consisted of a series of interconnected, covered corrals and holding pens sprawled across nearly three acres. Most of the week it was empty and silent. On Thursdays, trucks laden with hogs and cattle began to pull in to leave their cargo for the Saturday auction. By Friday, at least half of the pens were full. Saturday morning was a mad house. Trucks jostled for position in the parking lot. Animals of all types bellowed, mewed, screamed, and neighed to one another. People shouted, horns blew, and the loud speaker blasted.

Animals entered a large pen surrounded by worn, wooden bleachers all covered with a great tin roof which was by far the largest structure in the county. Men bid on the beasts by tipping their hats or waving at the auctioneer whose job it was to attempt to speak continually without breathing. The unspoken wisdom of using an auctioneer was that people bid more when they thought they were in a hurry or someone else was about to take the object of their desire. Faster talking meant higher bids. For as long as anyone could remember, Fred Trotman called the auctions for the Sale Barn. Fred sat next to the gatepost leading into the center ring. He must have weighed as much as most of the beasts whose features he extolled. I never saw Fred stand, walk, or do anything but sit on the bench with the microphone buried in his thick, red beard. Between every sale, he spit tobacco juice into the ring and took sips of coffee. He kept a John Deere cap pulled low across his face. Despite the speed and vigor of his voice, he never moved the whole time he called the auction. If you failed to notice the microphone, you would be hard pressed to tell whose voice blared from the speakers.

Nearly every week, at least a few animals escaped. The owners always caught the cattle, horses, and larger hogs. Less valuable animals, especially goats, if not immediately caught were often abandoned. As a result, the woods around my house teemed with feral hogs and goats. My brother and I stalked, trapped, and occasionally shot them. We ate the hogs fast, not having a way to freeze them or a brine trough to cure them. The goats, we tried once, but could not stomach the taste or thought of it. We mostly trapped and sold them, shot the big ones that tore up people's gardens and were too strong for us to handle safely.

This evening, animal noises filtered down from the Sale Barn as we approached home. When Daddy and I stepped onto the front porch, it squeaked just as it had thousands of times before, always sounding as if it might finally give way. The noise made knocking and doorbells unnecessary. Daddy opened the screen door and we went inside.

Mama stood in the kitchen frying chicken. Smoke and steam from it spilled over into the short hallway. She had propped open the back porch door to let out some of the heat.

"Take your boots off on the porch," she shouted. It was as much of a greeting as my mother ever gave us.

We sat on the worn sofa and unlaced our boots, knowing she knew we had already tracked some of Georgia's best red clay into her living room.

"Katrina's still at the hospital," Mama shouted again. We could hear pots and pans clanking. "Says she might not get home 'till eight. We won't wait supper for her."

My sister graduated from high school two months earlier. She worked as a nurse's aid at the county's only hospital. But like most of the recent female high school graduates of Stephens County, she already had her hook in a man she would likely marry before the year was out.

"Don't hurry on our account," Daddy said. "We had watermelon not half an hour ago."

Momma mumbled something we could not hear, probably about us ruining our appetite. To this day, no amount of eating has ever ruined my appetite.

Our house sat at the base of a small hill. It and four others like it belonged to my great-aunt, Mae. I never met Aunt Mae, only heard of her. I think she lived up near Clayton. We had a living room barely big enough for a chair, sofa, and television; a kitchen, two bedrooms, and a dining room. At one corner of the dining room sat Momma's sewing machine, one you pedaled rather than plugged in. I never once saw her use it, but I'm told in her younger days she made all of her own and most of Daddy's clothes. I guess she got overwhelmed by the prospect of making clothes for the two of them and their six children.

I went into the children's bedroom to change clothes. Two sets of bunk beds occupied most of the room. We had a dresser, one drawer of which was mine. The single closet held hang-up clothes for the three older children. The younger two girls, ages four and six, slept in baby beds on either side of Mama and Daddy's bed. My older brother and I joked that we hoped the girls discouraged more baby making between our parents. Ben, three years my senior, now lived in Carnesville, a town even smaller and less significant than Toccoa. He worked at a chicken processing plant by day and attended North Georgia Technical Institute at night. He did not visit much, but called home daily.

We had another brother, named Bret, six years my senior. Two years earlier, Bret went to Vietnam and never came home. The story we were told by the Marines was he had been lost in action near Laos, that Vietcong had overrun his squad. They never found his body. A rumor spread that Bret had actually defected to North Vietnam. I never knew how it got started. Older people would say things like "it's in his blood" or "not surprised." I never knew exactly what they meant until much later, after I learned of Nana's great secret. The paper did not even run a story about his dying like they did about other local boys. They just listed his name in a column with other Georgians who had gotten killed that week.

I still remember the Marine Colonel coming to our door, Momma crying, Daddy shaking the man's hand like he had done us a favor. I never felt like Bret was gone. In my mind I could not close the door on him, like he might show up some day. We held a small memorial service at the National Guard Center the next week where a couple of dozen people showed up. Then it was over, Bret was gone like he had never existed. We never talked of him. The only sign he had ever been part of the family was Christmas when Mamma would hang a sock with his name on it on the mantle with the rest of us. She would take the sock down before Christmas morning and never say a word about it.

By the time I came out in shorts and a tank top, Momma already had supper on the table. Momma was a good cook, even by the rigorous standards of rural North Georgia. But she had a repertoire limited to five meals, four edible. One was fried chicken with mashed potatoes and green beans. Spaghetti and loaf bread was our favorite. She fixed Irish stew, or that's what she called it, and hamburgers. Her favorite, the thing that made the rest of us cringe, was salmon patties. I had never seen a salmon, but I often wondered if the stuff she scraped out of the cans had died of natural causes and had been dredged up with bottom sludge. She added her own crunchy touch with peanuts. I usually hid a couple of patties in my pocket and later snuck a peanut butter sandwich. I never saw Momma make a salad or casserole. In fact, I was out of college before I even knew what a casserole was. But with eight mouths to feed, Momma concentrated more on quantity than quality, a priority we all encouraged. God never created a small Davis.

Daddy sat at the head of the worn, wooden table, Momma at the other end. My little sisters, Kari and Katlin sat on one side. Had Ben and Katrina been home, they would sit on the corners. Daddy told Kari to ask the blessing and she recited the same rhyming prayer we had heard every day of our lives. She finished and started gobbling. Like always, Momma corrected the girls' table manners constantly, kept dabbing at their messy chins with a cloth. She told me to sit up straight, even without looking at me.

We talked about the day's work, gossip Momma heard from town, and local sports. August in Toccoa is a slow time, too early for football, too hot to fish much. Tennis and soccer never caught the people's eyes around here much. In August we mostly waited for September. Momma kept talking anyway, as if we were listening. The girls teased one another and made a wish on the wishbone, which Kari won. I kept waiting to see if Daddy would violate Papa's prohibition on speaking about the grave. He did not. It weighed heavily on me. I wanted to tell everyone, describe it in detail, and have everyone join me in speculating who it really was and what it meant. But Daddy did not speak of it and I dared not.

"Katrina's meeting Corrie tonight," Kari said.

"How would you know?" Momma said in a scolding voice.

"I heard her talking on the phone," Kari responded. Momma shoved a large spoon of mashed potatoes in her mouth, effectively silencing her for the next minute.

"I don't like her hanging around that boy so much," Daddy said. "He's up to no good."

To Daddy, anyone from our class of the working poor who did not try to go to college or join the military was up to no good. It was acceptable in his eyes to be poor and work in a dead-end job, but you had to at least at one time in your life have tried to get an education that would open up new opportunities or have risked your life for the country. If you were content with your lot in life, you were up to no good.

"He's a good kid," Momma said.

The "kid" was twenty-four years old and worked as a machinist at Coats and Clark textile mill. He spent weekends laying roofs.

"Besides," she continued, "she's pretty serious about him. You might need to get real used to him."

Daddy rolled his eyes and speared another chicken leg. He dripped grease on the tablecloth, which Momma quickly dabbed at with a paper towel.

By the time we were settling into the living room for an evening of television, the Sale Barn was almost quiet. The buyers left with their purchases, most in great double-decker cattle and hog trucks. The sellers pulled out with empty trailers.

Our favorite Saturday show, *Gunsmoke* came on covered with speckles and lines. Momma stomped the floor, which jiggled the pocketbook she hung on the metal stem we used to change channel. The plastic knob from our TV had long since disappeared. For some reason, the metal rod it once sat on needed a little weight to keep it tuned to the station. We had tried just about everything to keep that knob turned just right. Nothing seemed to work as well as Mamma's pocketbook. Mamma stomped again. The pocketbook jiggled some more. The picture flickered a couple of times. She stomped again and it cleared up enough for us to see the black and white image of James Arness riding his buckskin horse across the rolling hills outside of Dodge City. Then the races started.

Just up the hill from the Sale Barn, sharing its parking lot, sat the Toccoa Speedway. Except in the deep of winter when the dirt track froze, every redneck in Stephens County who ever rebuilt a junked car came out to race on Saturday nights. Sometimes we walked over to watch, especially if they were running a demolition derby. Most times we just listened, even when we did not want to listen. The race was loud but the warm ups were louder. We had to turn the television up so high, my ears rang until bedtime.

Daddy cussed under his breath as he turned the volume up again. He had just sat down when a tractor-trailer rig barreled down the highway. It shook the house just enough to disturb the picture again, so Momma started stomping her foot. She kept stomping until the picture cleared. Nobody else tried to help. It only worked when Mamma stomped.

Katrina came in later, her lipstick smeared and clothes slightly ruffled. She pecked Daddy on the cheek, and then retreated into the bedroom. She knew she had privacy until the end of *Gunsmoke*. I watched the rest of the show, then came back myself. Katrina was already in bed. I changed into the pajamas my grandmother sent me, blue cotton with sailboats on them. I knew Katrina would turn away without me asking just as I did for her when she got undressed. As I lay down, I thought I heard her crying, a light sob, then a stifling sound. I acted as though I had not noticed it. Katrina cried a lot in those days, mostly over boyfriends. Seems she was always breaking up or making up with some boy who was always at least four years older than she was. We grew used to it and rarely ever asked her about them. For her part, she kept them away from us like she was ashamed of us. More than likely she was afraid Daddy would say something embarrassing, maybe threaten them if they offended her questionable honor.

Chapter Four

The next morning I slept late, Katrina later. Momma fixed eggs in a great caste iron skillet, which left them with black speckles. It was Sunday, the day most decent folk go to church. It felt holy to me, the sun brighter, and the air crisper. It did all my life even though we did not go to church. Daddy had a falling out with a distant cousin who presided as unofficial matron of Big A Baptist Church. It happened before I was born and I never knew the details, but Papa always said it ruined Daddy for church. Papa went rarely himself, mostly when a relative's child was being dedicated or was singing a solo. The only church service Daddy ever attended in my memory was Easter sunrise service, held at a graveyard just down the road. He would always wake the children and pack us into his car for the five-minute ride. We would stand there in the cold while the high school band played and a preacher gave a sermon, usually on things I did not understand. Daddy stood there, watched the sunrise, listened to the preacher, and bowed his head on cue. Otherwise, he showed no tendency toward religion at all and I was simply not given options on the subject—except when the itinerant preacher came to town.

I got visited by deacons once or twice a year, usually after revival week when they had been inspired spread the gospel to those few of us in Toccoa that did not attend church. They would come in pairs on Tuesday nights, the usual one for visitation at Baptist churches. They would speak to Momma and Daddy, then ask for a minute or two with me alone. They never asked for the other kids. I could understand ignoring the little ones, them being below what they called the "age of consent." Daddy would surely shrug them off and take Momma with him to sit on the porch, leaving me with the older men. They would speak to me of church being important for a young man like me, how they all thought I might be something special. But I heard something they never actually said. I heard them say I had a chance to be something more than most Davis'. Something a little less contemptible or low. Something visible. I listened, understood exactly what they meant, and for a while believed them. One year, I even went to Sunday School with a kindly man who said he would pick me up any Sunday I wanted. He ran a furniture store downtown and looked like he had never been excited in his life. He said I needed to go to church so I did. I went two weeks in a row, thought I was developing a pattern. The third week I waited on the porch steps in my best pants and shirt, but he did not come for me. I got dressed and waited two more Sunday mornings, but he still did not show. I never went to church again, though Sunday still seemed hallowed and the visits kept coming every spring. Like Daddy, I learned to shrug them off.

After breakfast, I went out and checked on the dogs. They yelped and jumped against the fence as I approached. We usually kept some beagles around for rabbit hunting. Always the short-legged kind, since they were easier to catch and less prone to jump fences. The dog pen was nothing but chicken wire nailed around some pine trees just inside the woods. I took them dry feed and water, pet all four one at a time, then closed the gate and walked back to the house. They yelped a couple of more times then turned to jostle one another for the food.

When I got back I was not surprised to see that Daddy's car was gone. I never knew where he went on Sunday mornings and it never occurred to me to ask him. Momma always made a bad face as she watched him go, like he was going out to do something she disapproved of. But he always came back by dinnertime.

"You got something to do today?" Katrina called out from our window.

I could not see her.

"Nothing special," I replied. "Thought I'd see if we can get the gym opened up and play some ball later. We might wait until tonight, though, see'n how it's so hot."

"Could you do something for me?" she asked. I still could not see her. I leaned against the wall outside the window.

"Sure."

"Go with me to the Wigwam after dinner?" she asked. When she talked to me like this I felt like I went back in time when we were the best of friends, then the only friends we had. She never used that voice when others were around and she knew that I could deny her nothing. I also knew that there were real risks for me in going with her.

"I'll go," I said.

Katrina developed relationships fast, pursued them intensely for a short time, and then found a reason to end them. Men and women suffered the same fate. Sometimes the jilted friend or lover made trouble, most times not. When Katrina feared trouble, she used me to act tough.

Though I had grown tall fast, the fact was I was getting skinnier by the day and could not win an arm wrestle with our head cheerleader. But, most people believed I could still hold my own with anyone in the county not carrying a weapon. In reality, I hated fighting, hated the thought of confrontation of any kind. I had to act tough around men, because that's what invisible, redneck boys in Toccoa did. I had to act as though I would fight without any hesitation, act like I wanted someone to start in on me so I would have an excuse to punch him. If not, someone would push you, take your girl, as if I had one to lose, or steal your pride, make it his own. I hated this part of life here, but I had one advantage besides being tall. I had a reputation.

One evening after a football game, two linemen ganged up on a smaller boy I knew. It happened in a parking lot with bad lighting, so no one could really see what happened. I came upon them as the bigger boys pushed my small friend against a car. As far as I can tell they picked on him for no particular reason except that he was small and available. He stumbled and struck his head on the bumper opening a two-inch gash over his left eye. He rolled over, blood covering his face. I stepped over to help him, accidentally bumping into one of the jocks. He pushed me, cussed, and then took a poorly aimed swing at the back of my head. I never saw it coming.

The punch glanced off my right ear. It hurt, but caused no real damage. I tried to apologize, tell him I just wanted to help my friend, but he did not want to hear and neither did his companion. The other boy lowered himself into a football stance, grunted loudly, and then lunged at me. This time, I saw him coming, stepped to one side, and pushed him forward into the same bumper that injured my friend. His forehead struck the bumper with a loud thud. He collapsed in a heap on top of his bleeding victim. The other boy swung at me again, this time he missed badly. While he was off balance I landed a solid right to his jaw. I felt something snap as I struck him. He too went down, clutching his face and screaming. A couple of dozen onlookers surrounded us by the time the fifteen-second fight was over. I helped my friend to his feet and hustled away, hiding the fact that I was trembling.

The player who ran into the bumper still lay unconscious by the time an ambulance arrived. I was told that when he finally roused and screamed curses at me even as they wheeled him away. The other boy drove himself to the hospital. His parents later tried to sue my folks to pay for getting his broken jaw fixed. The only lawyer in town laughed, told them Daddy's total assets would not be worth the trouble. But the threatened suit added to the story. I had single handedly beat up and sent to the hospital two big linemen of our revered football team. Suddenly, I had a reputation. I never learned to use it properly, though Katrina certainly did. I spent most of my time avoiding the football team.

I spent the rest of the day sitting outside reading a Jim Kjelgaard novel I have gotten from the Bookmobile earlier in the week. Daddy came home for dinner. He looked pale and worried. We ate, talking a little about the younger children's morning antics and last night's races. Katrina kept looking at me and raising an eyebrow, a signal that I should eat fast so we could leave. I still did not know why.

While Katrina preened herself in the bathroom and the little ones ran around outside, Daddy pulled me onto the front porch.

"Make sure you heed your Papa about that grave," he said.

"I haven't told a soul," I said. "Why is it so important? You'd think people would be interested, us finding a lost grave of Grandma Wiley's daddy."

"Never you mind," Daddy replied. "You just mind what he says. I'm saying it too. No one needs to know about the grave. Our time's coming, just not yet. Understand? This is important. More important than you could ever guess."

I nodded. Daddy went inside leaving me standing on the porch bewildered. Suddenly I felt a sharp sting in my scalp. Katlin had popped me in the back with a sweetgum ball. I jumped off the porch after her as she tore off up the hill. Kari hit me from the other side and I turned on her. We staged a pitched battle for a few minutes before I surrendered. They piled on me, declared themselves to be the Supreme Rulers of the World and me their slave. I was saved when Katrina appeared on the porch and waved me to the car.

Chapter Five

Katrina drove our blue Chevrolet Impala down Big A Road past the Office. The road was named years ago by the shape of an intersection which veered into the main road just east of town. Someone cut a shortcut across the angle of the road, making it the shape of a capital "A." No sign posts used the name and no one outside of Toccoa would ever find it on a map, but that is what we called it.

I sat, white knuckled, in the passenger side wishing we had seat belts and maybe a helmet. Katrina maneuvered the car like an over-insured demolition driver. Daddy always said that any ride with her you could walk away from was a good ride. We passed the junkyard, a couple of garages and a fenced in building used to store fireworks. People waved, many still wearing their church clothes. Katrina did not talk. She just clutched the wheel and stared ahead. Her dark hair whipped about her face and every minute or two she would pull it from in front of her eyes. She had a mean look about her that day. Someone would catch hell, I could tell from the vertical wrinkle between her eyebrows.

Just past the Office and up a hill, perfectly spaced on four acre lots surrounded by oak trees, sat the homes of the four Kresse sisters. Lanona Kresse, oldest of the sisters, sat on her front porch watching lesser mortals pass her sacred domain. Her house, perched on the highest hill, had the largest white columns and the largest turkey oaks out front. From the distance I saw her watching us pass, even thought I saw her turn her head slightly as if to dismiss us. Some say she sat on her porch speaking to her long dead husband. Nine years earlier her husband had driven his car onto the railroad track and waited for the Monday morning banana train. The train was late that day and he had waited almost twenty minutes. A few cars even drove by and waved at him. He waved back, smiled like nothing was amiss. Finally, the train came and ended his miserable life. Most people say that if Lanona really was trying to talk to her husband, he likely was not listening unless the devils in hell made him do so as a part of his punishment.

The homes of the three other sisters fell along side Lanona's like servants, slightly lower and slightly less grand, as though they had to bow to the grand matron. Bell, Celeste, and Prudy all sat around an old apple tree as far from Lanona as possible. The old spinsters huddled around an object, probably a large pot in which they tossed stringed beans. From the distance they could have been witches brewing an evil potion. Their heads bobbed up and down with animated conversation. All of their husbands were dead, none of them missed, likely none of them sad for the passing. I watched them as we drove by, distracted occasionally by Katrina's sudden swerve into a passing lane that did not exist.

The Kresse sisters owned almost six miles of the land from their homes into town and leased it to the storeowners and hamburger joints. Their family had owned it since the Civil War, the plots passed down by decree from mother to daughter. Each generation placed in their will that the next could not sell the land they inherited, only pass it along. Fortunately for Lanona, the Kresses bore only one or two children apiece and only the girl children survived. All took their husband's last name until the men died, then again became Kresses. The land stayed together, generation after generation, getting more and more valuable. A good part of Toccoa paid rent to the Kresse family, like tribute to royalty. People who crossed them, even in little ways, suffered, lost their leases, lost their businesses, sometimes mysteriously lost their lives. Davis' never interacted with them at all, not from overt spite, just from not being worthy of their notice. That was just fine with me.

Katrina pulled into the lot of the Wigwam and parked next to a red Mustang. An old classmate of hers, known to me only by the nickname "Slob," leaned his flabby torso back in the reclining seat and propped his feet on the dash, Steppenwolf music blaring from the eight track. He raised a chubby index finger toward us to acknowledge our presence, and then closed his eyes, lost in the music. Slob rarely spoke, never to girls. His father worked at the local steel plant until last spring. Union shopkeepers had him fired for working too hard and replacing three members of the local chapter. He now drove a pulpwood truck, having sworn off the confusing ways of factory jobs.

Slob worked with him. They never had much in the way of money and were so repulsive to women it's a wonder their bloodline ever survived this long. But a happier pair of men, I've never known. When Slob sat behind his rusty old truck, he had a look about him you would expect on a sailor with fair winds. He was in his element, master of his ship, and content with the world. At the moment, he was content to hear Steppenwolf make an entire song from a single curse word.

This early in the day, only a few cars nestled around the parking lot. Above us rose the twenty-foot white cone that gave the hamburger joint its name. Waitresses, all in short white skirts, all cheerleaders from past and forgotten high school classes, roamed about the cars taking orders. By nightfall, the lot would be packed. Nightlife in Toccoa was predictable and focused, with the Wigwam at its center.

Katrina looked around for a moment, waved off a waitress, and then started the car.

"Hey," I said. "I want a milkshake."

"I'll get you one at Bell's," she said.

Pebbles pelted the driveway as Katrina screeched away north. We passed the drive-in theater, a used car lot covered mostly with old golf carts, and Buck's Drive-In before we came to the other teen hangout. Town kids mostly avoided the Wigwam and hung out at Bell's where you could either sit in your car to eat or go inside to one of eight booths. Rural kids used the Wigwam. Unofficial rules stated that country kids like us could come to Bell's as long as we actually ate something and did not go inside.

At the far end of the parking lot where someone passing casually by would not notice, sat a yellow Camaro with black racing stripes, oversized rear whitewalls, and dual chrome exhausts. Katrina had found her man, or so she thought. Corrie was not there.

We pulled up to the empty car. Katrina parked, walked over to the car, and then spit inside. She came back to me and again started the engine.

"I don't suppose I'm getting a milkshake?" I asked.

Katrina glared at me.

"Drop me off at the Wigwam," she replied. "You can have the car."

Katrina was going bird-dogging.

Every evening the local boys drove their cars to the Wigwam where they turned around slowly, perused the selection of girls who were without dates, then drove to Bell's Drive-in. Unless a girl caught their eye and she responded to whatever line he threw at her, they turned around at Bell's and repeated the route. For reasons no one ever thought to question, the activity, both from the girls' and the boys' perspective was called "bird dogging." Girls often did it to punish unfaithful steady boyfriends. Boys did it-- well, because that's what boys do. A girl on a punishment bird dog was precious beyond price, good for a few minutes of passionate making out, but never for a real date. I kissed my first girl while she was on a punishment bird dog. Had my first real fight over it, which I lost badly. But that was before I had a reputation.

When I dropped Katrina off, the Wigwam was still only half full. She got in the car with Dixie Collier, head majorette of the Stephens County Indian Marching Band. Dixie was bird-dogging too. In fact, Dixie had been bird-dogging for a record two years running. She was a pretty girl with long, auburn hair, big teeth, and a slim body that looked great in her shiny majorette uniform. She carried a reputation as a girl easy to kiss but nothing more. No one ever asked her for a real date, they just picked her up bird-dogging. Any girl who bird-dogged more than a week or two was generally considered damaged goods. Any boy who dated her looked desperate and lonely, a nearly universal trait we all worked hard to hide. Once Dixie passed her first summer of uninterrupted bird-dogging, she had no chance of finding a boyfriend in this town.

I ordered a milkshake and drank it while driving to the high school. Hopefully, a few of our basketball team would be there and we could get up a game. Sure enough, two cars sat in the lot, so I parked and went inside.

A two-on-two game was already in progress, so I sat on the wooden bleachers next to Pop Fisher. Pop, best known as the football team's starting center, was also a second string postman for our basketball team. He was also one of the few football players who did not want to kill me. He greeted me with a mindless grin and a punch on my shoulder. Pop's father strung line for the Power Company. He lived in Toccoa's only subdivision, the Indian Village. Like his father, Pop carried broad, powerful shoulders upon which a small head sat devoid of any indication of a neck. His short fingers and meaty hands, made to recover a football not shoot a basketball, twitched when he spoke.

"What's the score?" I asked.

The game was gentlemanly, no shouting, little serious contact. I knew that would change when Pop and I entered.

"Six to six," he said.

An unwritten rule stated that games went to eleven baskets when people were waiting.

George Peterman passed to a black boy I did not know. Immediately the black whirled around and powered past his defender for a layup.

By the time the game ended, Pop and I had warmed up on the side with our own game. Pop was strong and quick but had slippery hands. I could shoot better and move laterally better. I won easily. He did not seem to mind. Pop was one of those boys destined to happiness regardless of his lot in life. Toccoa had many such boys. I longed to be one of them.

We played three on three for another hour in the August heat. Sweat poured from us and made slick puddles on the wood floor. We switched teams around to match up by height and played like the state championship depended on us. Finally, Coach McGee stuck his head in and shouted for us to wrap it up so he could lock the doors. We walked out exhausted and at least five pounds lighter than when we started. It was a good sweat, one that made you strong.

Earlier in the summer, Coach McGee told me I might actually start for the varsity this coming season. No Davis ever excelled at anything, so I felt a call to make his prediction come true. I worked out, ran, hopped up and down stadium seats, and played every chance I got. Best of all, I grew.

Seems some days I could feel myself grow. I never got to wear the same pants more than four or five months in a row. Momma took to buying them without hems so she could let them out as the year went by. I went from six feet, to six-feet four inches the next year and then six-six the next. I ate constantly yet never felt full. This year, I finally felt my gangly limbs start to respond in a timely fashion to the instructions my brain sent out to them. I could move, shoot, rebound, and block shots. I was ready for a glorious year. The Toccoa Tribune even ran a story about my progress. First time they ever noticed a Davis for anything except marriage or death.

When I got outside, I noticed a car across the road and up the hill next to the cannery. I saw the outline of heads but no faces. They were turned toward the gym a hundred or so yards away. By the time I got into the car, they had pulled down the hill, slowing near where I was parked. Two black men I had never seen sat up front. In the back seat sat Franklin Pearce. Franklin's flabby neck bounced as the car moved across the road's many potholes. He wore a green John Deere cap, a red checked shirt, and coveralls with the suspenders pulled down. It was the only outfit I had ever seen him wear. Franklin pointed something out the window. At first I feared he intended to shoot me. Franklin was known for such things, having gotten away with several well-known killings. But after I ducked behind my car door I saw it was only a wood walking cane, the kind men at the Sale Barn used to prod cattle.

I had no idea Franklin knew who I was, much less why he took notice of me. The best I knew, my family did not owe him money like many farmers did. I once got into a tussle with his second son, a transgression that earned Daddy a couple of threats. But that was three years ago, surely long forgotten. Franklin eyed me, kept the stick pointed at me as they passed. The black men up front did not even look at me, just kept looking straight ahead like they were chauffeuring the president of something. I saw Franklin laugh at me, then say something to the driver who sped away.

When they had passed, I got in the car and went to find Katrina. I found Corrie instead. By now darkness had settled on Toccoa. Tree frogs squeaked in time and fireflies filled the roadside. Corrie sat in his car, still parked behind Bell's. Belinda Kessler lay wrapped around him, the two of them smashed up against one side of the back seat. I knocked on the front door window.

"You seen Katrina?" I asked. I looked at the road, acting as though I had not noticed the two of them making out.

Corrie sat up and pushed Belinda away.

"No," he said sharply.

Belinda made a loud huffing sound at the way she was suddenly discarded. Corrie reached up and opened the door, then stepped outside. He put his hand out toward Belinda as if to signal her to be quiet for a moment. Belinda took out a mirror and started patting her face with a powder puff.

"I told Katrina I'd meet her here earlier, but she never showed," he said.

"I was with her. We saw your car. She went off with Dixie."

Corrie shook his head. Corrie knew you did not go with Dixie unless you intended to bird dog.

"Listen, Roy," Corrie said. "I've been thinking of breaking up with Katrina anyway. No need for you to tell her about me and Belinda."

"Don't think I need to tell her anything," I said. "I'd guess she'd about figure that one out for herself. But you see you treat her right now. No need to let her on."

"I'll be the one decides what's letting on and what's not," Corrie said. He wrinkled his brow and jutted out his jaw. "You mind your own."

Corrie was almost a foot shorter than me, but I had worked with him on some roofing jobs enough to know he was strong, tough, and quick. If he wanted, he could likely get the best of me. But neither of us wanted to find out.

I turned and walked away.

"Mind your own or I just might mind it for you," Corrie shouted behind me.

I found Katrina later, still at the Wigwam. She sat in the back of an old pickup next to Dixie and two guys from Raburn County.

"You want to go home?" I asked.

"Go ahead home, Honey," Dixie said. "I'll give her a ride."

"I'll be fine," Katrina said. "Thanks."

Katrina smiled. Her dark hair flowed across her shoulders, dancing occasionally when caught by a gust of wind. Her smooth skin, darkened by the summer sun, seemed to glow. In the shadowy light of the parking lot, I was reminded of how pretty she was. Slim, smooth, but mean to the bone. I pitied the poor boy who finally stayed around long enough to hitch to her. He would know ecstasy and terror. She was some woman, that sister of mine. At that moment, I wanted to tell her how beautiful she was, but brothers do not say such things to sisters. I wanted to tell her about Corrie, tell her he did not deserve her, but the words would not come. Katrina would have to sort this thing out herself. She had probably intended to maneuver Corrie and me into fighting anyway and I would do just about anything to avoid that. I told myself I wanted to protect my hands for basketball, but in reality I thought Corrie would pound me in the ground. I turned and left the four of them giggling.

Chapter Six

I drove toward home down Big A Road alone. Only a few cars passed me, mostly headed toward town. We had only a few streetlights back then, none in this stretch of road. Only the lights of houses and a few stores divided the darkness.

When I topped the hill above the Office, I saw a light on in the back. Daddy's truck sat beside the building. I pulled in to see if he needed help with something. Lately, someone had taken to breaking in at night and stealing tools. Thievery was rare in Toccoa, rarer still on farm plots where people generally trusted their neighbors and thought locks a terrible waste of time and money. But the close proximity of the Office to the Sale Barn brought plenty of outsiders by who could steal a set of ratchets and not have to explain to nosey neighbors how they came to posses them.

I parked, walked around back where cement steps led down to a wood porch behind the Office. We stored stacks of folded cardboard egg crates and barrels on the porch, nothing valuable. Daddy was not there. I tried to open the door, but it was locked from the inside.

"Daddy," I yelled. "You there?"

No answer. I went to the side door.

"Daddy?"

The door gave way. A low buzz came from a single fluorescent light suspended from the ceiling. I smelled cigarette smoke mixed with the odor of chemicals and feed sacks. Daddy smoked a lot when he was alone. I have seen him use one cigarette to light the next. I knew he was around by the smell of it.

The place was quiet. I felt a tingle on the back of my neck like cold breath. I wanted to run and almost did. But Daddy was here. He had to be. I saw his truck and smelled his tobacco. I stepped slowly through the door and peaked around a stack of feed sacks toward the front. Nothing moved. A few moths slipped past me and headed for the light. I thought I saw a mouse slip under a rack of seeds. I crept in slowly until I could see the whole room.

I saw Daddy sitting in the rusty metal chair, his head on the counter top next to the cash register. Papers and pencils, other things from the counter top, lay scattered across the floor. Daddy's right arm lay across the desk on top of some papers at an odd angle to his shoulder. My heart jumped to my throat when I saw his left hand hanging limp toward the floor.

I ran to him and rolled his head to face me. Lifeless eyes stared back at me. I wished I had not seen that face. For years afterwards, I would think of him and want to remember his face and voice. I wanted to see him alive and smiling. Instead I would see the pale face I saw that night. His lips hung open, blood pooled at the corners. I felt his neck, no pulse. Daddy's hand swung back and forth. I shook him, tried to force him to look at me, make him be alive. Blood oozed from his chest in dark globs. He slid from the chair onto the floor. I tried to stop him from falling, but he was too heavy, too limp. I was able only to let him slide down on his back, his head in my hands. He kept staring up at nothing, no real expression on his lifeless face. I do not know how long I knelt there with my dead father's head in my hands watching blood ooze from his chest. It could have been an hour. It could have been a few seconds. It did not seem real.

I barely remember the rest of that night. I do not remember calling the sheriff's office or the hospital. I recall how the deputy asked me a lot of question, seemed not too interested in my grief and shock. I saw Momma come running in, apron flying loose, hair frizzed out like she had been hit by lightning. I heard her scream when they showed Daddy to her. A lady from Eastanollee Baptist Church was there, kept pulling Momma to her, trying to calm her. I do not know who she was or how she got there, only that Momma would not calm down.

I sat on a turned up bucket and watched everyone like they were in a play or something. I could not feel anything, could not think straight. I had no idea how I was supposed to act, what to say. I did not know how to be responsible, which is really what I wanted. I wanted to be responsible for making this night go away. But I just sat there watching. Finally Momma found me, wrapper her chubby arms around me and sobbed. She went limp in my arms and I thought she had fainted. I pulled her up, hoping she did faint for fear I could not support her bulk and keep her from hurting herself on the concrete floor. She looked up at me with a face contorted with shock and grief. I pulled her over to a stack of feed sacks and made her sit. She resisted, made me drag her along. But she finally sat down and buried her face in her hands. Her round form shook in waves as she sobbed and moaned.

They wheeled Daddy out to a big station wagon the local undertaker used as a hearse. Momma heard them and looked up. She screamed again. Sheriff Bowers arrived just as the hearse pulled away. A big man, almost as tall as Papa, the Sheriff wore khaki pants and a white shirt with his badge pinned over the pocket. An automatic pistol swung back and forth as he strode into the building. He gazed about as if he expected everyone to stop what they were doing and look to him for direction. That is exactly what we did.

He motioned the deputy to him. They spoke in whispers for a minute, looked back at me a couple of times and then pointed to various parts of the room. The Sheriff patted the deputy on the shoulder, and then strode over to me and Mamma.

"Good evening, Mrs. Davis," he said in a somber tone. He nodded toward me. "Roy."

Momma nodded and then began sobbing again.

"I cannot tell you how sorry I am for your loss," he continued.

I sat there motionless, too numbed to cry, too shocked to speak.

"The deputy tells me it looks as though your husband was shot," he continued.

Mamma stopped sobbing and looked up at him. The Sheriff swept his white hair back, took a deep breath, then continued. I assumed Momma had seen the blood coming from Daddy's chest. I knew of nothing but a bullet could do that. Daddy was a big strong man. Somebody with a knife would have had a hard time killing him where he sat.

"You didn't know?" he asked.

Mamma shook her head then looked at me.

"He was shot, Momma," I said to her. I had assumed someone had told her how he died. It did not occur to me that she would assume he had died some other way.

Mamma began sobbing again.

"Any idea what happened, son?" he asked.

I shook my head.

"Any reason to think he did this to himself?" Bowers asked.

I stared at him, unable for a moment to respond.

"He did not kill himself," I said slowly and deliberately so as to leave no doubt in his mind.

"Ok. I know this is a bad time to discuss such things," he said. "But if someone murdered your daddy, we'd best find out all we can as quick as we can. Easier following a hot trail than a cold one."

I nodded. The Sheriff went on asking questions. No, Daddy had no enemies. No, Daddy did not have any money on him. No, the cash register is emptied every day. No, I do not know why he came to the Office tonight. We kept saying "no" until we stopped listening to the questions. Sheriff Bowers kept on asking, writing things in a little pad. The deputy poked around the store, lifted up papers, opened boxes and drawers. Momma watched him as she answered the Sheriff's questions.

Mamma pulled herself away from me, straightened herself out and faced the Sheriff.

"You find who killed my husband, Sheriff," Momma said sternly. "You find you did this terrible thing. He never did wrong to nobody. I don't know why anybody would want to hurt him. Nothing much here worth stealing, surely nothing worth killing over. I can't say why someone would do this thing, but you find them. Make 'em pay, Sheriff. And get that snoopy deputy out of our store."

She made a face and flung her head toward the deputy. She then turned and went out the door. I saw the pickup leave, going away from the house, probably following the hearse. The sheriff and deputy watched for a minute then turned to me. They stood looking at me like I knew something.

"I got no idea why anyone would do this," I said. "Don't pay Momma no mind. You look around all you need to. I'll stay here and lock up when you're done. Right now I got to call my Papa."

Chapter Seven

Within minutes, Papa's truck had pulled in front of the Office. He ran into the store as if his presence could somehow save his only son.

"He's already gone, Papa," I said to him. When I saw him I finally started to cry. "Took him to the funeral parlor, I suppose."

Papa nodded. He looked a strange combination of angry and sad, suddenly much older. He bent over like he had something pushing on his shoulders. To this day, I remember that moment and the way he looked. If I try hard I can see his face and in hindsight read what he thought. At the time, I believed Papa must have felt grief and I am sure it was at least a part of what I saw in him in that brief instance. But I sensed something else in him that night. Something that later on I understood was grief mixed with guilt. However, at the moment I just saw a curious form of sadness cross his face. Later I would know why. Later on I would have a dark secret of my own that I shared with Papa. A secret born of that terrible day.

The sheriff and deputy approached as if to begin questioning him.

"I know you want to ask me a bunch of fool questions," he said. "Right now I got no answers for you, Bowers. Maybe you'd better finish up here and leave. I got a dead son to check on, grandchildren to manage, and a wife near dead with grief up the road. Got no time to help you fill out reports. You finish what you need here then leave. I'll come on down tomorrow and tell you more than you want to know."

The sheriff started to speak but stopped when Papa raised his open palm toward him and cast him a glowering look. No one messed with Papa.

"We're about done here, Deputy," the sheriff said loudly. "Put police tape around the building when they're gone. We'll see if the lab people from Gainesville can come over tomorrow. Mr. Davis, you and the boy better leave too. Can't go messing up a crime scene."

"I own this property clean," Papa said defiantly. "I'll go when I'm damned ready."

The sheriff hesitated.

"Wait for him to leave, then tape off the whole building," he said to the deputy.

Sheriff Boyle left, slamming the door behind him. Papa glared a minute at the deputy, then he left too.

"You found your Daddy?" Papa asked.

I nodded.

"Sitting at the counter?"

I nodded again.

"Any boxes, containers nearby?"

I shook my head, no. Just receipts and normal papers.

Papa looked out the window. The deputy sat in his car talking on the radio. Papa went over to a stack of dog-feed sacks in one corner. He pulled a couple of sacks off and moved them to one side. Behind them sat a wooden box slightly smaller than a loaf of bread. It looked old and fragile, held together with new twine. I had never seen it before.

Papa looked around to see if anyone besides me was watching. Seeing no one, he put the box into a burlap bag and handed it to me.

"Keep this behind you when we leave," he said. "Don't want the deputy asking any questions about it."

I nodded and we walked out. Papa stayed between me and the deputy as we got into his truck. I put the box on the seat between us. The deputy sat in his car eyeing us suspiciously. Papa started the truck and drove me to our house. He did not speak at all, just kept looking in the mirror like someone might follow him.

We pulled into our drive and Papa stopped but kept the motor running. He waited for a minute and kept looking up and down the road.

"Take this box with you," he said. "Find a place in the woods, under a stump maybe. We won't get rain for a couple of days yet. Hide it and don't tell anybody about it. I'll explain later."

"This got anything to do with Daddy getting killed?" I asked.

"Not now, boy," Papa said, a little too quickly, like he was annoyed with me. "Just do like I said. You'll find out soon enough what's going on. Go hide the box now. Don't even go inside first. Go hide it and mind you don't tell anyone about it. You understand? Don't tell your Momma, your brothers or sisters, or nobody. I can't tell you how important this is but you've got to do as I say."

I nodded and then stepped out of the car. I stood and watched Papa drive back up the road, the red taillights of his truck getting smaller, then disappearing around a curve. I had never seen so dark a night.

Chapter Eight

I stood holding the box, barely able to see the ground from the shafts of light which came from our house's windows. Inside, my young sisters slept, still thinking they had a father. It looked like before she'd left Momma had turned on all the lights in the house except the ones in her room where the little ones slept. She had not returned from wherever they had taken Daddy and the girls slept alone in an otherwise empty house. In those days we did not worry so much about that sort of thing. I could see light peeking out from the numerous cracks in the walls, under the door, around the windows. I thought of how easy it was for mosquitoes to get in and bite us in our sleep. I thought of how looking from outside like this made it easy to find the cracks and maybe we should try caulking the house someday. I thought of the most simple and unrelated things as if my mind was searching desperately for something to dwell upon other than the pale and lifeless face of my father.

Daddy was dead. A car passed and blew the horn, probably some students who recognized me, the tallest and skinniest boy in town. I was easy to spot, even in the dark. The dogs barked at me when I did not go inside, like they always did if you do not stay in the pattern they recognized. Some dogs are like that, especially hunting dogs. If you act like you belong they wag their tails. It does not matter if you are robbing the house or killing the family. Act like you belong and they will just stand and sniff. If you act different from the people they are used to, they bark a warning. I think sometimes they bark just because something feels wrong. They barked a lot that night.

Back then, I usually did not notice the tree frogs and crickets that sang throughout the night. The sound was too common so my ears did not register them. Sounds are like that. Cows bellow and everybody hears them except the dairy farmer. Live next to a railroad track and you may not even hear the train the kills you. That night, the crickets seemed louder than normal, the tree frogs closer. I heard individual creatures call from the trees and grass, hundreds of them, maybe thousands. I heard each one. The sound seemed to bounce around in my head and make it swim in circles. I thought how terrible it would be if I heard the nights sounds like this forever. I wondered if Daddy's death would drive me crazy. Daddy was dead. I wondered if the earth under my feet would ever feel the same again, if the sound of doors closing would ever be familiar, if the crickets would ever shut up for me again. Daddy was dead and the dogs were barking. I yelled at them and they quieted down. For a few seconds, the crickets stopped too.

I walked around the house into the woods. Papa would have a pretty serious reason for me to hide this box. If it was dangerous, I surely did not want it near the girls. The dogs whined when I passed the pen, but I hushed them. My eyes adapted to the faint starlight that filtered through the trees giving me hints as to my whereabouts. I had played, hunted, and explored these woods since I could walk. Even without the light, I could find my way. I followed a wide area between older trees that once had been a logging road. The familiar shapes of trees I recognized guided me. A couple of hundred yards into the forest, I came to a fallen sourwood tree. Pushed over by storm years ago, the tree still lived, sending green shoots straight up along its now horizontal trunk. The umbrella of roots formed the roof of a damp cave. I played there often in years past, made forts from it and hid valuables in it. I got on my knees and crawled the few feet to the back of the cave. It smelled of rotting leaves and damp earth. I liked the scent. It smelled safe.

I pulled the box out of the sack and held it on my knees. I could not see it, only feel it. The box was rough and the wood soft, held together by old leather bindings and twine. I felt its outline as I took it from the bag. I felt around its surface, felt a lock and some hinges. I put it back in the bag and sat it on my lap for a minute. Mosquitoes buzzed in my ear and I felt something crawl across my neck. I ignored them while I absorbed the safe feeling of the shallow cave and the darkness. No one would find me here, not in the dark, not in this light. It would be good to stay here on a night like this. This secret place was secure, known only to me. Whoever killed Daddy would never find me. Papa, with his strange demands, would never find me unless I wanted him to. But I had family to tend and the night would only last so long. I tucked the box, still wrapped in burlap, into a crevice and piled leaves over it. While I hid the box, the crickets and frogs stopped, or so it seemed. I heard them again when I stood up.

The woods were dark and loud. I started back toward the house. Within a few minutes I could see the lights peaking through the trees.

Momma pulled into the drive just as I got back to the house. She took my hand and led me inside. She looked bad, like she had cried so much something inside her had broken. Like she might grieve herself to death. For just a second, I wondered how I would manage the girls if Momma died too.

"Let the girls sleep," she whispered as if she could tell that I was thinking about them. "We'll tell them in the morning."

I nodded. Momma squeezed my hand. She turned out the lights then stood in the black hallway. I think she did not want to go to the empty bed with a dent in one side shaped like Daddy. His clothes were still scattered on the floor, the smell of his hair oil still in the air. She stood there like she did not know what to do or where to go.

"We'll find out who killed your Daddy," she said. "I think Papa already knows."

Again I nodded. I was not sure if she could see me and would rather she could not. I was crying again.

"Do you know where Katrina is?" Momma asked.

"No, Momma. She was driving around with Dixie Collier last I saw."

"I swear," Momma said softly, as if I would not hear. "You'd best go find her, bring her home. We need to be together tonight."

I squeezed Momma's hand. She squeezed back, and then pulled me to her again. We stood there, Momma's soft roundness seeming to melt around my hips, her head barely to my chest. I smelled her sweat and felt her tears soak through my shirt.

"I'd better go find Katrina," I said. Momma held me a moment longer as if she would not let go. Then she stepped back, rubbed her hands up and down my arms. I was glad I would not see her face again that night.

Some boys at the Wigwam told me where Dixie and Katrina had gone. I found them up on Curahee Mountain on the flat rocks looking out over the town. I pulled up next to the empty pickup at the edge of a black void. I knew the area well, having explored it and camped on it many days and nights. The Smokey Mountains loomed over us from the west. To the east lay the rolling hills of what my Georgia history teacher called the Piedmont Plateau. Toccoa sat in the transition, dots of lights against a sea of now black foothills. The granite face of the Curahee looked over the town like a giant sentinel.

I stood for a moment gazing at the quiet beauty of the Appalachian night. The mountains and foothills felt like home, safe, familiar. They washed up from the flat lands to the east like gentle surf. I ran through them, hunted them, lost and found childhood treasures in the hills, always within sight of the Curahee, grandfather of all the foothills, child of the larger mountains to the west. They were warm and moist, inviting mountains, not like the harsh

Rockies I saw in movies and books. The Smokies were blunted and harmless, most of the sharpness worn down by unmeasured time and the penetrating fingers of countless trees. These were mountains that sustained us, threatened us rarely, and hid us from enemies and sometimes the truth. They were home.

A chill swept over me as I looked out from the top of the Curahee that night. I knew these hills and mountains. Any other night would feel safe, familiar. But tonight, someone had killed my Daddy a man of great strength and quiet kindness, the kind of man who deserved to grow old peacefully. The murderer was down there now. Likely come daylight, I could see his house, even see him or her step out to their car. Like many small towns, controlled violence was a way of life in Toccoa. Not the kind that kills you or causes riots. Our kind of violence usually only costs you a few teeth and your pride. It is hidden in the culture of the town, spoken of openly only by the young and strong while they are still young and strong. It was the kind of violence that makes us throw rocks at the bus of visiting football teams if we lose the game, or punch out someone who seemed too friendly with our girl. Never random, never unexplainable. Small town violence was like the nipping of wolf pups settling small, unimportant disputes and creating social order. Tonight was different. Someone had killed my Daddy, a man who would not harm anyone, even if he had reason or opportunity. They had done so anonymously and fled into the same night that surrounded me. It was a violence I did not understand, did not fit with the town I had grown up in. The songs of crickets and frogs came back, louder than ever.

Katrina did not answer me the first time I called her, probably wishing I would leave her alone. Teen romance bloomed year round on the Curahee. I knew she could hear me. If I shouted loud enough on a quiet night like this, people miles away could hear me.

"Something bad has happened, Katrina," I shouted. "It's Daddy."

Katrina appeared out of the dark trailed by one of the boys from Raburn County. Her blouse was wrinkled and her hair matted with twigs.

"What?" she asked.

The boy put his arm around her and pulled her toward him. She pushed him away and shot him a disdainful look. He let her go and stood watching as she came to me.

"Someone shot Daddy," I said.

I had no gift for delivering such news. No real experience at it. People in our family died infrequently. When they do, they are so old it seems more blessing than curse. I do not believe I ever told anyone any news worse than about the death of a dog. At that moment I wished I had someone to pass the task to. Preachers are good at that sort of thing, I think. If not, they should be. At that moment, I wished we had one so he would tell Katrina about Daddy.

"Is he dead?"

I had to say it again, for the third time that night.

"Yes," I answered.

Katrina got into our car without another word. She did not start crying until we were off the mountain and headed home. She leaned over, buried her head into my shoulder and cried all the way back. We passed a few cars on the dark roads. I looked them over carefully, thinking one of them might be Daddy's killer still roaming around, maybe looking for the rest of us. But nobody stopped or even slowed up when we passed. We were invisible, likely not to be noticed again until the town heard of Daddy's murder. Morning would come in a few hours and people would talk, people would know about it. For a brief time, we would be the object of everyone's pity. I hated the thought. The story would change, take on a character of its own, and spread across the town like fog. Likely as not, Daddy would end up sounding like he had done something to deserve killing. People would try to make sense of it like that. They would tell each other such an ending had to be somehow the victim's fault, at least a little. They had to or else they would be vulnerable, just as likely to meet such an end themselves. I already knew nobody would ever really consider the possibility that Daddy could be completely innocent and did not deserve in any way what happened to him. Unless the killer was found and revealed to be a complete villain, people would need to cast the hint of blame on him or us. Here in Toccoa, there was no other way for them to feel safe.

We passed the Office. The lights were still on inside. The deputy and sheriff had put yellow tape across the door.

Momma met us in the yard, embraced us both, and then pulled us inside. We sat around the bare dining room table, spoke of Daddy and what he would want us to do now. In reality, there was not much to do at all. We just sat and waited for morning. Sunrise was still four hours coming. We sat in the dark, cried, talked, cried some more. I avoided looking at Momma's face.

A car pulled into our driveway, turned around, and then headed back toward town. In the distance a lost goat bleated. Daddy was gone. Killed. Papa might know why. This night did not seem real. The crickets and frogs did not sound real. Someone had killed Daddy. It felt even worse when Papa pulled up.

Chapter Nine

That night was the only time I ever saw Papa embrace Momma. They hugged and sobbed in our swept dirt yard under a giant hickory nut tree while all around us lightning bugs flashed to one another. Momma cried, asked why? Papa cried but did not talk. I saw Nana sitting in the truck alone, a dark, still figure. Katrina got in the car with her.

When Papa finally let Momma go, he came to me. Momma went to speak to Nana.

"You hid the box?" he asked, glancing around like someone might overhear him.

I nodded in the dark. I had wanted him to console me, tell me things would be fine, that they would get Daddy's killer, that I would not feel this bad all my life. I felt again like I had when my dog had died and he ignored my grief. He asked me about the box and I answered him, hid the extra pain he caused by not asking me about myself.

He shook his head. "Good. Don't tell anyone, even your Momma, about it."

"Papa," I said. "I don't like this, keeping secrets from Momma. If it has to do with Daddy dying, she deserves to know."

"She'll know everything in time," he said. He lowered his voice, looked up and down the road. "Everybody will know everything at the right time. I need to count on you, Roy."

I felt dirty and sick inside, keeping things from Momma like that. I needed to mourn my Daddy. Something about the secret box interfered with it, took something from me that should have been used to mend my hurt.

"What do you want me to do?" I asked.

Papa looked around again, a thin wraith in the dark. It could have been Daddy's shadow, could have been his voice.

"Nothing now," he said. "Just do not tell anyone about the box. Could get 'em in trouble."

I nodded, not knowing if he could see me or was even looking in my direction. A minute later, Katrina and Momma got out of the car. They sniffed and wiped their faces with white linen handkerchiefs. I would speak to Nana later. I knew what she would say. Same thing she said when my Aunt Eileen died.

"Not right that a mother should outlive her children," she had said. "I should go before them."

I did not want to hear it.

I knew that Daddy's death would make Nana withdraw further from us, if such a thing was possible. She would grieve alone, like hers was a deeper despair than the rest of us felt. Not getting out of the truck was the start. She would faint at the funeral, refuse to eat for days, and sit on her porch dipping snuff and moaning to herself. Nana knew how to mourn. She was born to it, trained for it all her life. I expected it of her, though I dreaded seeing it.

We all slept only a couple of hours that night. The next morning, Momma fixed breakfast like she would any other day. She kept quiet and stayed in the kitchen while Katrina and I ate. Ben arrived just as we finished. He came in, hugged Momma who broke down and cried again.

"Papa called," he said when Momma finally released him. "You guys holding out ok?"

Ben spent a summer in New York City. It was there he learned to say "you guys" rather than "y'all." I declined. My composition teachers always corrected me when I refused to use the ambiguous second person pleural pronoun. I considered the term "ya'll" one of many corrections Southerners have made of significant deficiencies in the English language. New Yorkers of seemingly higher intellect had convinced Ben otherwise.

"Fine, Ben," I said. "Glad you're here."

Katrina hugged him briefly, and then sat down looking out the window. She and Ben were never close. Only one year separated them. She dated his friends and he dated hers. They knew too much about each other's lives outside the family to feel comfortable with one another in it.

We left Momma in the kitchen and went to sit on the front porch steps. Trucks and cars went down the road and rattled the window panes. I thought a few of them turned to look at us. No one ever seemed to notice our houses before, like they were trees or something else of no consequence. Likely word of Daddy's killing had started to spread. Murder was a rare thing in these parts. When it happened, people usually knew right away who did it. Spouses killing spouses were most common. Occasionally someone walked up on a working still or a drifter tried to break into a house and got killed. A real murder where the killer was still free the next day had never happened in my lifetime. People would look now, look at our house, see us like we had just set foot in town. We were not quite as invisible as we were yesterday.

"Any idea who killed Daddy?" Ben asked me.

Katrina already knew the answer. She went into the kitchen to help Momma.

"I don't know," I said. "Maybe Papa does, but he's not saying right now."

Ben did not seem surprised. Papa was a gregarious sort, though closed. A secret to him was something to be hoarded, not shared. In that regard, as with many others, he was quite unlike his wife.

"Any idea what Daddy could be into so's anybody'd want him dead?" Ben asked.

"He hadn't been up north for almost a month, nobody's shipping eggs right now," I said. "He goes off for a half day at a time, like always. You know that. Mostly we've been clearing out the land behind number seven and nine chicken houses. Papa wants to fence it off."

Ben shook his head and looked at the ground. A flicker swooped in front of us, almost close enough to catch with our hands. It settled on the ground, pecked a couple of times at a clump of grass, and then flew away. In the distance we heard mockingbirds chatter and screech, likely trying to chase a snake from the tree holding their nest. In days past, Ben and I would follow the sound and try to catch the snake to put under the Office and eat rats. Today the sound barely registered in my mind. A few spots of sun poked through the trees to the east. The morning was cooler than usual but humid and still.

"Makes no sense," Ben said. "Daddy's got no real enemies. No real friends for that matter. Nothing worth stealing. Why would anybody kill him? You sure you don't remember anything else he could be into?"

"Same old stuff," I replied. "The Martins are a little upset that we won't let their goats over into the field behind the Office. I think Papa pelted one with some birdshot a few weeks ago and they had words. A couple of feed vendors made noise about our accounts. A couple of farmers made noise about their accounts. Nothing new."

I thought of the grave. I started to tell Ben, not knowing if it was important or not. But I remembered Papa's command not to speak of it. I had not even told Momma or Katrina. But this was Ben, my big brother, now the oldest man in the family. He needed to know and I decided to tell him.

"There is one thing," I said. I hesitated again. Going against Papa did not come easily for me. I finally decided this was not the time for secrets. Daddy was gone and Papa be hanged if he expects me to keep important stuff from the rest of the family. If it had anything to do with Daddy's killing, Ben deserved to know.

"We found a grave out in the field we were clearing," I said.

Ben looked up at me as I continued. He brought his eyebrows together just like Papa, just like Daddy.

"An old grave. Headstone said it was Ebenezer Wiley."

Ben's eyes got wide.

"*Our* Ebenezer Wiley?" Ben asked.

"Can't say for sure," I said. "Papa's pretty worked up about it. Said I shouldn't tell anybody. Wouldn't be too keen on me having told you."

"You say it's an old grave? Old enough to date back to the Civil War?" he asked.

"Sure looks it to me," I said. "Got dates on it that say it's from the War."

We talked some more about the grave, Papa's strange reaction to it.

"Show me," Ben insisted.

"Not now," I said. "Later. No use making Papa any madder'n we have to."

I started to tell him about the mysterious box, but Ben did not wait. He went around back, probably to greet his dogs, while I went into the kitchen to help Momma. The kitchen, contrary to its normal state, was immaculate. Every cabinet glowed, every pan cleaned and hung. Even the ever-present dishtowels were folded and put away. Momma still piddled in the corner, trying to get an ageless stain off the refrigerator door. It was her way, when things were tough. She cleaned, folded, pressed, and scrubbed. If the girls were awake, she would scrub them too. I was glad to be too old for her to clean.

I remembered the week she thought Daddy had left her for a waitress in Lavonia. The place looked like she was going to sell it. She washed all of our clothes and pressed them over and over. The collars of my shirts were so stiff they rubbed my neck raw. For the first and only time, I saw the real color of the wood on our dining room floor after Momma spent a whole day scrubbing it. When Momma got upset, things got cleaned. This morning, the kitchen was spotless from Momma trying to put her life in order.

I watched her scrub. The flabby part of her upper arms swaying back and forth, her head down close to the stain, inspecting it for signs of a surrender it would never give.

"We're going to be alright, Momma," I said. "We'll take care of you and the young ones, Ben and me."

Momma stopped scrubbing but kept her face close to the stain. She breathed hard, her considerable chest moved up and down and pulled at the seams of her blouse.

"We'll be fine," I repeated.

"I know we will, Roy," she said as she started scrubbing again. "You're a good boy. So's Ben. After your Dad's buried, I'll look for a job. Could sell clothes at Belks. Maybe start sewing again. We'll make it just fine. Sure wish your Daddy'd saved a little though. We don't even have enough to pay for the funeral. Papa said he'll help."

Momma stayed bent over scrubbing the unresponsive stain on the refrigerator and babbled on. She talked about life insurance and how Daddy thought it was a scam. She talked about the rent, car payments, social security, and her own mother, now six years dead. Momma talked and scrubbed as if scrubbing could clean up the mess in which she now found herself.

Momma had been brought up in relative luxury. In my later years, I would have called her family middle class. In the mind of a poor Georgia child, her younger years sounded like royalty. Momma's father wore a coat and tie to the steel plant, which meant he managed rather than produced work. Her mother was a stately beauty with flowing black hair and piercing blue eyes, who wore pearls and large hats covered with feathers and plastic fruit. They played bridge and golf. They traveled to Florida, stayed in hotels, and owned their own house. Few Davis people did such things. I never knew the man everyone referred to as Granddaddy Jack Perry, him having died when I was two. Momma Perry, I remember well. She was flamboyant and proper at the same time. She taught me how to shuffle a deck of cards, play poker and gin, and how to properly cut honeydew melon with your fork. She smoked constantly, always had either a cup of coffee or a beer in hand. One day, while playing bridge with some friends in Birmingham, Momma Perry keeled over with a stroke. A day later she died.

When Daddy married Momma, he was a Marine private preparing for a tour in Korea. I saw pictures of him, tall and straight in his uniform. The war ended before he had to go. They lived near the Marine base in Beaufort, South Carolina until Daddy left the Corps to help Papa with the farm.

They had big plans back then, a time when small farmers did not have to compete with big corporate farms. They had a feed mill where they ground great trucks of corn and millet into laying mash. They had a route to deliver feed to the other small farmers in the area. Daddy would drive a bulk truck under an auger and we would drop two or three tons of feed inside. He would then drive to the chicken farms and we would crank a handle that swung the truck's auger over large funnel shaped bins. Daddy and I would stand and watch the feed flow like water. He would take a board and tap the sides of the bin to hear how full it was. When he was through, I would climb up and shut the cover of the truck hold. When I think of my younger years, I still smell ground dry corn and the dust of feed sacks.

The feed mill burned down during a slack time where Papa had let the insurance lapse. Corporations who ground their own feed began buying up small farms. Papa tried other kinds of farming. He had bought a couple of small plots of land to raise grain for his feed mill. These he sold off one at a time, complained each time that someone was treating him poorly. He always told me he never sold a piece of land that he did not regret later. But, it kept the bills paid most of the time. Nana inherited the land on which the office and chicken houses sat. She could not have sold it had they wanted. Her mother bequeathed it to her with the stipulation that it be passed on to her children. At the time, I had no idea of how important that queer fact played in the lives of my family. Later, it was the key to the biggest secret a Davis or anyone else in Toccoa ever kept.

Daddy and Papa worked the land but Nana actually owned it. Daddy talked about it like it was his, family holdings being what they are to people like us. Hard to tell what anyone owns. It's a good thing, not common among the rich. It ties the family to the land, makes us more a part of each other.

When her mother died, my Mama inherited some fake jewelry, an old car, a few pictures, and a really nice pot. Despite not inheriting land, something about the way she talked about her childhood left me with the impression that Momma always thought she had married beneath her station. She hinted of it at Davis family reunions. Mama Perry had often spoken openly of how many more suitable pairings she had envisioned for her oldest daughter. Daddy had always just laughed at her when she said such things. He loved Momma dearly, thought of her as a great treasure he did not deserve. Momma, on the other hand, constantly hinted that she had made a mistake marrying Daddy. I think she loved him, but she hid it well when bills came, roofs leaked, and the house smelled of old leather and livestock.

That morning after Daddy died, Momma alluded to all this, still scrubbing, still bent over, her massive backside hiding most of the refrigerator door. I let her ramble on without interruption. Better let her do it now all at once or she would dribble it out for weeks. Momma kept scrubbing and talking for half an hour. When she finally took a breather, I went outside, her still scrubbing away, the stain looking much the same. I thought I should go check up on the Office, see if the police needed inside or the lights were left on.

Chapter Ten

It occurred to me that Daddy had been beside me the last time I had walked this road. I cried a little, thought of his deep, gruff voice. Daddy was gone, killed maybe by someone who wanted that box Papa had me hide in the woods. I passed a muscadine vine laden with black fruit, early for these parts. Normally I would stop and shake a few down, eat them on the way. But today I kept going, having no desire for such things. Daddy was gone and for now he had taken the taste for such things with him.

Except for the side entrance, yellow tape still covered the doors and windows of the Office. An empty sheriff's car sat outside. I walked to the window and gazed inside. Sheriff Bowers dug through a stack of papers on Daddy's desk. Every drawer lay open. Most of the feed sacks lay randomly across the floor. Even the pesticide boxes were open. The Sheriff looked disheveled, sweat dripped from his flabby face as he leaned over the papers, glancing at each one, and then tossing it to the side.

I considered knocking on the window, yelling at him to leave things alone. But he was the Sheriff. I assumed he needed and had the legal right to search for clues, though what clues Daddy could have hidden in his invoices and bills, I could not fathom.

"You best be going home, boy," the deputy said from behind me.

He startled me and I whirled to face him. He looked cock-sure, held a shiny black baton in his right hand, tapping the outside of his leg.

"This is my Granddaddy's store," I said. "Got every right to be here."

I knew I should not push the deputy. Sheriff Bowers' department had a reputation for beating up locals who gave them lip. The deputy took a step toward me, now holding the baton in both hands.

"This is official business now," he said, his face now inches from mine. I smelled coffee and tobacco on his breath. "I could arrest you for interfering with a murder investigation."

"Why is the Sheriff trashing our place? He's got no right," I said.

I pulled myself up, tried to look bigger. I looked down on the deputy, at least eight inches shorter than me. He tapped the baton even harder against his leg. He looked up at me with a smirk on his face.

"He's got every right to search a murder scene," he said, not backing off. "You hiding something, boy?"

He placed the tip of the baton on my chest, gave a little tap.

"I want my father's killer caught more than anyone," I said. "Just don't see why you have to trash the place looking. Where are the G.B.I. people from Gainesville? If there's evidence in there, seems to me the sheriff is messing it up."

"Shows what you know about investigations, boy," the deputy said again.

This time he tapped my chest a little harder. I grabbed the baton, pulled it from him too quick for him to react, tore it from his grasp and held it at my side. I intended to toss it in the grass, but he did not give me the chance.

"You trash," he shouted, backing up with his hand on his holster. "You best drop that weapon and step away."

"You watch who you're calling trash," I shouted back. "Weren't my momma what left me for a textile trucker. That badge don't make you better'n me."

I knew I had pushed back too hard by referring to his mother like that. But I had never had trouble with the law and had never given him reason to call me trash. The second I said it, I regretted it. I had had enough of people saying tacky things about my family without cause, knew how that hurt. To have things said that you know are true, that must hurt even more. I wanted to apologize, but he never gave me the chance. I felt that same feeling I always felt when Katrina forced me into a fight I did not want. I hated it, spent most of the times looking for ways out of it.

"You little bastard," he said drawing his gun. "I said drop the weapon."

I stood looking at the gun. It seemed small, hardly deadly at all. The deputy's hand trembled. He lifted it with both hands, and aimed at my face. I dropped the baton and stood transfixed by the gun. I should have been afraid.

But what I felt was not fear, more fascination. I had never seen this end of a gun in someone else's hands. I mostly wondered how much a bullet in the face would hurt, how it would feel, how it would leave me looking. I stared down the barrel, for a second thinking I would see the bullet come out like a cheap 3-D movie.

"I ought to kill you where you stand," he said. "You're trash, your daddy was trash, probably killed doing something trashy. Your Granddaddy's trash. We're better off without all of you. You think you can resist the law? Touch me, touch my stuff? I'll just rid the world of one more of you."

I did not want to apologize any more. Gun or no gun, he was about to find out what a Davis was made of. I took a step forward. He pulled back on the hammer and braced himself. I was about to die, but I was not about to back down. I stared back at him, tried to look mean. He squinted down the sights.

"Put down the gun, Roddy," the Sheriff said from the side door. He stepped out, wiped his face with a dirty white handkerchief.

"He assaulted me," the deputy shouted, still pointing the gun at my face.

"I said put the gun down now!" the Sheriff shouted. "Go up the hill, see if there are any recent car prints going to the barn."

Deputy Cobb lowered the gun, snarled at me, and then stomped away. He kept glancing over his shoulder as I watched him leave. I felt certain I was not through with him. Sooner or later, this day would come back on me and the deputy would do what it took to put me in my place. I would be careful, but it did not matter. Some day he would find a way to arrest me or possibly just humiliate me in front of some friends. I put him down with Corrie and the football team on the list of people I needed to avoid.

"Don't you go messing with the equipment," I shouted after him.

"Don't push your luck, boy," Sheriff Bowers said to me. "He'll be around long after this thing with your father's over. You don't need enemies right now."

I looked at him, tried not to hint that I knew he was right.

"What are you looking for, Sheriff?" I asked.

"Clues, son," he responded. "That's what we do when someone's murdered. We look for clues."

"Where's the G.B.I. lab people you talked about yesterday?" I asked.

"Come and gone," he said.

"Then what are you still doing?" I said.

I tried to hide it, but about this time I began to shake, the image of the gun still fresh in my mind. I could see how it would have played out. Boys in Toccoa do not step down when they're insulted, especially if their family is insulted. It's been pounded in me since I stood on the playground at Big A Elementary School. I could no more back down after the deputy insulted my dead father than I could fly, no matter that he was the law and he had a gun pointed at my face. I was going for him. A couple of seconds later, I would have made another step. Deputy Cobb grew up with the same schoolyard training. He could not step down either. He would have shot me dead, made up a story of being attacked. I would lay there against the wall while the Sheriff and Deputy talked over their stories, made them fit each other. The way things go here in Toccoa, he would stay Sheriff, I would stay dead and forgotten, and the deputy would let the story grow with time. A few years later, every chance he got he would tell people how he had shot it out with the Davis boy. In his story I would have a gun, maybe two. He would try to talk me out of it, but in the end he would kill me in self-defense. Except for family, no one would remember me for anything else.

I moved around, looked in the window, trying to keep moving so he could not see my legs shake.

"Looks to me like you're making a mess I'll have to straighten out," I told the sheriff. "We keep sales receipts, invoices, stuff like that in Daddy's desk. No need for you to throw them around like they's garbage."

The Sheriff walked slowly up to me and sighed deeply. I thought he was about to apologize. Suddenly, he grabbed me by the throat and pushed me against the window. My elbow flew back, shattering one of the panes. I could barely breathe. I grabbed his arm, tried to pull away. He was too strong. He pulled me down to him and bent me at the waist.

"You listen to me, boy," he said, his face almost touching me. Slobber splattered my face as he spit the words at me. Blood rushed to my head and I thought I would pass out.

"I'll look where I want, question who I want, and dig where I want," he said. "You got that? I don't normally touch your kind. But just this once, I wanted you to feel how helpless you really are. You know anything about your Daddy's killing, you tell me, hear? You see anything, you let me know. You hide anything from me, and I'll bury you. Got that?"

He released my neck, and then shoved me again. I slouched against the wall trying to catch my breath. The Sheriff wiped his face again and propped one foot up on the windowsill.

"Anything you need to tell me, boy?" the Sheriff asked, bending over me.

I shook my head.

"You sure now?" he asked again. "You best take me for my word, boy. You hold out on me, you'll get hurt. Maybe that slut sister of yours too."

"You can't..." I tried to get up. The sheriff backhanded me across my face. I fell against the wall again and felt blood trickle from my nose.

"One more time, boy," he asked. "Just one more time. You hiding anything? Your daddy tell you anything important before he died? Did he give you anything unusual?"

I thought of the box, tried not to let on that I knew something. I shook my head.

Sheriff Bowers stood up, straightened his shirt. I could not tell if he suspected I had lied to him. No matter what, I would not tell him about the box anyway. No matter what he did to me, I would never tell him anything. Right then I was thinking of ways to kill him and get away with it.

"You think of anything, you tell me right away. Got that?" The Sheriff turned and walked to his car. The deputy stepped from behind a stack of wood flats where he had been waiting. They got in their car and pulled up beside me.

"You remember what I told you, boy," the Sheriff said. "Don't go holding out on me."

He pulled out fast, his tires sending a shower of pebbles toward me.

I stood with my back against the cool cement block wall, my face still stinging. When I saw them disappear around the corner, I went inside. Papers and gardening debris covered the floor. Sheriff Bowers even cut open the sacks of feed and potting soil. I stacked the papers on Daddy's desk, then began sweeping the feed and soil out the side door. Daddy's blood still stained the desk and floor. I wondered if I should clean it up. The Sheriff said the lab had already been there, so I guessed it was all right. I filled a bucket with water and soap, got a sponge from the bathroom and started scrubbing. Maybe it was Momma in me, but I needed to clean that bloodstain, make it go away. Seemed strange, almost like something I had no right to do, cleaning up my father's blood. But I had to do it. The counter came clean just fine, but the cement floor absorbed the blood. I kept scrubbing in great circles, but the stain just got darker, maybe even bigger. I gave up and tossed the blood stained water out the back.

Chapter Eleven

Ben pulled up just as I finished. I told him what happened with the Sheriff.

"I never trusted that son-of-a-bitch ," Ben said. "Everybody knows he's paid off by the liquor runners and poachers."

"He's after more than just a still," I said. "Daddy was into something big. Papa maybe too."

"We both know Daddy would stretch the law if nobody got hurt," Ben said. "But Papa? No way. If Papa's involved, it's by accident."

"Don't matter if it's an accident or on purpose," I said. "Sheriff Bowers is liable to can us all. Maybe trump up some charge, plant drugs on us or something."

I thought again about the box. Should I tell Ben? Could just make trouble for him too. No, I thought, best keep it to myself for now. Papa would tell him later, I hoped. The longer I held out on him, the madder Ben would be at me. I hated being in the middle like this. Sooner or later, someone would blame me for leaving them out or letting them in.

"Let's go talk to Papa," I said.

If Papa told him about the box it would be fine. I had been in enough trouble already. We got into Ben's old Pontiac and drove toward town. School was still out for the summer. Even though the Wigwam had not yet opened, few cars sat in its parking lot. Further down the road, in front of the Mr. Bee's grocery store, Sheriff Bowers sat in his cruiser and watched us pass. Ben flipped him a finger. The sheriff just watched, never moved, like he either did not notice or was just storing things in his head to hold against us later.

"That was stupid," I said.

"Maybe," Ben responded. "But it felt right."

Nana and Papa sat on the screened porch overlooking Holly Road. We parked under one of dozens of dogwood trees that lined the street. Nana rose as we came in the door.

"You boys want something to drink?" she said.

"No, Nana," Ben said. "Please sit down."

Normally Nana would stay up and push Cokes or ice tea at us until we took it. But today she slumped back into her cane rocker and looked across the street. She wore a long black dress that seemed to come straight from an old photograph. It buttoned almost to her chin and, despite the heat, had long, two-button sleeves. Her short grey hair clung close to her scalp. She made little sighing noises every time she exhaled like even breathing hurt her.

They had raised my father and aunts in this house, seen them play in the same front yard she looked at right then. Not much changed, not the view, not the house across the street, not even their own home. Only the trees got bigger and the children got older and died too early. Nana looked at the same view she had been looking at for almost fifty years, looked like she would see something new. Maybe she saw my Daddy rolling in the grass or coming in from school. Tough to tell with Nana. She mostly stayed hard and closed.

"Morning, Papa," Ben said. He pecked Nana on the cheek, then pulled up a short stool. I stood by the door. Nana kept looking toward the yard.

"Sheriff Bowers searched the Office today, Papa," I said.

Papa nodded, did not seem surprised.

"Find anything?" he asked.

"No, sir," I said.

"You tell him anything?" Papa asked.

"No, sir," I responded.

"Good, Roy," Papa said. "He'll find out sooner or later. Later's better. Good to see you, Ben."

Papa leaned back, rocked slightly and looked across the yard. Maybe he saw what Nana saw. I looked too, saw nothing.

"Good to be home, Papa," Ben said. "Do we need to do anything about Daddy's funeral?"

"All taken care of," he said.

"Papa," Ben said. "Roy hasn't told me much yet. But I can tell something's going on. Something that got Daddy killed and Roy beat up."

"Somebody beat you up, Roy?" Papa asked.

"The Sheriff slapped me around a little," I said. "I'm ok."

"Son of a bitch," Papa snarled. "Same snotty thug he was as a kid."

Nana glared at him briefly for his language, then turned to stare into the yard again.

"Roy's fine," Ben continued. "What's going on, Papa?"

Nana sighed loudly, looked at the sky, then turned to us.

"You boys better look out for that sheriff," she said. "He'd as soon shoot you as look at you. That no good deputy too."

"We can handle the sheriff," Ben said impatiently. "Now what's going on?"

Papa and Nana exchanged looks. Nana nodded, giving Papa consent to tell us something we both knew would likely not be the whole story.

"Roy told you about the grave?" he asked.

Ben nodded.

"I could have guessed as much. Did he tell you about the box?" Papa asked.

Ben looked at me. I raised my eyebrows and shrugged.

"Guess not," Papa continued. "Don't be mad at your brother. He kept his tongue because I told him to. I dug up the grave. Found something when I did."

"Ebenezer Wiley's grave?" Ben asked.

"It was Ebenezer's sure enough," Papa said. "I proved it."

"You boys remember who Ebenezer Wiley was, don't you?" asked Nana.

"Your grandfather," Ben said. "Daddy told me about him. Told me you forbid him to speak of him to you ever."

"Years ago, your father found out things best left alone," Nana said. "He got interested in our family tree, especially ancestors from around the Civil War. Dug up some stuff about Ebenezer and Jane Wiley."

"Jane Wiley, Ebenezer's wife?" Ben asked.

"You shut your gums a minute and I'll tell you," she said. "Ebenezer left my grandmother, Jane, to go fight the Yankees. Family first thought he had been killed in battle. Found out later he was hung a traitor and deserter. No matter why. He never came back."

"People in Toccoa took desertion of the Confederacy seriously," Papa said. "Held their own trial, them thinking Ebenezer was already swinging on a tree up Richmond way. Tried and convicted him. Run Jane and her three daughters off the farm. Confiscated the land, all the way from Oggs Creek to the Big A fork and past the railroad line."

"That's half of the Toccoa," Ben said.

"Only half worth having," Nana said. "They left Jane fifty acres. Most of it's been sold off. What's left is under the chicken houses and the Office. She left it to my mother who left it to me. In her will, my mother made sure I could never sell it. I think now that she knew about the grave. What she knew, we'll never know."

"So if he was hung up in Richmond during the war, whose grave is that?" I asked. "Did they bring him all the way back here to bury?"

"I told you it's Ebenezer buried up there," Papa said. "I got the proof."

"That's all interesting family history, Papa," Ben said. "But what's that got to do with Daddy's killing?"

"Could just be some folks around here don't want the truth about Ebenezer known," Papa said. "Could cause trouble for some folks."

"What sort of trouble?" Ben asked. "And what truth about Ebenezer?"

"Can't say right now," Papa said. "I'll tell you for sure when I know for sure."

"Papa..." Ben started to protest.

"Don't push me, Ben," Papa said. "I've told you everything I know for sure. When I know more for sure, I'll tell you that too. For now, you boys stay away from the Sheriff and don't tell anyone, even your mother, about any of this."

"But Papa," Ben said again.

"Not now," Papa said sternly. "After you father's funeral, I'd like you boys to go visiting with me. Could be we'll learn something about all this mess."

"Who're we visiting, Papa?" I asked.

"We're going to go visit the Kresse sisters," he said.

Chapter Twelve

Daddy's funeral was sad in many ways. We lost our father, son, and husband; reason enough to be sad. Relatives who otherwise never gave us the time of day showed up and made great show of their grief. The colder the relationship in life, the louder the moans and sobs at the funeral. Daddy did not hold the Davis family together, but he was constant, always present when someone needed a shed built or stump pulled. I never recall him getting the slightest help from family other than Papa. Distant relatives from Royston, Seneca, and as far north as Charlotte drove up in dark sedans. The women wore black dresses and white gloves, the men their darkest suits. This many of the Davis clan gathered only for funerals.

The few close friends that Daddy made walked in, spoke to Momma, then slipped out the side before the service began. Some of them still wore work clothes. Many, I knew, had nothing fancier to wear at all. As I listened to the pastor lie about my father's deep Christian conviction, I noticed only a handful of people from the town. It saddened me that a man as steeped in simple kindness as my father could pass from the life of Toccoa and so few people take notice. In a month or two, no one outside the family would recall him, no one but those in our direct family would mourn his passing.

I saw Rita Brown come in, slip into a back pew. Rita, a black girl who lived off Whitman Street, had been hit by a car outside the Ice Company one Saturday a few years back. Daddy and I had just pulled up, intending to get a block of ice crushed up to make ice cream. Rita, only six years old at the time, stepped in front of a yellow station wagon. We all knew Dr. Reiter's daughter drove the wagon. Not wanting the town's only surgeon mad at them, no one ever formally accused her. Rita was knocked back onto the sidewalk and the doctor's daughter just sped away. She lay still for a minute and I thought she was dead. Daddy saw people standing around, looking at the girl. Likely they thought she was dead too. Daddy ran over, picked up the girl, and put her in the front seat of the car. She leaned against the door and sobbed occasionally. Blood poured from her forehead. She still bore the scars. All the way to the hospital, all I could think was how I could get the blood off the seat without touching it. It was a black girl's blood. Unless they worked for you, you did not talk to black girls, did not touch them, certainly never let them in your car. In those days a black girl and a white boy kept as much distance as possible from one another, more than white girls and black boys. I never made much sense of it, but those were the rules. I kept thinking of her blood ruining our car seat. No matter the seat looked as if someone had used it to for a stable floor. Rita's blood just kept coming out and dripping on it, adding more stains. She glanced back at me, great watery brown eyes looking like she did not want to be near me either. Even through the blood and tears, I realized at that moment that Rita was beautiful.

Rita's momma found out Daddy had taken her to the hospital, carried her inside, then signed papers so he would be sent the bill if the girl's parents could not pay. They paid the hospital bill themselves so we never saw it. Mrs. Brown's a fine cook. Brought us blackberry cobblers every season from then on. Daddy seemed to never even understand why she was so grateful, but he took the pies, thanked Mrs. Brown, and asked how the girl was. He never even knew her name. Rita sat in the back corner of the funeral home and cried over the man who had cared for her that day. I cried some more. Our eyes met briefly. In that instant, I felt a kinship with her that I could never admit. She knew my father as the kind man he was. She bowed her head slightly at me, giving me all the acknowledgement I needed. She turned and left. I wish I had said something to her, told her how I appreciated her coming. I have no gift for such things so it was likely better I did not. She hesitated at the door and looked back at me and again I noticed her beauty. I saw how her eyes caught the light and how her cheeks flickered a small dimple when she smiled as she did right then at me. I nodded toward her and she left. It was all either of us needed.

I saw the Kresse sisters slip in the door, speak to Momma, then make their rounds to the other people. They dressed as they always dressed, all gray and black. The smiled as they spoke, terrible smiles of snuff-stained teeth and gaudy lipstick. Smiles that spoke of empty lives and disdain.

"They never miss a funeral," Uncle K.C. said to me. He tucked his shirt in, an action his great bulk and poor fitting clothes required constantly.

He was bald, fat, and jolly most of the time. He laughed like Papa and had Papa's eyes but not his build. I did not know what the initials stood for as all the other relatives also referred to him as "K.C." and I never saw his name written. I nodded and continued to watch the sisters. They glanced at me, then took obvious pains to move away and avoid shaking my hand. Papa saw them, hesitated, then began maneuvering toward them. When Lanona saw him, she whispered to the other sisters. They all retreated to the door and left before Papa could get to them. Papa stood at the door and watched them leave.

Nana fainted a couple of times before we left the funeral home. We all expected her to and thought she had done a fine job of it. Aunt Fanny caught her both times, fanned her face, stroked her hair a little. Nana came out of it and resumed her mourning posture. She refused to sit down, forcing Aunt Fanny to follow her around, arms ready for another faint.

We laid Daddy to rest at the same graveyard where he always attended the Easter Sunrise Services. I thought how he would not miss another one. We sat under a green awning, listened to the pastor, who Daddy had actually never heard preach in life, and spoke to one another in whispers. Momma and the girls cried, we consoled them, all playing our roles as best we knew how.

The Sheriff's car guarded the entrance to the graveyard. Next to him sat Franklin Pearce. They watched the family motorcade pass, nodded at Momma and the others, then followed us as the cars went different directions. Nana had not gone to the gravesite. Instead she cleaned her house and set out the massive piles of food relatives and neighbors had left for her.

We drove back to Nana's house, past the Office, past the school, past the Kresse sisters back on their porches watching us. For the next two hours we ate, spoke to the people who came and left, and took turns hugging Nana and Momma. I thought it odd that hardly anyone spoke of Daddy. We learned of the businesses, family affairs, and local sports, yet no one spoke of missing Daddy. When I could take no more of it, I went to sit on the back porch steps. A great pecan tree shaded the steps and a cool north wind blew from the mountains. I pulled off the tie Ben had insisted I wear and used a paper napkin to wiped the sweat from my face. A few minutes later Ben joined me.

"I've done some checking," Ben said as he sat beside me. He too had removed his tie and opened his white shirt. "I don't think the Sheriff is really investigating Daddy's killing."

"How'd you find that out," I asked.

"I have a buddy whose father works at the G.B.I. lab in Gainesville. I asked him to check on what they've found out so far. He said they weren't even on the case. He lied to you when he said they'd already been to the Office."

"The Sheriff's in this," I said.

Ben nodded.

"Seems that way," he said. "I've already called G.B.I. headquarters in Atlanta. They'll send someone up later today. Say's they'll do it without telling the Sheriff."

"Think Bowers killed him?" I asked.

"Maybe," Ben said. "If he didn't it's likely he thinks he knows who did. Could be he's covering up for a friend. Maybe that slimy hoodlum, Franklin."

I told Ben about Franklin showing up at the gym, pointing his stick at me like it was a gun. He nodded, seemed even more convinced Franklin had done it.

We heard the screen door creak open. Papa stepped out, handed us glasses of ice tea, then pulled off his tie too. We made room for him on the steps and he sat down with a great sigh. We looked across at the Curahee Mountain barely visible between some houses. I told Papa the rest of the story about Sheriff Bowers threatening me at the office and Franklin Pearce's strange behavior at the school. He nodded like it meant something to him.

"When you boys finish your tea, we'll go make that visit I told you about," he said. We guzzled the tea in seconds. We had both had enough of sitting around. We wanted answers. If Papa thought the Kresse sister had them, the Kresse place was where we were going.

Chapter Thirteen

Papa drove past the younger Kresse sister's places and turned into the drive for the main house. Lanona Kresse sat on her front porch, still dressed in the black dress she wore to the funeral parlor. She rocked back and forth, looked at her hands, and did not raise her head when we drove up. I felt quite uneasy being on her property. It smelled different, felt different, almost holy, maybe evil. Sometimes the difference is hard for me to tell.

Papa got out and walked toward the house. Ben and I got out and stood on the other side of the truck, still close enough to hear. Papa stopped at the brick steps, propped one foot on a cement pot from which sprouted an assortment of dying flowers.

"Afternoon, Lanona," Papa said.

Lanona just sat there rocking, looking at her hands.

"Afternoon, Duncan," she said. She still did not look up.

A few cars passed in the distance. Other than that, hardly anything made a sound. I wished for a breeze.

"You know why I'm here?" Papa asked.

"Your boy's not even cold yet and you've come to accuse an old woman," Lanona said.

"I haven't accused you of anything, yet," Papa said. "Just need some answers."

Lanona kept rocking.

"If you're not too particular about the answers, I'll not be too picky about the questions," Lanona said. She chuckled to herself, an awful, snuff stained smile spread across her face. Her laugh sounded like an old laying hen.

"What do you know about Ebenezer Wiley?" Papa asked. It was not what I expected. We thought he would ask her about the Sheriff, Daddy, or Franklin Pearce. Ben and I eased closer, stood with our backs to a great pear tree.

"Only what my Pa told me," Lanona answered. "And what the rest of the town knows to be true. You know about Ebenezer and Jane Wiley. Why are you asking me?"

She stopped rocking.

"And what exactly is it that we're all supposed to know about Ebenezer?" Papa asked.

Lanona turned slowly, squinted her eyes toward Papa as if trying to make out his features, maybe read what was in his mind. Her wrinkled face contracted, adding more wrinkles. The air stood still as death, like she had willed it to be so. A few bugs buzzed around pears rotting on the ground at my feet, otherwise the world was silent.

"Same as Estelle's Pa told her," Lanona said. Her voice penetrated the humid air like a spark of electricity, seemed unnaturally loud and close. "Mr. Wiley was a coward and a traitor. Hung by the Confederate Army for treason and desertion."

Papa took off his hat and wiped his brow.

"How about Stenton Kresse?" Papa asked.

Lanona raised her brown and nodded as if giving approval at the mention of a fine name.

"Stenton Kresse was a patriot of the South, a hero," she said. "You know all this as well as I do, Duncan. What's on your mind?"

"That's all you know about him?" Papa pressed further.

"He weren't no traitor like that Ebenezer," she said. "He never acted like no woman, no cowardly assassin. Never hid like an animal. He was brave and good. Stuff your type don't understand."

"Your family inherited all your land from Stenton, that so, Lanona?" Papa asked.

"A grant made during the war," she said. "Legal, binding. Tested in the courts six times before the turn of the century."

"Who owned the land before Stenton?" Papa asked.

"Can't say," Lanona responded. "Don't matter much now, does it?"

"Maybe," Papa said. "Maybe not. But I think you do know who owned the land."

"You saying I'm lying, Mr. Davis?" Lanona asked. She brought a white shawl up from her shoulders and pulled it over her gray head. Hot enough to boil eggs in the sun and Mrs. Kresse was pulling up her shawl.

"Who owned the land?" Papa pressed on. "It wasn't Indian land. It wasn't open, unclaimed land now, was it, Lanona?"

"Told you, I don't know," she said, turning her face away from Papa. I looked at Ben. He shrugged his shoulders. He could not guess what Papa was up to any better than me.

"You worthless, shriveled up old hag," Papa said. "You'd sooner die than admit anyone other than you got ancestors worth speaking of. You know and I know. Now I've got proof and everybody'll know soon."

"You got nothing," Lanona said. She turned hateful eyes on Papa. "You are nothing, you've got nothing, you're worth nothing. I'll waste no more time on you. Now get off my property or I'll call the Sheriff."

"I'll go for now, Lanona," Papa said. "But you think having my boy killed's going to save you and your precious land, you're wrong."

"I don't need your kind dead or alive to keep what's mine," Lanona said. Her voice cracked, reeked of hate. "You tell that woman of yours her bastard mother had no claim to the land and neither does she. Her born with Ebenezer long dead and buried. She had no claim to her own land, much less mine. You want the truth? Listen to this, boys. I'll tell you the truth."

Lanona raised her withered hand and pointed to Ben and me. Her voice seemed to come from everywhere.

"Your grandmother's mother was a bastard child. Her father was never known. Jane Wiley never spoke of it. Tell them, Duncan. Tell them!"

Papa stood motionless. He stared at Lanona like he wished staring could make her disappear.

"It was probably some Yankee scum Jane Wiley took up with, sold out the people around these parts," she continued, still pointing at us. "People remember. I remember. You should too. You're dirt. Nobody. Got no history worth remembering, no blood worth saving. You remember that. Now get from here."

Papa looked at us, saw how confused and scared we were.

"We'll go for now, you old hag," Papa said. "But we're not done with this. Not done at all."

Papa turned and started toward the truck.

"Better yet," Lanona said as she stood up and walked to the front door. "I'll just shoot you myself."

"Save yourself the effort, you old cow pie," Papa said. "I'm going."

Lanona stopped at the door, kept her hand on the knob. Papa got in the truck and drove away. I half expected her to pull a shotgun out from behind the door and blast the car with it.

Ben and I looked at one another, waiting for Papa to explain himself and Lanona Kresse's curses. Her words "got no history worth remembering, no blood worth saving" echoed in my mind. To someone like her, it was the greatest of insults. Papa did not speak and I could stand it no more.

"What was she talking about, Papa?" I asked.

Papa sighed and kept driving.

"Tell us what she's talking about," Ben said. "Is she right? Do you know who Ma Davis' daddy was? Was it Ebenezer?"

Papa looked like he was considering whether or not to tell us what he knew. He sighed again, then spoke.

"Your great grandmother, Ma Wiley was born the year after the war ended," he said. "Found that out a couple of years ago while your Daddy and me were going through some papers."

"After Ebenezer was hanged?" Ben asked.

Papa nodded. "Hanged or not, it was long after the war records showed him dead. Too long after for him to be Ma Wiley's father."

"And we don't know who her real father was?" Ben asked.

"Maybe," Papa said. He kept his eyes on the road. He was silent for a minute, like he had decided not to tell us anything else. Ben would have none of it.

"Enough now, Papa," Ben said. He sounded stern, not like we usually talked to Papa. Papa turned and gave him a look of warning. Ben did not back down.

"Time to tell us what's going on," he insisted.

Papa shrugged, sighed again. It was hard, getting things from Papa that he saw no need to share.

"Your Nana made me and your Daddy swear not to speak of it again," he said. "But we found out her Momma was really almost two years younger than the family let on. It made up for the years after Ebenezer was reported hanged. She started school earlier, celebrated birthdays like she was older. That way nobody'd ask fool questions like you're asking now."

"You mean Lanona was telling the truth?" I asked. "We don't know who Ma Wiley's father was?"

"You pay no mind to what that old bag of bones says," Papa said. "Celia Wiley was a fine lady, finest I ever knew. Spent most of her life being reminded by the Kresses and people like them she didn't have a father. Even a few family members tried to keep her from inheriting any of the family land, her land."

"We didn't mean anything by asking, Papa," Ben said. "I was seven when she died. I remember her a little. Kind lady. Good on the dulcimer and piano."

"Folks used to gather from miles away when your Ma Wiley sang," Papa said. "Could've made a living at it if things had been a little different."

"But we really don't know who her father was, that right, Papa?" I asked. Ben elbowed me in the ribs. I guess it was an obvious answer, but I needed Papa to say it outright.

"We know Ma Wiley was a good woman, no matter whose blood she carried," Papa said. "And I know Jane Wiley was a God fearing woman. Not bent to shaming herself or her family."

"What's all that to do with Daddy's killing?" Ben asked. "Time to tell us everything, Papa."

"I'll tell you and show you, Ben," Papa said. "I'll show everybody soon."

Chapter Fourteen

Papa drove us to our house. He refused to say any more. We begged and threatened, but he had said all he would say.

"You boys settle in here for a little while," Papa said. "I'll be back."

He drove off leaving Ben and me standing in the yard, still wondering what was going on. Papa would not tell us what he suspected. Who killed Daddy, and why? What was the mysterious box? I was tempted to go back in the woods and look in that box. I wanted to know what Lanona Kresse and Ebenezer Wiley have to do with any of it. Ben and I went inside, changed into our work clothes, and waited like we were told. We talked and speculated for a while, then we sat silent, listening to road noises. Far off we heard cows bellowing to one another, getting ready for the night. Dogs barked. The air was still and heavy. The house creaked occasionally. Ben and I whispered for no reason, like it was dangerous to talk out loud.

I jumped when the phone rang. Momma was on the other end.

"Katrina's staying with a friend tonight," Momma said. Something in her voice did not sound right. She sounded put out with Katrina. Likely she wanted her to stay home, be comforted by her own mother rather than some other teenager.

"The girls and I will stay with Nana," she continued. "You boys'll be alright, won't you?"

Somehow I got the impression she was talking about more than supper.

"We'll be fine," I said. Ben had his ear pressed against my head to listen too.

When Momma hung up, Ben settled into the kitchen while I went to feed the dogs. We got a series of phone calls from a few feed customers saying they heard what happened and they hoped they fried whoever did it. Ben and

I sat on the sofa and watched some television. Ben stomped as skillfully as Momma to keep it in tune.

Darkness came fast to the foothills, even in late summer. One minute you looked outside and notice the light was failing. The next minute all was dark. I looked through the window and about a quarter of a mile away I saw our nearest neighbor back his truck under a metal carport and pull out his work light. Hawthorne Able spent almost every evening working on his pickup. It ran smooth as silk, but Hawthorne always found something to adjust before every supper. He was, what many people here called, a "Tooner," someone who tuned his car daily if it needed it or not. Tonight he let the engine run with the hood up, listening for sounds no one else could hear let alone decipher. Hawthorne considered himself more of an artistic mechanic than a Tooner. I watched him switch off the engine, then lean under the hood to tinker with something.

"Got no history worth remembering, no blood worth saving."

Lanona's hateful words kept coming back to me. They summed up the feeling I had when people ignored us at a restaurant or refused to give us a car loan. We were invisible, not easily oppressed into servitude like some poor black folks, so not even useful. Not a threat like some families with their wild, thieving children. We were nothing, just in the way. Not worth remembering, not worth saving. Not even being good at basketball in a small town where sports figures are worshiped could heal the wounds those words opened. A bad season, injury, or just a few years pass, and they would forget me again. I knew that they already begun to forget Daddy. I hoped against hope that Papa and Nana really had something, something worth folks around here noticing. Maybe even something Daddy would have thought worth dying for, though I could not imagine what that could be. I hoped they had something big. Maybe then we would be something. Maybe then people would notice when one of us passed on or just moved on. I did not want to be important, just something more than a shadow, more than invisible.

We lost interest in television pretty fast, so we went outside a while to get cool. Bats flitted about just above the treetops. I tossed stones up and watched the bats chase them to the ground. Cars passed, and filled the air with sound and light, then disappeared into the night. Ben talked a little about school, how he hoped to go back and finish college someday. Now with Daddy gone, he wondered if he needed to come home to help support Momma and the rest of us. I felt a little embarrassed that he could not think of me as capable of handling the man's chores for the family. I think Ben sensed that he had insulted my pride and changed the subject.

"Any idea what Papa's up to?" he asked.

"You know Papa," I said. "He'll tell us when the time's right, not a minute before. Hope he knows what he's doin', though. Whoever killed Daddy's not likely to hesitate taking on an old man. Us either."

"Lanona has something to do with it," Ben said.

I could not tell if he was asking me or himself. While I was thinking, Papa drove up. He got out of the pickup carrying two shotguns and a box of shells.

"Go get your Daddy's Browning," he told me. "Bring some buck shot or slugs if you've got 'em."

"What kind of trouble are you expecting, Papa?" Ben asked as I hurried inside.

I stopped on the porch to listen. Hawthorne's distant light, the stars, and fireflies provided our only light. Papa was a dark outline against the haze. He was hunched over, more than usual and he turned his head constantly as if looking for danger. I was glad I could not see his face.

"Someone's going to come callin' tonight, boys," he said in a hushed voice. "We'd better get ready."

"Who's coming?" Ben asked.

"The man who killed your Daddy," he said.

Chapter Fifteen

I ran into the house and fumbled in Momma's dark closet until I felt the cold barrel of Daddy's shotgun. He kept shells on top of some white shelves in the hallway. I pulled down four boxes and carried them all to the living room. Ben and Papa had already come inside.

"Do you know who it is, Papa?" I asked.

"I've got some ideas," he answered in the dark. "But I think whoever it is will come looking for that box I gave you to hide."

"What box?" I heard Ben whisper. I could not see him but I could feel the look of betrayal he must have thrown me.

"Papa gave me a box to hide in the woods," I said. "You going to tell us what's in it, Papa?"

I hoped to divert Ben's attention away from my deception. I knew he would bring it up latter.

"Something I found in Ebenezer Wiley's grave," said Papa. "Something valuable and dangerous."

"I've about had enough of this, Papa," Ben said loudly. I saw him outlined against the window as he stood up. "I'm not squatting here in the dark waiting for some killer unless you tell me what's going on."

"Get down, Ben," Papa said loudly.

"I'm not doing anything until you..."

A loud boom interrupted Ben. A window shattered and I saw the outline of Ben's form fall backwards into a floor lamp. He grunted and lay moaning on the floor.

"Ben!" I shouted. I tried to get up but Papa pushed me to the floor.

Another shot rang out, shattering the window in front of me. Glass pelted me in the face.

"Ben!" Papa whispered loudly. "You alright?"

"Hit in the shoulder, Papa," Ben said. "Hurts like hell, but I'm alive."

"Then get back over here against the wall," Papa said.

I heard Ben slide along the floor as glass crunched beneath him. He cursed under his breath.

"Can you hold a gun?" Papa asked.

"I think so," Ben responded.

I heard Papa slide something toward Ben.

Papa lay on the floor and squirmed over to me. He raised his head slowly over the edge of the window.

"Who's out there, Papa?" Ben asked.

"Can't see a damn thing," he said.

Papa squinted toward the dark window.

"Can't say for sure," he said. "But you can bet your boots it's the same people who killed your father."

Papa fired his shotgun out the window, not bothering to aim.

"Just wanted to get their attention," he said. I think I heard him chuckle a bit.

Another shot pierced the wall next to me and shattered the television.

"I don't think I care much for their attention," I said.

Papa laughed out loud this time.

"Who's out there?" he shouted toward the window.

"You know what we want," came a voice from the darkness. I could not place it.

"Can't say's I do," Papa responded. This time he laugh louder.

"I don't see anything funny here, Papa," I said. "Ben's shot, we're trapped in a flimsy house that can't stop birdshot. I can get to the phone, call for help."

"Who're you going to call?" Papa asked. "The Sheriff's office?"

I did not answer.

"Listen, old man," came the voice from outside again. This time it sounded familiar. "Throw out the diary and we'll let you be."

Papa chuckled again.

"You sons of bitches," he shouted. "You ain't gettin' nothing from me. Now get out of here before we blow your heads off."

Another shot shattered the window frame and sprayed us with splinters.

"What diary?" Ben asked.

Papa did not answer him. Instead he turned to me.

"What diary?" Ben said insistently.

"Not now," Papa said. "Later. Know any way out of here?" he asked.

"You know this house as well as I do," I answered. "You can see the porch door from the front. All of the windows are in plain view of anyone around back. We're trapped."

"This house isn't on a slab, is it?" Papa asked. "Don't you play around in the crawl space?"

"Used to when I was younger," I said.

"That floor around your bath tub still rotting out?" Papa asked.

I nodded. We all kept betting on who would be in the bathtub when the floor gave way. I bet it would be Momma.

Another shot rang out. This time a window around back shattered. We were surrounded.

"Come on, boys," Papa said.

Papa crawled across the floor and into the short hallway into our bathroom. Ben and I followed. Ben moaned with every movement.

"Show me the weakest spot," Papa said to me.

I felt around in the darkness until I felt the legs of our old bathtub. At the end toward the toilet several gaps in the wood had begun to widen. The tile had long since peeled away. I put my hand into one of the gaps and pulled. A piece of the board came up. It made a loud creaking sound that I feared the intruders outside could hear.

Papa joined me and we pulled a board completely out of the floor. We tossed it in the tub and pulled out two more. A hole, dark as a cave, lay beneath us. Papa gestured for me to go down. I eased myself into the hole until I felt the ground touch my feet.

"It's ok, Papa," I said. "Hand me a gun and I'll guard the door to the crawl space while you and Ben come down."

Ben groaned loudly as he eased down toward me. I prayed that the men were not close enough to hear. Papa joined us. Another shot rang out and we heard another window somewhere in the house shatter. I gave them back their guns.

"Where's the door?" Papa whispered to me.

I did not know how to tell him and he could not see my hands to point.

"Follow me," I whispered.

I waddled across the dusty crawl space, wondering if my old red wagon and other toys were still there. Papa and Ben followed. My own breath sounded loud enough to attract attention and my heart pounded in my ears. I heard Ben breathing fast behind me. Papa was silent.

We eased past several cans and piles of garden tools until we came to the door. The ground sloped down at that point and I could sit upright. The door to the crawl space consisted of a wooden frame covered with plywood. It was not hinged, but rather sat in the metal frame. I eased the door from its frame and leaned it against the foundation wall outside. This noise too, I felt sure anyone nearby could hear.

We all three squatted at the door and listened. Nothing but silence. A car passed. Its lights silhouetted one intruder behind a tree between us and the road. Peepers squeaked their love songs to one another and crickets chirped. In the distance, heat lightening lit the sky and a faint rumble moved through the trees. Lightening like that sometimes brought rain. This late in the summer, mostly not. A rain would have been good, though. Would have hidden us better.

"Try to make it to the woods," Papa whispered. "If we get separated, meet me at the north side of the Stonesifer pond."

"You going to make it, Ben?" I asked.

Ben did not speak, though I thought I could see his head nod.

I eased through the door and stood flat against the wall. Papa and Ben soon joined me. We all three then bolted for a large hickory nut tree halfway between us and the woods. I had never wanted to get into the woods as much as I did at that moment. I did not look to either side, afraid if I did someone would be there with a gun pointed at us. We ran fast, me the fastest.

We were almost to the tree when a voice bellowed from behind and to our right.

"Stop or we'll shoot," the voice shouted. Again, it sounded familiar.

I kept running. I think Ben and Papa kept running too, though I did not look back to see.

"I mean it, Duncan," the voice sure and threatening.

I stopped, Ben stopped beside me. Papa stood a few feet behind us. We heard movement to our right toward the road.

"They're over here," a man shouted.

Just then a shot split the darkness. I saw a flash of the barrel ahead. A man grunted behind me, then I thought I heard him fall.

"Run this way!" a different voice shouted, one I was glad to hear.

It was Hawthorne. We only saw the faintest outline, a shadow from where his voice came. We ran toward him, almost in his back yard.

"Heard the shots," he said. "Who's after you?"

We passed him, barely slowed down and headed to the great hickory tree.

"Let's talk about this later," Papa said. "That man was not alone."

We ran toward the woods. When we reached the trees, the darkness grew even denser. I looked back. Hawthorne was not with us. I heard another shot, then two more close together. I started to turn back, see where he was, but Ben grabbed my arm.

"Let's go!" Ben whispered loudly.

He pulled me into the black forest.

After a minute or so of groping, I began to see the outlines of a trail. I was sufficiently familiar with the woods that we could walk fast. Starlight and the dim flashes of the heat lightning filtered through the trees allowing me to see more and more of the landscape. We crossed several downed trees, slid down a bank and crossed a shallow creek. On the other side we stopped to listen for signs of pursuit.

"You think Hawthorne's alright?" Ben asked Papa.

"Hope so, son," he said. "Hate to see any more people get hurt than already have."

"Who were those people, Papa?" Ben asked.

Papa sat for a moment, listened to the darkness.

"I think the Kresse sisters want us dead, or at least silenced," Papa said. I could barely make out his silhouette. "I think they sent these men to do the job."

"What about that diary he asked for? What's that all about?" I asked.

"Why haven't you figured that out yet?" Papa said. I heard him chuckle softly. I found the hint of his laughter comforting. Papa was himself. Strangely humorous, but confident enough to retain his wits.

"It's Ebenezer Wiley's diary, of course," he said.

"Is that what's in the box you had me hide?" I asked.

"Sure enough," he answered. "I think someone killed your Daddy trying to find it. But he didn't even know about it. I found it in the grave, never even got the chance to show it to him."

"So you really did dig up Ebenezer's grave!" Ben exclaimed. "Ain't that against the law, desecrating a grave."

"Well turn me in later, boy," Papa responded. "Roy, where's the box?"

I stopped for a second to get my bearings.

"We'll have to go around this rise and head back toward the house," I said. "Shouldn't be so close the people at the house will see us."

"Let's go get it," Papa said.

Chapter Sixteen

We followed the creek downstream until it emptied into a natural pond beside an overgrown abandoned pasture. We then crossed back, headed up a steep bank, fought our way through a laurel thicket, and back into the clear woods. I whispered to Papa that we were close to the house and we began to move slower and quieter.

I found the box where I had left it. Papa signaled for us to follow him. We eased through the woods from one tree to the other. Early dew softened the fallen leaves so we walked with barely a sound. We could hear the dogs barking and people talking loudly to one another. Three shots rang out, followed by a hurt yelp.

"They shot the dogs," Ben said. "Damn 'em to hell."

When we were close enough to see the entire yard, Papa stopped us behind a cluster of blueberry bushes. Two cars sat in our driveway. All of the lights in the house were on and we could see people passing the windows to our bedrooms.

"They're looking for the diary," Papa whispered.

"Who is it?" Ben asked.

"That's what we've got to know tonight or we might not find out until they kill us," Papa said.

"Any sign of Hawthorne?" I asked.

Papa shook his head. Ben pointed to Hawthorne's house. The truck was gone.

"Hawthorne made it," I said. "Nobody else could start his truck. He's got a hidden switch for the starter."

"You boys stay here," Papa said. "I've got to get closer to see who these people are."

I put my hand on his shoulder.

"Papa," I said. "I have played, hid, and sneak around these woods and this yard all my life. I am faster than you, quicker, and have better hearing. Let me go."

Any other time, Papa would have threatened to wail the tar out of me. He never would, of course, but he would sure threaten me. Times being like they were, I could get away with saying something so obvious. None the less, I expected Papa to resist. I was wrong.

"No need to get too close," he said. "Just close enough to identify one or more of the people. We'll find the rest later."

I turned around and headed to a fire break that the Whitening family had build on the north side of the woods. I knew it would lead me to the top of the hill from which I could see the entire front yard. I trotted quietly along the recently broken earth, stopping often to duck under branches and vines.

When I reached the end, I slowed down, and eased from tree to tree until I was overlooking the front yard. If I wanted, I could easily pick off anyone who tried to get into their cars. I resisted the temptation to do so and laid the shotgun to the side.

I heard shouting from the house, curses going back and forth, and the sound of glass breaking. An old Chevy sedan sat closest to the house. Someone sat in the back seat, hidden in the darkness.

A few minutes later, Franklin Pearce stepped out on the porch.

"It's not in here," he shouted to whoever sat in the Chevy.

The person in the back seat responded, but I could not hear what was said.

Franklin turned, pointed his cane toward someone in the house.

"Torch it," he said.

I reached for the gun, intent on stopping them from destroying our home. Someone grabbed my arm from behind.

"Not worth the chance, Roy," Papa said. "They'll get theirs later."

I leaned back against the tree. The sound of more shouting filtered up to us. I was amazed that my elderly grandfather could sneak up on me so easily. Probably let me underestimate him on purpose, then showed me I was wrong. Papa was like that.

"They're going to burn the house down," I said.

"I heard," Papa responded. He stuck his head out, spotted Franklin, then pulled back behind the tree with me.

"You'll lose a couple of fishing rods, clothes, and some family pictures," he said. "Things that have value, but not worth risking your life for."

I knew he was right. We did not even own the house.

"We flushed up a real bad covey here didn't we?" Papa said, chuckled again.

"Guess we know who killed Daddy," I said.

"We know Franklin is involved, even if he didn't pull the trigger," Papa said.

"Should we tell the sheriff?" I asked.

Papa shook his head.

"Look yonder," he said, pointing with his shotgun down the road.

Just where the road bends to the right, barely within sight, sat a car. I could see the outline of the sheriff's blue light on top of the car.

"What're we going to do, Papa?" I asked. "If the Sheriff's in this, we can't even get out of the county alive."

"Don't you worry none, boy," Papa said. Again he chuckled. "I didn't stir up this nest by accident. We ain't leavin' the county. Hell's bells, boy. We own most of it."

Daddy dead, Ben shot, the house about to be destroyed. I was in no mind for Papa to be talking in riddles. Granddaddy or not, if we were not in danger of being seen, I think at that moment I would have slugged him one. But Papa kept chuckling as we watched the first light of fire dance across the dining room window. A couple of minutes later, flames began lapping at the upper doorframe and the roof started smoking. It was an old house, all dry wood. It did not take much to get it going.

"We'd better get out of here before the fire gives them enough light to see us," Papa said.

"Where to, Papa?" I asked as we back tracked to find Ben.

"First, we send the women and children to Atlanta," he said. "Then we go to the court house."

Chapter Seventeen

It took us half the night to double back across the woods to the highway. Papa had stashed his other car down a short dirt road four miles from our house. Papa looked at Ben's shoulder and told us it looked like a long buckshot ball had hit him, likely a ricochet. It entered and exited the part of his shoulder muscle right where the nurse gave us vaccinations. Papa put strips from his shirt on it and held pressure for a few minutes before binding it with more strips. When the wound stopped bleeding, Ben swore he did not need a doctor, so we all piled in and drove south toward Lavonia. When we crossed the county line, Papa pulled over to a gas station and called Nana from a payphone. They spoke for almost ten minutes. Ben and I sat in the car under the lights of a closed filling station just waiting for the armed men to find and attack us. The sodium light hummed over our heads. We slumped down every time a car passed and prayed it was not Franklin or the Sheriff. Papa got back in the car and started back toward Toccoa. I could not believe it.

"Nana already had the women and children packed," he said. "They'll be out of town within the hour. They'll stay with your Aunt Frances for a while."

"Where're we going, Papa?" Ben asked. Neither of us liked the fact that he was heading us back toward town.

"Like I told you," he said. "Soon as it opens, we got business in the courthouse. Right now, I want a place to sleep. Could use a bit of food, too. How 'bout you boys?"

We both nodded. I suddenly felt tired

"When are you going to tell us what's going on, Papa?" Ben asked. "You keep anything else from us and I swear, I'll take Roy with me and head to Atlanta with the family."

"I've told you plenty already," Papa said.

"You've told us Ebenezer Wiley's diary was in his grave," Ben said. "You've told us the people who killed Daddy would come for us tonight. They did and they shot me. We've found out Franklin Pearce was involved and you think Lanona Kresse put him up to it. You've as much as told us they killed Daddy trying to find the diary. But you have not told us why. What about that diary makes it worth killing for? I want to know everything you know and I want to know it now or we're leaving. Just stop the car right now and we're out of here."

I did not like it much, Ben speaking for me like that. But he was right. We had been put in harm's way for whatever Papa was up to and we deserved to know why. Papa did not respond at first, kept driving down the road, chuckled just a little to himself. I really hated it when he did that.

"You going to leave me too, Roy?" he asked me.

"I don't see a need to keep stuff from us, Papa," I said. "People shooting at us 'cause of something you done, seems we got the right to know why."

Papa took a deep breath.

"Ok, boys," Papa said. "I'll tell you what I know and some of what I just suspect. Lanona Kresse and her sisters own most of the west side of Big A Road from the Drive-In to town. You know that, right?"

"Sure, Papa," Ben said. "It's better'n two miles of frontage road."

"Well, Lanona got it from her momma, who got it from her momma. Lanona's grandmother got the land as a grant from the State of Georgia, at the request of the Confederate Army, in reward for her husband's service during the war. Odd as it may seem, that grant carried weight even after the war ended and the South lost. Acts of the Confederacy would not be recognized, but the State of Georgia never lost its legal standing, even when they were rebelling. What most people don't know is that the land was originally settled and owned by Ebenezer Wiley."

"Nana's grandfather?" Ben asked.

"None other," Papa responded. "Not a year into the war, Ebenezer was tried and hanged by the Confederacy for treason. They claimed he surrendered his company to Yankee troops and deserted from the battle field. They confiscated his land and gave it to Lanona's family."

"Why's that?" I asked.

"Seems Lanona's great grandfather supposedly infiltrated enemy lines, attacked the Yankees from behind, and was credited with winning the same battle where Ebenezer was accused of treason. Got himself killed in the process but saved thousands of his troops," Papa stopped chuckling.

"Toccoa was even a smaller town back then," he continued. "Folks took the war hard and personal. They kicked her out of her house but they let Jane Wiley keep just enough land to support her and her two daughters. You've worked that piece of land all your lives, boys."

"But how can that be, Papa?" Ben asked. "You said Ebenezer was hanged one year after the war began, right?"

"You finally noticed, eh, boy?" Papa said. He chuckled again.

"Noticed what?" I asked.

"The grave stone gave the date of his death as 1866, a year after the year the war ended," Ben said. "Isn't that what you told me."

I nodded, then it came to me.

"They didn't hang Ebenezer?" I asked.

"They hung someone," Papa said. "I've even seen a lithograph of the execution. But it sure as hell weren't Ebenezer. The dates in the diary confirm it was him in the grave, but it couldn't have been him swinging from that rope."

Papa chuckled. I looked at his face, barely visible by the lights from the car console. He was smiling, his head bobbing with suppressed laughter. His oldest son dead, killed, and this old man laughed.

"So Ebenezer could well have been Ma Davis' father after all and Lanona was wrong," Ben said.

Papa nodded, chuckled some more. It felt good, to know that but I do not know why. Nana, me, and Ben were the same people, no matter who sired Nana's momma. But it felt good knowing it was Ebenezer. In reality, it would have felt good just knowing anything about who it was that fathered Ma Davis. It felt like we had gotten another root down in the ground and it made us more stable. Something about knowing your family's past makes the future less intimidating. Earlier in the day, we had lost a root, Lanona saying those terrible things about Nana. Papa had let us think it too. Now Ebenezer was back and it felt good. But that did not answer but one of the dozens of questions we had. I knew Papa would be good for only a few, brief answers before he clammed up again.

"If they didn't hang Ebenezer, who did they hang?" I asked.

"That's the last piece of the puzzle, boy," Papa said. "Find that out and we have it all."

"Who do you think it was?" Ben asked. We both knew Papa would not answer and he did not. Just kept driving, chuckled every once and a while. We asked a few more questions he did not answer.

It was now only a couple of hours before sunrise. We did not see another car. All the houses were dark. Papa drove us to Hershel Cobs' place, just outside of town at the base of the Curahee. Hershel and Papa had been friends since childhood. We hunted deer and fished the streams on his property that backed up against the Chattahoochee National Forest. His pastures sat right up against the forest line and ancient trees hung over the edge of his pastures. He fought a constant battle to keep the deer from ruining his crops and we helped him as best we could. It was a rocky farm, rolling and jagged. Polk weeds lined the fences between cedar trees planted by bird droppings. Numerous rocks poked up from the ground, the beginning of the stony slopes of the Curahee. It was rich land, though hard to handle and requiring much work. Hershel lived for such work, seemed content to do nothing but tend the land and survive on what it produced and he could sell.

Hershel never voted, did not really even understand the concept. He assumed it was somebody's job to run the country just like it was his job to mend fences and run water to his cattle. He read volumes, mostly nature magazines and books, but never newspapers. He did not have a television, owned only one small radio, which he never used. Hershel and his wife were an island unto themselves, connected to the rest of the world only through his reading and the few people he knew well enough to let them hunt or fish on the farm.

"We'll spend the rest of the night in Hershel's tack barn," Papa said as he pulled into the rough dirt road.

I got out and opened a low metal gate and Papa drove through. A couple of hundred yards further we came to a small tin roofed barn with open stables attached to one side. Several horses neighed and blew at us as we pulled around back. We were plenty far from the road not to be noticed, but Papa was afraid an errant trout fisherman would see his car and mention it to someone. Papa pulled around back, next to a monument to Hershel's most visible bend toward oddness.

A score or so years ago, Hershel had opened a *National Geographic* magazine to unfold a flattened map of the world. As he studied the map, noticeably missing Toccoa, he discovered what to him was another significant oversight on the part of the mapmakers. He saw no designation of the center of the world's surface. Thinking he had come upon something the rest of the civilized world had to date missed, Hershel decided to fix the problem himself. He reasoned that since the center of the world's surface had to be someplace, and the location of that place was somewhat arbitrary, he might as well fix its location before someone else did. So Hershel gathered all the cinder blocks he could find and built a twelve foot pyramid behind his tack barn. He took pains to smooth it out with clay and cement, and then painted it blaze orange. On each of its three sides he painted CENTER OF THE WORLD.

Very few of us were fooled into thinking the Center of the World actually happened to be in Hershel's pasture. But Hershel was pleased with the result, thought it anchored the rest of mankind to a known reference point that would eventually be recognized by geographers the world over. He repainted it every few years, but mainly left it to the kudzu and honeysuckle vines which crept across its surface, sometimes this late in the year nearly hiding it from view. When we pulled up, only a few orange patches peeked through the blanket of green, though the title was still readable. We had come to the Center of the World, or at least the center of Hershel's world.

We went inside the barn and found enough bales of hay and horse blankets to make beds. I loved the smell of hay and leather, mixed with old horse sweat and the hint of manure outside. No place that smelled like that could harm you. All three of us settled in and were asleep in minutes.

Chapter Eighteen

We woke a few hours later to a bright North Georgia morning. We all groaned and stretched, sore from our run through the woods and our uneven beds. Papa opened the door to let in enough light to inspect Ben's shoulder again. The bullet had grazed him and made a shallow groove in the skin. The most painful thing was the bruising it caused in his muscles and surrounding skin.

"You want a doctor?" Papa asked.

Ben shook his head. "Got hurt worse playing football plenty of times. I didn't go out of the game then. Not coming out now. I'll be fine."

We sat back on our hay beds , listened to the birds and farm animals. In the distance a tractor started. Minutes later we heard the churning sound of a bush hog. Papa cocked his head, listened for a minute.

"Hershel's cutting the field below his house," Papa said. "He won't come up here for a while, maybe not all day."

Ben and I nodded. Ben told him how the sheriff had not really notified the G.B.I., but his friend had. Sometime today, the officers from Gainesville will start asking questions.

"That might just keep 'em occupied for while we find out a few things," Papa said.

"Like what?" I asked.

"Like what really happened to Ebenezer Wiley," Papa answered.

"Papa," Ben said. "Seems we should find out about Daddy's killing before we go off looking for someone over a hundred years dead."

"You still don't get the whole thing, do you?" Papa answered. "Whoever killed your Daddy did it just to keep us from finding out the truth about Ebenezer. Maybe the truth about who they actually hung in his place."

"You still haven't told us why that's so important," Ben asked.

Papa thought a minute. We could tell he was considering closing up on us, holding out again. If he did, Ben would leave. I would likely follow. I think Papa knew it.

"Lanona Kresse's grandfather was Stenton Kresse," Papa said. "History records that he was a hero."

"We know that, Papa," Ben said impatiently. "Lanona reminds everyone about it every chance she gets."

"Don't push me, son," Papa said crossly. "Like I said, Stenton was a hero. To reward him, the people of Toccoa recommended to state officials that he be rewarded the land that originally belonged to Ebenezer Wiley, land they confiscated claiming he was a traitor."

Papa stopped for a few seconds, listened to Hershel's tractor. We listened too, thinking Papa had heard something threatening. Finally, he shrugged and continued.

"You'd think the Confederacy couldn't confiscate land and give it to someone else, them having lost the war and all," he said. "But that's exactly what they did. Jane Wiley never asked the United States government for help getting it back. Folks always assumed she was ashamed of the way Ebenezer died and she couldn't see herself benefiting from the South losing."

"You mean she just let them keep it?" Ben asked. Obviously Jane was not like her granddaughter, Estelle.

"Never made a move to get it back," Papa said. "A few other family members went to court, tried to return the land to the Wiley family. It had belonged to the Wiley's ever since it was a land grant from King George himself. But none of them had sufficient claim on it. Only Jane had a chance and she refused to talk. Refused to name her youngest daughter's father, too. Never spoke of it to anyone."

"So if that really was Ebenezer Wiley's grave Roy and Daddy found and you can prove it, you think finding out who was really hanged might get Nana all that land back?" Ben asked.

"T'aint the land I care about most," Papa said. "It's the people. Been so long you'd think the wounds would be healed by now. But they ain't. Your Nana's family has suffered for generations over what people said Ebenezer done. Most of the Davis' didn't believe it, still don't. They took the name calling. Even took it quiet like when they stole their land. Left 'em with just enough to live on. But they stole your grand mamma's honor. She's never forgiven the people in these parts for it. Never forgave the South for losing the war, Yankees for winning it. Didn't hurt her much as a youngster. Young people like you have a way of shedding such things, not letting them soak in and stain you. She did just fine with it in the early years. Didn't seem to bother her at all. Later it did. Year after year thinking on it, having the family stew over it, took the sweetness from her. I saw that sweetness when she was young. Fell in love with her like that. You should have known her then, all laughing and sparkling. But time and the wagging tongues of the likes of Lanona Kresse wore her down, stole the spark out of her, just like it did her mamma and her momma's mamma. Generations later, your grandmamma still feels the shame. That's what we're after, boys. I want the spark back in the woman I married."

Papa looked at his hands, twisted a shank of milo around and around. He did not laugh like I wished he would. Ben and I looked at each other for a moment. What Ben said without words, I agreed to. We would help Papa find Nana's spark.

"How're we going to find out about a Civil War hanging?" Ben finally asked.

Papa chuckled.

"Boy, don't you know?" he said. "Your momma's a member of the Daughters of the Confederacy. Don't nobody have more records of such things as them."

"Why did you have to wait till now to search those records, Papa?" I asked.

Papa pulled out the box I had hidden in the woods, held it up for us to see.

"Before now, I didn't have this," he said. "Until I got this diary I didn't know enough, didn't know where to look. We didn't know what Regiment Ebenezer was in. We assumed it was the Georgia Seventh Infantry. Most folks from Toccoa fought in the Seventh. Ebenezer himself wrote in this here diary that he was transferred from the Seventh Infantry to the Tennessee Reconnaissance Battalion."

"Tennessee?" Ben asked. "No wonder you couldn't find it. You mean we got to drive all the way to Tennessee?"

"No need, son," Papa said. "Some years back the Daughters of the Confederacy raised enough money to put all those records on microfilm. Got'm stored down at the Courthouse."

"Great," Ben said. "Sheriff Bowers can see the Courthouse from his office. What're the odds we can get in and out of there without being seen?"

"Better'n even, I'd suspect. Don't reckon they'll be looking for us in the middle of town," Papa said. "Besides, with all those people around, I don't think Bowers or Pearce will try anything, even if they do see us. Only trick'll be seeing them first so's we can get out with any information we find."

Ben looked at me. I do not think he was convinced, but he would go along. So would I.

I did not have a watch, but it could not have been but a little after six or seven in the morning. Papa said the Courthouse would not open until nine. We lay back on the hay, not talking, listening to Hershel cut the top off his lower field. I envied people like Hershel. They never seemed to wonder who they were or where they were going. I lived in a rented house, now burned down. We lived from chicken flock to chicken flock, hoping the market swung up in time, hoping the fields stayed just wet enough, hoping no one tried to under price us on feed or tools. I wondered every day that he was gone if Daddy would come home from his trips to New Jersey. Sometimes I wondered if Momma would be home at the end of the day. Now I wondered if we could stay alive or if Sheriff Bowers would kill us. Meanwhile, Hershel bushhogged, less than half a mile from the center of his world. My world now had no center.

I went back to sleep. Later I woke up to Ben shaking me. We drove into town, me barely awake. A second sleep hangs on to your mind longer than the first, like it's looking for a night that never happened.

The Courthouse could have been any one of hundreds scattered across any other Southern state. It sat in the center of town, where four roads converge to make a square. Old magnolia trees surrounded the white two-story building topped by the traditional dome and flag pole. On top of the pole hung three flags; the United States', the State of Georgia's, and the Confederate Battle flag. We parked by Harper's Five and Dime. Bobby Holland swept the sidewalk but never looked up. We crossed the road quickly, and opened the old double doors at the front of the courthouse. Only a few early merchants walked around, none of them seemed to notice us. Being socially invisible was sometimes convenient.

Papa directed us to the basement, just off the main hallway. Someone had already propped open the door to the Archives Office. We went in and found no one there. Papa sat on an old wooden bench to the side while Ben and I paced. Twenty minutes later, Paula Dean, or so her name tag identified her, came down the stairs. She wore a very short skirt, something a woman of her immense size should have avoided. We could hear the sound of her hose rubbing together on her thighs even before we heard her footsteps. She had a puffed up hairdo that swayed and threatened to fall every time she moved. She opened the counter door and went inside, not bothering to acknowledge our presence. When she did look at us, she brought her sketched-on eyebrows together into a frown. I looked at Papa and Ben and could see why. We were dirty, scratched, and every piece of clothing we wore was tattered. The stubble of Papa's gray beard had begun to show through. We did not look like people who would come to the courthouse.

Papa stood up and went to the counter.

"We want to look something up in the Daughters of the Confederacy's archives," he said.

Paula did not answer, just pushed a sign-in book toward him.

"We want to look up something about a Confederate soldier," Papa said.

Paula only stared at him.

"You speak English, young lady?" Papa asked. "Or do we need someone else here to translate?"

Paula stuck out her already overly pouty lower lip. I could see where the deep red paint ended and her own lip color began.

"When did he serve, sir?" she asked.

"Well, my guess would be sometime during the Civil War, wouldn't yours?" he said.

Again Paula poked out her lower lip.

"The microfilm readers are in the corner back here," she said. "We have an index of materials in the cabinet beside it. If you find what you want listed, you give me the registration number and I'll get it for you."

"Thanks, Miss Dean," Papa said. He motioned for Ben and me to go with him.

The archives were organized according to rank, battalion, regiment, state, county, and name. We went straight for the name list and within seconds, we found Ebenezer Wiley's. Ben gave Paula the numbers and she brought out a couple of microfilm sheets, mostly of newspapers.

The first paper listed Ebenezer's name along with others from Toccoa who had volunteered to fight the "Yankee aggressors." The second carried a short story of his trial and hanging.

December 2, 1862, Ebenezer Wiley, of Toccoa, GA, pleaded guilty to treason against the Confederate States of America. He was tried by a military court in Spartanburg, South Carolina, where overwhelming evidence of his guilt prompted his plea. He was discovered to have sold military supplies to Yankee raiding parties who had killed at least two hundred civilians. A second trial was held in his home town. While the second trial carried no weight of law, his wife and three daughters found it so emotionally trying that Jane Wiley fainted and had to be carried from the Courthouse. The disgraced Mr. Wiley was taken to a military prison in Wilmington where he was executed by hanging.

"Nothing new here," Papa said. "Let's look for something on the Tennessee Reconnaissance Battalion."

Ben flipped through the archive index until he found the Battalion's name. Beside it, dozens of record numbers appeared. He took a piece of paper and jotted them all down. A few minutes later, Paula handed Papa the requested microfilms.

They flipped through several clips about the formation of the Battalion and its members. Sure enough, on the list was Ebenezer Wiley. They continued to search more clips, but the papers usually reported only that the Battalion was engaged in covert operation behind Yankee lines.

More microfilm sheets contained copies of orders, requisition forms, and other daily records any military unit maintained. One by one, the three of us searched the orders looking for Ebenezer Wiley's name. Hundreds of orders, dozens of campaign outlines passed before our eyes. I got so drowsy, I started having trouble focusing on the screen. I feared in my sleepiness I would let an important passage slip by. Fortunately, Papa and Ben looked at the same screen and seemed as alert as ever.

We took a break around noon and went across the street to the drug store. Papa ordered sandwiches and Cherry Cokes from a man behind the counter. We all ducked when the Sheriff's car passed, but he did not see us. Ben slipped out to check on the car. It too was untouched and seemingly unnoticed. We sat for a while and enjoyed the cold drinks and the feel of the ceiling fans blowing down our necks. Papa brought us here often, especially during times when Daddy was off driving trucks. It felt good to sit with him and Ben again. The man who served us wore all white and had a cloth hat with his name on it. People passed, some stopped to look in the window. No one seemed to notice us. Things were normal and we were as invisible as usual.

Chapter Nineteen

We went back to the basement and passed Paula at her desk painting her fingernails. She did not speak to us. She did come back later in the afternoon to tell us that she was closing at three. We were about to give up on finding anything about Ebenezer's service in the Reconnaissance Battalion, when Ben let out a whoop. He pointed to a copy of orders, most of which we could read, some of which was cracked and had not copied well.

Sgt. Ebenezer Wiley is assigned to infiltrate political groups in Chicago, Illinois. During this assignment, Sgt. Wiley will make regular reports to V.R.B. He will also engage in subversive actions against U.S. Regular troops and specifically arrange to disable munitions factories in the area. Highest priority will be given to disabling factories responsible for manufacture of repeating rifles. A cover story will be created and carried out prior to this assignment. Sgt. Wiley will neither receive nor should he expect direct support during this assignment...

"He was under cover," Ben said. "Fighting up north. Look here."

He pointed to the screen.

"The date is November 9, 1862," Papa said. "Less than a month before he was supposedly arrested for treason. Keep looking boys. We need more."

We kept searching. When three o'clock got near we started to hear Paula clear he throat loudly. It was Ben who again spotted something about Ebenezer. This time, it was a commendation.

In acknowledgment of service above and beyond the call of duty, the Confederate States of America commend Sgt. Ebenezer Wiley for actions taken while serving in the Tennessee Reconnaissance Battalion.

"Look at that date!" Ben said loudly.

Papa shushed him, looked back to see if Paula heard.

"Look," Ben said again. "May 16, 1864. Ebenezer was alive in 1864. A live hero, not a dead traitor."

"What does it say he did?" I asked.

Ben read on.

While engaged in covert operations deep behind enemy lines, Sgt. Wiley did courageously and without regard for his own safety disrupt railroad lines, destroy a munitions factory, and provide surveillance information. Such was the value of his service that the Confederate Forces at the Battle of Bull Run would certainly have been destroyed without Sgt. Wiley's brave and self-sacrificing actions. Be it known this day, May 16, 1884, that the Confederate States of America and all its Citizens are eternally grateful to Sgt. Wiley. A small expression of that appreciation is manifest by awarding Sgt. Wiley the medal of Hero of the Confederacy and awarding him a commission as an officer with the rank of Lieutenant. Sincerely and with gratitude for a job well done,

Gen. R.E. Lee

We sat, stared at the document. All these years, my folks, Nana's folk thinking Ebenezer was a traitor. Now turns out he was a hero. Also turns out he was alive when Nana's grandmother was born, making almost certain he was her real father. Why was it secret? I could not fathom why anyone would hide such a thing and allow their name to be smeared, their land stolen, and their children disgraced.

"Write down those reference numbers," Papa said to Ben.

"You mean they didn't hang anybody?" I asked Papa.

"They hanged someone," Papa said. "I saw the reports years ago while searching these very same archives. If I'd known about Ebenezer's transfer to the Tennessee Regulars, I'd have found it then. People saw someone hanged, almost two years before General Lee signed this commendation. I think I just might know who. We'll have to come back tomorrow to try and find out. Right now, we'd better slip out quietly and head back to Hershel's barn for the night."

Ben wrote the numbers on a yellow pad Paula had left for us and stuffed them into his pocket. We then headed for the door. Paula was gathering her nail polish and other stuff. She still ignored us.

"We'll be back tomorrow," Papa said.

Paula grunted in response and did not look up.

We stopped at the Courthouse door and looked outside. A couple of dozen people strolled the sidewalks and looked in the windows. We walked casually out, turned down the street, and went to Papa's car. When we were safely out of town, Ben quickly turned down a side road rarely used. We all knew it would eventually lead us back to the highway near Hershel's place.

"You know, Papa," Ben said. "I don't mean to be disrespectful, but I just don't think it's right for you to hold anything back on us now. I want to know who they hanged, or who you think they hanged. Don't matter to me if you're right or wrong. Just tell me what you think."

Papa nodded, chuckled to himself.

"You're right, boy," he said. "I think they hanged Stenton Kresse."

Ben raised an eyebrow but kept driving. I was sitting in the back listening.

"Ebenezer's diary told me what he did on that mission," Papa continued. "Seems Ebenezer collaborated with a few dozen Confederate sympathizers around the Illinois border and really raised some hell with their supply lines. He didn't mention many details, but enough to know what he'd done. General Lee's letter of commendation filled in the rest."

Ben waited, just like me hoping that for one time, Papa would get to the point without prompting.

"That box I found in the grave had some letters in it too. Ebenezer had written them to Jane during the first few months he was spying," he continued. "Says for her to watch out for the Kresse family. Seems the people up north knew the Kresses to be Yankee spies, selling information and contraband. Ebenezer learned some of it from his own band of Yankee sympathizers, could not tell anyone at the time for fear he would betray the whole group.

"Folks around Toccoa took up the cover story of Ebenezer's treason, let it grow. I suspect the Kresses were behind it. People in Atlanta learned about Kresse being the real traitor. Worst thing Kresse did was try to kill Robert E. Lee himself. Letter says he dressed up like a woman and stood in a crowd of people watching the General and his troops cross a bridge somewhere in North Carolina. Ebenezer had warned them about Kresse. People spotted him and turned him in. That's probably why General Lee himself wrote that commendation letter."

"But if they found out and hung him, what's all this talk about him being a hero," I asked.

"Can't say for sure," Papa said. "But it's pretty clear he weren't no hero. Somehow the Kresse family managed to sell a story about him being killed in action and the like. Don't know how, but it had to happen that way."

"And poor Jane Wiley, knowing all the while that it was all a lie couldn't say anything for fear it would expose her husband and get him killed," Ben said.

Papa nodded, chuckled, nodded some more. After a few seconds he laughed out loud.

"That's the way I figure it," he said.

"But after the war was over, wouldn't she tell them the truth then?" I asked. "Get her land and honor back?"

"Maybe, maybe not," Papa said. "You got to remember, Roy. The South lost that war. Southerners who fought for the South were rebels ready to be pardoned. Northerners who fought for the South were traitors, don't matter if the war's over or not. One of Ebenezer's letters was hand delivered, never bore a postmark or nothing. In fact, it introduced the bearer of the letter as a friend and comrade. Tell's Jane to never speak of Ebenezer's work as a spy or nothing, else dozens of people who had fought with him and had saved his life on many occasions would certain be tried and hanged."

"I still don't know why you think they hanged Stenton Kresse," I said.

"Right now it's just a hunch and you asked me to tell you what I suspected," Papa said. "But it's something Lanona said the day of your Daddy's funeral. Said Stenton never acted like a woman or an assassin. These are things Ebenezer was never accused of doing. Those are things Stenton was said to have done. I think Lanona knows Stenton was the real traitor and her family somehow covered it up all these years."

"Why would the paper report Ebenezer being hanged if it was Stenton?" I asked. "Seems the army would tell 'em who it was they just hanged."

"The dates of the hanging are the dates Ebenezer was on his spy assignment," Papa said. "I think the Army allowed people to think Ebenezer was hanged so Ebenezer could go off for a few years on his spy mission without people back home asking a lot a dangerous questions."

"So when they hung Stenton, they told people it was Ebenezer," I said. "Think Jane knew the truth?"

"I think she knew it weren't Ebenezer," Papa said. "The letters show he wouldn't let her think him dead, but nor would he let her tell anyone else he was alive."

"And the land?" Ben asked. "She just let them take it?"

"Probably thought that when the war was over they'd get it back," Papa said. "She didn't know that even after the war was over, Ebenezer couldn't tell anyone what he'd done for fear of getting all those people who'd saved his life killed."

"How'd Ebenezer die?" Ben asked.

Papa clinched his jaw. I saw the muscles of his face working hard.

"The body I dug up had a bullet hole in its skull," he said. "Someone killed him at close range."

"You don't think Jane Wiley would let her own husband be murdered and still not speak out?" Ben asked.

"Hard to say," Papa answered. "She couldn't go and betray those people Ebenezer swore to protect. Probably couldn't get anyone to consider her story. The war was over. People were tired of it. They needed heroes, not traitors. It's not hard to see how she just let it go, tended her small plot and her children. In her place you might do the same."

"Then Ma Wiley was born," I said. "Born to Jane and Ebenezer, Jane not able to tell people her own husband fathered the child."

Ben nodded, chuckled like Papa. I never noticed before how much alike they looked. Ben was shorter than Papa, had more hair. But the long nose, prominent chin could have been a young Papa. Made me think of Daddy. Made me wonder if people saw him in me.

"Also explains why the Wiley family always had it in their wills that the land behind the chicken houses couldn't be sold, had to be passed to the next generation," Papa said. "Nana didn't know about Ebenezer's grave, but her Momma likely did. Jane for sure knew. They wanted somebody, someday to find it, find the diary and letters. They wanted Ebenezer vindicated."

We pulled up to Harrison's Grocery Store. It was a small store, even by standards of the time. White paint covered what once was red brick walls with a high façade and metal sign on top. Red-lettered signs painted on the front windows announced the specials of the week—the same specials he had every week. Mr. Harrison had two cash registers, though only one had ever been used. Had a line more than two deep ever formed at the store, I am sure he would have manned the other. But as it was, one did just fine. Ben and Papa went in to buy some food and drinks. I sat in the car with the motor running.

Normally I liked going into this store, though it was on the other side of town from us. The owner, nicknamed "Chinless Harrison," could do amazing things with a cigarette. Years before I was born, Mr. Harrison, distraught over his wife having run off with a Chinese drifter, tried to shoot himself. He managed to blow off his chin, exposing his front lower teeth. The blast also destroyed his left eardrum, hence enabling Chinless the ability to perform his wonder trick. Chinless could blow smoke out his ear. He did it on request, when he thought people were considering going to another store, or when he wanted the attention of a woman. His ever exposed lower teeth and absence of a chin guaranteed that otherwise no woman would look at him.

Today, I would miss the show. While I waited, the Sheriff's car passed. I watched as he slowed, then turned at the next road. I could not see if he went on or was turning around.

"Come on, now," I said to myself. "Come on now."

I tried to see Ben and Papa, tell if they were close to finishing or not. I saw Ben at the produce stand. I could not see Papa.

A woman in an old Dodge pulled up beside me, blocked my view of the road where the Sheriff's car had turned. She got out, left a barking Bluetick hound in the car. It saw me, rocked the car jumping from front to back seat, and howled. I normally liked the sound of Bluetick hounds, reminded me of rabbit hunting and nights around a fire listening to dogs tree coons. But right now I did not want anyone to notice me. A black boy across the street looked at us and laughed at the way the dog carried on. Another car pulled up across from us. I thought I recognized the man who got out. Maybe it was someone who bought feed from us. He looked at the dog, then at me, wrinkled his brow and got back in his car.

"Come on," I said to myself again.

Finally, Papa and Ben came out of the store with a couple of bags of groceries and got in the car. The hound bellowed at them.

"The Sheriff just passed," I said. "Don't know if he saw us. He turned down the next road."

"Let's just go to Hershel's," Papa said. "If he saw us, he'll follow us and we'll see him. If we need to, we can try to lose him around the river."

Ben took the driver's seat and pulled us out to the road. No sheriff's car in sight. He continued toward the Curahee and the relative safety of the Center of the World. I kept looking back, but saw only normal traffic. No one seemed to notice us.

Papa pulled a copy of the Toccoa Record from one of the bags. On the front was a picture of the charred remains of our house.

"FIRE DESTROYS HOME OF RECENT MURDER VICTIM."

Papa read the story to himself and gave us the condensed version of it.

"They say you boys are being sought for questioning," he said. "Don't say why."

"Bet that slimy sheriff's made up some story on us," I said. I rubbed my face where he had slapped me.

"It'd be just like him," Ben said. "Him being the only law around here, we don't have much of a chance. I think we should go to Atlanta or Gainesville. Go to the State Patrol or the G.B.I."

"Soon enough," Papa said. "Let's check on the women."

Chapter Twenty

Ben pulled over to a hamburger joint off Whitman Street. Only blacks sat in the parking lot. Some sat on the hoods and trucks of cars talking, while others leaned against the wall. None looked too happy to see us. We went inside, only blacks sat at the tables and bar. No one smiled. Papa chuckled as he took us to a booth to sit.

I had passed this place hundreds of times. No name hung in the window next to the Coke signs. It was simply known as the "black drive-in." Segregation in the schools ended years ago. I never recall the "Blacks Only" signs my parents knew. But like much of the social order of small towns like Toccoa, the unofficial rules were kept as vigorously as any written law, never mind what the Supreme Court said. I never saw a black person at Bell's Drive-In or the Wigwam, not until many years later. Likely, we were the first white people this place ever served. I did not like it. Felt like I was trespassing. Or more like I was hunting on someone's land who I had run off of ours. I wanted to leave.

"Not likely to look for us here, are they?" Papa said laughing.

People turned and stared for a second, then went back to talking. A young black girl, about my age, came up and asked us for our orders. We all three ordered cheeseburgers, fries, and a Coke. Jackson Five music blared on the speakers. People kept turning around, looking at us.

"You boys wait here," Papa said.

Ben and I looked at each other in mild panic. Papa called us "boys" with affection. Likely he did not know that calling someone "boy" here would get us beat up or killed. I started looking for a back way out. If they did not have a back door here I considered the possibility that I might need to give them one.

Papa went to the man at the cash register and handed him a couple of dollars. The man smiled and laughed at something Papa said. We relaxed a little. Papa had a charm about him that most people found disarming. If he broke some hidden protocol of speech, he was apparently forgiven and the cashier handed him a fistful of change. Papa went to a pay phone in the corner near the bathrooms and dialed. A minute later we saw him talking, shaking his head. He stopped, added some more coins to the phone, then talked again for a minute or so. When he came back to the booth he looked worried.

"Your Nana's been visited by Franklin Pearce," he said as he got in the booth with us.

"How did he find her?" I asked.

Not many people knew we had relatives in Atlanta, much less how to find them.

"Don't know," he answered. "Could be he just followed them. Nana, your Momma, and the little ones are at your Aunt Frances' house. Last night they saw Franklin sitting in a car with a black man, just watching the house. Didn't try to hide or anything. Just sat there and watched. They called Aunt Sue and Uncle Peter. Peter'll take care of 'em, no problem. He's also friends with some local policemen. They've got lots of protection. Might even get old Franklin in trouble, him being off his own territory and all."

Uncle Peter lived about fifteen miles north of the suburb where Aunt Frances lived. I do not think he was actually related to us, but we all called him Uncle just the same. I wondered what his relation to us was, but could never bring myself to ask. He was a big, burly man, as able to bust up a bar as to shoe a horse. I could not imagine anyone bucking him. Just the same, I did not like the idea of the likes of Franklin being around Momma and the girls.

"What'll we do next, Papa," Ben asked. "Even if you could prove that Ebenezer was a hero and Stenton Kresse was the one they hanged, what does that accomplish?"

Papa laughed.

"I'd think a smart boy like you could figure that one out," Papa said. "If the Kresse family owns all of Big A Road because of a grant based upon Ebenezer's treason and Stenton being a hero, seems to me the Kresses got a big problem holding on to their land."

This time Ben laughed.

"You don't think that all these years later, some judge is going to give Nana all that land, no matter what you prove, do you?" Ben asked.

"Listen, boy," Papa said. "I done checked with a lawyer. Same one that got those Indians clear title to hundreds of thousands of acres up near Dalton. Government can't give away land without reason. We prove the government acted in bad faith, we got the land back. It don't matter when the land was taken."

"But the land was taken by a government that doesn't even exist now," Ben said. He spoke loudly, causing a few heads to turn in our direction. Papa scowled at him.

The waitress brought our food. We waited until she left and the other patrons were about their business.

"That's even better," Papa said. "What Lanona said about their ownership of the land being tested in court was true. The State of Georgia, not the Confederate States of America, granted the land to the Kresse family. The United States government never recognized Georgia's succession. They could legally give the land away and make the grant stick, but they couldn't do it under false pretenses. If the government took Ebenezer's land without what the lawyer called 'due cause' the land belongs to your Nana. In fact, the lawyer says the State of Georgia owes us what they called 'compensatory damages' for what they did. Ebenezer's conviction was a hoax to cover up his undercover operations performed during the war. It was never even really official, just reported in the secret papers. He was never hanged. We proved that for sure. I think the Kresses are in trouble. I think Lanona knows it and she's got Bowers and Pearce after us to cover it up."

Papa shoved most of a cheeseburger in his mouth, chuckled and chewed while Ben and I looked amazed at one another.

"Since we can already prove the land belongs to Nana, why do we need to prove Stenton Kresse was the one hanged?" I asked.

"Clearing Ebenezer's gets him his name and us the land," Papa said after he swallowed. "Proving Stenton Kresse was really the traitor gets us justice."

What he did not say was that justice might get Nana back the spark Papa missed so much. Ben looked at me over a handful of burger. We both knew what Papa was after.

We finished our food and then paid the man at the register who frowned at us over his glasses. Several patrons mumbled things we could not hear, probably about letting them have their own place. I wanted little else than to give it to them.

We drove toward Hershel's farm while Ben grilled Papa on what the lawyer had told him. Seems all we have to do is sign a representation agreement with the lawyer and he'll do the rest. Says we can expect years of appeals but he has no doubt that Nana really would end up owning the land. Papa laughed like I had never seen him laugh before. Several times he had to push his dentures back in, he laughed so hard.

"Just wish your Daddy'd been able to see this," he said, then he stopped laughing.

We drove the rest of the way without speaking. When Ben finally turned into Hershel's property the sun was setting behind the Curahee. The sky was pure red, not even a streak from a jet or high cloud. A sky like that meant it would be hot tomorrow, muggy and still tonight. High above, the night hawks came out and flitted in and out of the shadows, silhouetted against the sky. The Curahee loomed over us, outlined in red. This close you could almost feel it, a hard presence blocking out the sunset, pressing against the lowlands and farms.

Ben and I went into the tack barn. Papa said he wanted to go down and speak to Hershel. Ben talked nonstop about the land, how the Kresse sisters had always looked down on the rest of Toccoa. I do not know that Ben ever spoke to any of the Kresses. I think he mostly piled on them what he felt about the rest of Toccoa's social elite. Even those people never seemed particularly harsh or haughty to me. Mostly they seemed indifferent. As Ben went on and on, I got the feeling it was not that he hated the status the Kresses enjoyed as much as the status we never had. He did not like being looked down on, that's for sure. But more than that, he did not like looking up to anyone else. Moments like that, he sounded a lot like Nana, the Papa in him pressed back inside. Some of Mamma's feelings about marrying below her station crept into his words. I stopped listening.

"History not worth remembering, blood not worth saving." I kept thinking of Lanona's words, how they'd hurt, how if Papa has his way they would come back to haunt her.

"'After all'," Ben said, mocking Lanona's creaking voice. "''Our property was granted to our family for heroism.'"

I still could not fathom how Nana and Papa could have gone all these years without finding all this out. It was the grave that Daddy and I found that was going to right a hundred year-old wrong. It was the grave that got Daddy killed, our house burned down, and now the rest of the family threatened by the likes of Franklin Pearce. Jane Wiley planned for us to find the grave, planned all this to come about. She set up her will so her children could not sell the land, had to pass it on to their children. I had found the grave just like she had planned. Now her vengeance on the Kresse family was coming to pass. Somewhere she must be sitting back, content that all her contriving had worked out as she wanted. The tree frogs and crickets got loud again.

Ben ran out of things to say and shortly afterwards thankfully stopped talking. Every once in a while he grunted as if a new thought had come to him. I lay back against the sweet-smelling hay and thought about Daddy. He likely died not knowing exactly what his killer wanted from him. The morning of his death, however, I recalled how he'd found me, told me to do like Papa said and keep the grave secret. He said how important it was, hinted even that it was dangerous. Daddy was gone now, fallen victim to his grandmother's plans for revenge on the Kresse family. If whoever shot him asked him about the things Papa dug up, Daddy would not have known what he was talking about. I was sure Papa never told him, never really had a chance to.

Chapter Twenty-One

An hour after dark, Papa still had not come back. Ben paced back and forth, kept looking out the door. Finally we heard footsteps approaching. We flung open the door, prepared to berate Papa for leaving us in the dark so long. It was Hershel. He jumped back and raised his hoe as if to strike us.

"What're you boys doing here," he demanded.

Before we could answer he stepped into the barn, shined a flashlight in Ben's face, then mine.

"Ben and Roy Davis," he said. "Little late in the day and early in the year to be deer hunting ain't it? What're you boys doing?"

"We're here with our Papa," I said. "He went to your house a couple of hours ago to speak to you."

Hershel wrinkled his sweaty brow. Hershel was a big man, soft around the waist, with shaggy gray hair which spilled out from under a gray-stripped railroad hat.

"Ain't seen your Papa," he said. "He drive or walk?"

"Walked," Ben answered.

Hershel sat on a bale of hay. He wore the only clothes any of us had ever seen him wear. The old coveralls had been patched so often there were patches on patches. He had a white tee shirt underneath and a red bandana around his neck. He kept wiping his chin and neck with the bandana.

"Shore hope nothings happened to him," Hershel said. "Folks have been looking for him. You too."

"What folks," Ben asked.

"Sheriff Bowers, a couple of Franklin Pearce's boys," he said. "Y'all ain't into nothing illegal now, are you? Can't believe Duncan would."

Hershel continue to ramble, seems he might have done so all night had not Ben interrupted him.

"We've done nothing illegal," he said. "The Sheriff's been after us for something personal."

"That sheriff's a bad one," Hershel said. "Keeps pushing me for money so he won't turn me in for the thumper."

Hershel looked at Ben and me, trying to see if we minded him running a thumper. When we did not react, he relaxed. Everyone knew Hershel made corn liquor. Only a few cared. He rarely sold much, just enough to meet expenses, he would say. The stills Hershel built were called "thumpers" after the sound they made. Steam laced with the raw alcohol pumped through the twisted tubes making a loud, rhythmic thumping sound. On still mornings around Hartwell Lake or this side of the Curahee, you could sometimes hear two or three thumpers at a time working off in the woods. Locals knew to stay away from the sound. Occasionally a nervous moonshiner would fire on an unsuspecting outdoorsman, usually just a warning shot. Sometimes more than a warning.

Hershel ran his liquor in unregistered wrecks he salvaged and fixed up. He never tried to outrace a policeman in a car. Instead, when stopped, Hershel simply abandoned the vehicle and ran into the woods on foot. That way the most valuable thing he lost was the tank of gas in the car. He was yet to be apprehended.

Hershel stroked his grizzly beard. Ben and I and anyone who knew Hershel could have told that he had a thumper running. Hershel thought it was bad luck to shave, so when the thumper was cooking, his beard grew. If it got busted up by the federal men, Hershel shaved. Right now he had at least a month's growth on his chin which meant things were going well for Hershel. We also had heard that Hershel's wife hated the beard and would not let him near her with it. If he was lucky at the still, he was unlucky at love.

"Help us look for him," Ben said to Hershel.

The old farmer, part time moonshiner grunted. Before we asked we knew he would.

We searched the fields around the tack barn in the dark. Hershel's wife brought us lanterns and flashlights. We called his name, no answer. Papa was gone, swallowed up in the dark. We did discover that Papa had taken most of the food he had bought. Seeing that, we realized he had gone intending to be away from quite some time. We stopped searching for the night.

"Your Papa's gone off on purpose," Hershel said.

We looked at each other and nodded our agreement.

Hershel told us to stay at his house for the night. We slept in old bunk beds in the room of his two boys, long since grown up and moved away. It reminded me of our childhood, Ben below me, whispering in the dark.

"Papa's alright," Ben whispered. "I'd bet he's gone off to find something else, try to get Daddy's killers. Probably didn't want us tagging along."

"He didn't seem to mind us tagging along when the men came, shot you, and burned down the house," I said. "What could he be doing now?"

"Papa knows what he's doing," Ben answered. "He's been right about everything so far."

"Hope he's right about leaving us behind," I said. "I can imagine what he'd find to do that could be more dangerous than what we've already been up to."

"Maybe it's not more dangerous," Ben said. "Maybe he just didn't want us around, thought we'd get in the way."

I did not answer. Hard to imagine we'd be in the way now, after all we'd been through. We were not in the way when Papa handed us a gun. Papa could often appear more open than he actually was, Ben knew that. He'd laugh, say a few things, but you always knew he'd only let on enough to get by, never tell you everything. Nana was the opposite and much worse. She'd tell you things you did not want to hear.

The next morning, Hershel's wife woke us with the rising sun. She'd already been up, made breakfast for us. She wore a quilted bed jacket and fluffy, pink slippers that slapped the floor when she walked. Even this early, her mountainous hair, an obvious and poor-fitting wig, rested just barely below the blades of the ceiling fan of her kitchen. We sat, answered just a few questions about the attack on our house, and ate. She put out fried eggs, link sausage, and pickled carp filet. Cannot say I cared much for the carp, but manners demanded I eat a little. She filled great ceramic mugs with the blackest coffee I'd ever seen and we topped them off with thick cream.

Hershel had already scoured the field for a couple of hours. He came in as we finished eating.

"Searched the entire area," he said. "Found a track across a section of plowed field next to the National Forest border. Duncan's gone into the woods, boys. He weren't by himself."

"What do you mean?" I asked.

"Somebody came after him later, stayed to the side a little," he answered. "My guess is, he was followed."

"You got anybody else staying on your property?" Ben asked.

Hershel nodded his head.

"She ain't staying by my leave, but the Cat Hag's put up a tent way down past the white rock pool," he said. "Done checked, though. She's moved on. Likely back to her place down Gumlog way."

"Sure she ain't the one that followed Papa?" I said.

"Possible," he answered. He tugged at his beard as if trying to pull the luck from it. "Men's boot tracks, kind of deep for an old woman as light as her. But she's been known to wear men's boots before. Maybe if she was carrying something that made her heavy, it could have been her."

"Can you follow the tracks?" I asked.

Hershel shook his head, pulled at his beard some more. His wife brought him a mug of coffee.

"Duncan headed up the side of the Curahee," he said. "Woods too thick, not enough open flats. Not many places he could go, though. He'd either head straight up the path and end up on the bald side of the mountain, or he'd have to follow the creek north to Wildcat Fork."

"How far's Wildcat Fork from here?" Ben asked.

"Better'n six miles the way he'd have to go," he answered. "My bet is he's gone up top."

Chapter Twenty-Two

We thanked Hershel and his wife then left to drive around to the top of the mountain. In the early light the mist hid some of the Curahee from below. The stone face shone with morning dew, not yet burned off by the heat. Great patches of moss formed patterns across the rock. As a child, I tried to find faces and shapes in the moss. Every year, the shapes changed. Today, I thought it looked like a buffalo. We drove around the south side of the Curahee through mostly government-owned land. We turned north up the side of a deep ravine. The road followed one of the many streams which flowed off the slopes. We kept working our way to the top of the mountain, still dreading seeing the Sheriff's car pull up behind us.

People who lived near the mountain differed from those who lived just a few miles away. They had things in their yards, wooden birds whose wings spun in the wind, plastic deer and geese. We passed several houses whose driveways were lined with half buried tires painted white. Some whitewashed the trees up to their first branch. Cars sat in the yards, overgrown with months of grass and vines. These were people who lived as if they never expected anyone to drive by, much less visit their homes. They shopped in nearby stores, most just small cement buildings sporting a single gas pump out front. Their churches sat at the end of hidden dirt roads marked usually by a single plywood sign. The county school was the only real link to the rest of the community. Even there, the children of the mountain tended to cluster in small groups, often dropping out of school to work the textile plant or road crews.

I knew a few families on the mountain, none well. They were as invisible as the Davises. I knew, however, that I could stop at any of these houses, ask for help, and they would lay their lives on the line to take care of us. Even if it meant bucking Sheriff Bowers. I liked the feeling of the homes we passed, secure and steady. Heartland if ever there was one. Eccentric, odd, and reclusive, but good people to know when you're lost in the woods or need a church built.

The last time I came up this road I was looking for Katrina, needing to tell her about Daddy. At the top of the Curahee, a few high school kids had camped out the night before. Their campfire still smoldered, forming patches of haze which hung low to the ground in the morning air. Scattered about the stone face, five or six boys, some of whom I knew, stirred in their blankets. I avoided them, not wanting to discuss the fire, Daddy's death, or least of all why the Sheriff was looking for us. Ben went around and asked them if they heard or saw any sign of Papa. None of them did.

Pop Smith came out from a pup tent, slapped me on the back of the neck and belched. I had not expected to see him. His beard, more advanced than any of our peers, poked through in reddish stubbles making him appear much older. He looked as though he had not slept in days. He also smelled of stale beer and tobacco smoke. I asked if he'd seen Papa. Pop had worked in our chicken houses a few years back and knew Papa well.

"Haven't seen your Papa," he said. "You got trouble you need help with?"

"We're fine, thanks," I answered. "He wandered off last night. We think in this direction. Listen out for him, would you?"

"Sure thing, Roy," he said, slapped my neck again. "But we'll be leaving soon. Just as well. I didn't sleep at all last night."

I started to leave with Pop still talking. I knew he would tell me in great detail of all the debauchery they'd done last night. I did not want to know.

"You should have heard the Cat Hag last night," he said.

Ben and I stopped, turned back to him. Seeing our interest, Pop continued.

"We heard her coming, making that cat crying sound she always makes," he said. "Scariest thing you ever heard. Comes up the mountain, screaming, moaning, and making cat sounds. We never saw her, just heard her."

"Where'd she go?" I asked.

"Can't say," Pop replied. "Just glad it was away from here. Near dawn, she just stopped making noise. Hope she's gone back to Gumlog."

We thanked Pop and then asked him not to tell anyone he'd seen us. He did not bat an eye, like our whereabouts being secret was the most natural thing he could imagine. We maneuvered our way around the other campers without having to speak to anyone else.

"Think we should look around more up here?" I asked Ben.

"Papa would have seen the fires and heard these boys up here," Ben said. "If he'd wanted help, he would have come to them. If he's down below, or on the side of the mountain we'll never find him without help of our own."

"We can't just leave him," I said.

"Get in the car, Roy," Ben said. "We'll find Papa, but not until he wants us to find him. Remember, he took food and a flashlight. He didn't intend to come back to Hershel's for us. Knowing he's not up here is enough for me. Papa's hiding and he's got good reason. We'll just have to leave it at that."

"What about the Cat Hag. Why would she follow Papa?" I asked as I got into Ben's car.

"Woman's batty as they come," Ben answered, starting the car. "Some would say she don't need no reason to do nothing she does. Some would say she has a reason to do every crazy thing she does. But she followed him. Maybe coincidence. Maybe not. Could be she was just curious. But she's not known to hurt anybody so I think Papa's fine. But batty or not, the Cat Hag may well know something about what Papa's up to."

I noticed that Ben's grammar had deteriorated dramatically since he'd been home. He'd started to sound like the old Ben, before he got sophisticated.

"Where to?" I asked.

"I think we should find the Cat Hag," Ben said.

Chapter Twenty-Three

I sunk into the seat, afraid he would say that. But I knew he was right. Papa was gone, disappeared into the woods. Only person to be near him last night when he left was the Cat Hag. If we wanted to find him, we'd have to deal with her.

Ben headed west, nearly thirty miles out of the way to circle around Toccoa. We came upon the Interstate almost to Athens, then headed north. We took the Highway 17 exit, which later became Big A Road. We stopped at Randall's Place, a general store and gas station. Maurice Randal greeted us from behind the counter as we went inside.

The store was twice as big as it needed to be because it had once been a one-room elementary school. The store sat in the middle of the incorporated town of Avalon, population twenty-six. Only nine of the citizens were registered to vote. Maurice paid five of the voters fifty dollars apiece to vote to legalize the sale of beer in the town. The vote passed and Maurice hit it rich. The rest of the county was dry. People now could either cross the river into South Carolina for beer or visit Maurice. Most gave the business to Maurice.

We bought some sweet cakes and cans of juice for later, filled the car with gas, and paid Maurice. He offered us a good deal on the pickled eggs and pigs feet, but we declined. Every country store in Georgia had great jars of pickled eggs and pigs feet sitting somewhere close to the register. Never in my entire life had I ever seen anyone buy or eat one. Whatever embalming method they used would rival the Egyptians since the jars always looked the same, the feet never wrinkled and the eggs never bloated. They just sat there, year after year, soaking in the mysterious red liquid. I suspect only the drunk or those trying to cover the taste of raw corn whiskey ever actually ate them.

Ben took the next turn past Maurice's place and headed toward Gumlog, another metropolis of less than a dozen families. Not a town, I could never tell exactly what the Gumlog was. It consisted of five or six houses scattered in the woods along a dirty creek, no light or even a stop sign to signify a community. Gumlog was an area, probably the remnant of an old family compound. We turned up a dirt road with no sign. The road turned rough and dusty, deep tracks cut into the red clay. A few abandoned cars sat to the side making piles of rust. Now and then we saw a Coke sign tacked to a tree for no apparent reason except to sell soft drinks to lost souls.

We came to the bottom of a hill so steep we were not certain the car would make it. Thick blackberry briars crowded both sides of the road, more like a trail. We left the car and went on foot.

Every boy in Toccoa had seen the Cat Hag's house at least once. Clubs and gangs used it to initiate members by forcing them to try and steal one of the Cat Hag's cats. Local legends abounded about what the Cat Hag did to those she caught. I stole my cat when I was invited into the Letterman's Club last year. A senior handed me my assignment in a sealed envelope in front of a committee of other seniors. I had hoped for something like climbing the gym roof or rolling the principle's yard. But such choice assignments were not for the likes of me. They were reserved for the town people, those with cars and girl friends.

Jaybo Crawford drove me to Gumlog, handed me a burlap bag, and dropped me off miles back down from where Ben and I now stood. I walked in the dark along the creek following the road to the Cat Hag's house. It had been a cold, windy night in late November. The trees had lost their leaves and their bare branches whistled in the sky over me. Shapeless clouds intermittently covered a half moon, making the shadows come and go. It was all together a spooky night, something like you'd read about in a horror novel. I kept hearing things in the woods, funny crying sounds. I've spent more time in the deep woods than most folks, seen and heard just about everything that lived in them. Maybe it was the night, maybe it was fear of the Cat Hag's reported witchcraft. But that night, my ears heard things that did not belong in the North Georgia woods. I could not see anything, though it seemed something moved out of sight, just at the edge of the little light that filtered through the branches. Thought a couple of times I saw someone. I yelled, hoped members of the club were out there trying to scare me. I knew they were not. They'd be just as scared to be out here as me.

It took me almost two hours to find the Cat Hag's house. I saw it from a distance, faint light coming through the woods from a fire inside. I crept up the hill to the edge of the clearing and watched for a while. I heard cats inside, smelled them. I just needed one cooperative one to wander out of the house to me. If it did not, I would have to go inside. The light flickered in the windows. I kept seeing movement inside, like someone dancing without music. The wind whipped the smoke down the roof and across the yard. It smelled funny, like she was burning treated lumber or something that did not belong in a fireplace. It sent a chill up my spine and into my brain that settled one subject once and for all. There was no way, no force on Earth, that would make me go in that house on that night and take one of the Cat Hag's animals. Lettermen's Club or not, it was not going to happen even in the unlikely event that my legs would cooperate with the effort. I kept watching, kept hoping for some face-saving miracle to happen and end this night. Half an hour later, the door opened and half a dozen cats ran outside. I saw the Cat Hag, only a silhouette against the firelight, watching the cats scamper about the unkempt yard. I could not see her face, but her hair scattered in all directions like it was alive. Whatever she wore whipped about in the wind and made her seem huge, even more foreboding than anything I could dream. She said something to them about coming inside soon, it being cold and all. Then she shut the door.

An orange cat with stripes ran straight toward me like she'd known I was there all along. She stopped a foot from me and looked up as if she was expecting something. I picked her up and ran. The wind whipped at me and swung briars and twigs in my way. I pushed through them. I kept hearing the strange sounds around me, thought even that they'd gotten louder. I dropped the bag, but I just kept holding the cat, running faster. Once I tripped on a root, fell forward holding the cat up so's not to hurt her. She stayed there, passive, like a warm glove. I rose, ran some more. When I got to the main road into Gumlog, I stopped and walked. Someone was supposed to meet me there, take me back to town. No one showed. I kept walking.

Toward four in the morning, a man going home from a late night in Atlanta stopped and gave me a ride. He was drunk, kept swerving around the road. I asked if he wanted me to drive but he declined. It was the most dangerous ride I'd ever had without Katrina at the wheel. He dropped me off in front of my house. I put the cat in a chicken coup out back and went to bed. The next morning the cat was gone, the chicken coop door still closed. I never made it into the Letterman's Club.

I never dreamed I'd find myself again at the Cat Hag's house. Ben and I walked another hundred yards until the road disappeared into the overgrown yard of an unpainted shack surrounded by dozens of chicken wire pens. Black locust trees hung over the yard and shack with their poisonous bean pods swaying in the gentle breeze. Scary as the place looked at night, it was worse on this gray day. I could not even say why. Lots of things look scary at night. But if it's scary in the light of day, it's truly a place to avoid.

I'd never spoken to the Cat Hag, seen her only that once. Ben claims to have sold her a sack of lime from the store a few years ago. He told me she was a black lady with gray-blue eyes that grabbed you when she talked. Said her hair was white, frizzed out in every direction and that her voice sounded like a man's. I do not know if he was joshing me or not, but today, I sure wished he would keep such things to himself.

Maybe it was the tension. Maybe it was my imagination, but I'd swear something unnatural hung over that house. I looked back toward the car and everything seemed normal. When I looked toward the shack, the trees were smooth, almost glossy. The sky had a slight yellow tint to it, the sparse clouds vague shapes of faces and figures. There was no sound. The cats, hundreds by most accounts peered at us from within wire fences and made not a sound. No birds, no katydids, no frogs, no sound. It was as if the sound was absorbed by the shack and the Cat Hag trapped it, made it her own. I felt silly for thinking such things. But I swear I felt something unnatural watching us. If Ben was not there I'd have high tailed it home and never come back. The look on Ben's face told me he felt it too.

People talked about her often enough that I felt I thought I knew what to expect. Far as I could tell, no one knew her real name, how old she was, or where she came from. They said she walked stooped over, gray hair hanging in her face, hiding her features. But no one knew if she was stooped from age or if she were born that way. She wore gray, tattered clothing and a white shawl. From her pockets always stared a kitten or two. She spoke constantly to them in whispers. Sometimes she seemed to hear them answer. She had the magic to steal your soul, local people claimed. They said you should not look directly at her eyes. You should never cross her. People let her wander around, camp a day or so on their property as long as it was well away from houses. No one complained when she took a chicken or some garden vegetables. No one knew why she left her house to live for long periods in the woods. No one questioned her. Most just let her be.

What business would she have following Papa? If she knew anything about where he was, would she tell us? I had my doubts and plenty of fear. Even Nana warned us to stay away from the Cat Hag. Said the Cat Hag did not like people to crowd her unless she invited them. She never invited anyone we knew.

Ben pulled at my sleeve, urging me to follow him to the house. He tried to hide it, but he was afraid too. I could tell by the way his eyes kept darting about, looking at the bushes as if the Cat Hag would jump out at us any second. We walked up to the house and stood at the base of the steps for a minute. We hoped the Hag had seen us approach and would come out on the porch. The sides of the house were bare, no sign of paint or stain. No color at all. A couple of metal lawn chairs sat on the porch. An old washing machine sat to one end. Water stains on the floor boards told us she used the washer. Over us hung a few wind chimes that swayed in the breeze, enough to move, but not enough to make sound. A black and white cat, so fat I could barely believe it could move, sat at the front doorway and watched us. Another yellow one sat on a window sill. It jumped off, approached us, then sat at the top of the stairs and looked down at us. I wondered if it was the one I'd stolen last year. When we just stood there, it lost interest and wandered off to the side.

"It's better'n twenty miles to the Curahee," I said. "You ever see her driving a car?"

Ben shook his head.

"Then how's she supposed to be back yet?" I asked, chiding myself for not having already thought of this excuse for leaving.

"Somebody's feeding all these cats," he answered. "If not her, somebody."

Sure enough, scattered about the porch and some of the pens sat dozens of flat dishes with fresh food and water. Someone had been here today, probably within the hour. How the Cat Hag covered twenty miles of rough woods in such a short time, I could not guess. Maybe someone helped take care of the cats, probably not.

Ben and I eased slowly up the porch. The place smelled terrible, like stale cat dung. A crow sat on a dead pine and called to us. I would not have been surprised if the crow spoke to us by name and warned us away. The old wood creaked with each step and the yellow air seemed to get thicker. I knew this was no place for Roy and Ben, but we kept going.

"What do you boys want?" asked a voice from within the house.

I jumped so hard I almost wet my pants. Ben stepped onto the porch and pulled me up with him.

"Sorry to bother you, Ma'am," Ben said. His voice quivered slightly and I was none too reassured by the sound of it.

"Our grandfather got lost on Curahee Mountain last night," he continued. "We heard you were around so we thought you may have seen him."

"Come in, boys," she said.

Chapter Twenty-Four

We still could not see her.

"That's ok," I said. "We don't want to bother you none. If you know anything about our Papa, just tell us and we'll leave you be."

Silence for a moment that seemed like an hour.

"You won't bother me," she said. The door opened. We could not see around it.

"Come on in and we'll see if we can't find what you're looking for," she said.

Ben pulled the door the rest of the way open and then cautiously stepped into the threshold with me behind. We looked into the house but saw only shadows and shards of light from the windows. A cat bolted past us.

"Like we said, Ma'am," Ben said. "Our grandfather wandered off Hershel Cobb's place…"

"What were you doing on Hershel's place?" she asked, not letting him finish.

We peered into the corner in the direction of the voice. We saw her vague outline in the shadows.

"We were fishing," Ben said.

The instant the words left Ben's mouth, a cat screeched. We jumped back toward the door and noticed for the first time it was closed. I didn't remember closing it.

"Lucy doesn't like it when people lie," she said.

"We were hiding," I said.

Ben elbowed me in the ribs.

The Cat Hag chuckled.

"Hiding from what?" she asked.

Ben started to answer, checked himself, and then continued.

"We were hiding from the Sheriff," he said. "We didn't break the law. He's after us for something personal."

"Sheriff Bowers is an evil man," she said. "Perhaps I can help you with this personal thing he is after you over."

Her voice was calm and deliberate. It reminded me of a news anchor woman, educated, sophisticated but with a touch of the common. It did not fit her image, seemed maybe not to come from her at all. She stood in the corner with window light shining over her shoulder. It lit her gray hair, made it glow like a halo. She stood crooked, still, and seemingly lifeless, like a scarecrow or Halloween decoration.

"We can handle all that," Ben continued. "We just want to find our grandfather."

"What makes you think your grandfather is lost?" she asked.

"He left us at the barn to speak to Hershel Cobb, said he'd be right back," Ben said. "He never came back and Hershel never saw him. We found his tracks crossing a plowed field near where Hershel said you'd spent the night. We saw your tracks going in the woods after him."

"That all?" she said.

"Some kids were camping on the bald face of the Curahee," Ben continued. "They said they heard you making noises in the night. Papa had to come that way. Did you see him?"

"Tell me more about why the sheriff's after you," she said.

"Not meaning to be disrespectful, Ma'am," Ben said. "But I don't see how that's any concern of yours,"

"Maybe it's not," the Cat Hag answered. "But I somehow think your grandfather would want me to help you."

"How would you know that?" I asked.

The Cat Hag sighed, moved into the light. The straggled hair hid her face as usual.

"I owe Duncan Davis," she said. "I owe him whatever he needs now. He would want me to help."

"Owe him for what?" Ben asked.

"I don't see how that's any of your concern," she said, echoing Ben's words back to him.

Ben looked at me, then back at the Cat Hag. I nodded. I could not see how telling her about the killing, the attack on our house, and about Ebenezer Wiley could possibly hurt. Maybe this old woman could find a way to help us. In any case, it was obvious she was not going to talk to us about anything she may or may not have seen last night on the Curahee until we talked to her first.

She directed us to some bent-wood rocking chairs and we sat down near an empty fireplace. She drug an old stool over, sat down, and leaned her bent back against the stones. Ben started with Daddy's killing. I filled her in about the grave, the sheriff, and our visit to Lanona Kresse. We talked for more than half an hour, her interrupting us only to ask a small detail here and there. She seemed particularly interested in what we'd found out about Stenton Kresse. We did not tell her about the diary. When we finished out story, we found that the room had brightened and seemed a bit less frightening. Light now hit the Cat Hag squarely in the face and I saw her eyes for the first time. They were not what I expected at all. I could tell from the way Ben stole glances at her that he thought the same. She had kind, gray eyes that sparkled when she spoke. She brushed her hair back and I saw a face wrinkled and pitted by years of hard, lonely living. It was not the face of the evil witch I had expected, just one that seemed molded by bone crushing loneliness.

"You boys' family might be the only ones in these parts who didn't know about Stenton Kresse," she said.

"What are you saying?" Ben asked. "The whole town has been keeping a secret for the Kresse sisters for the past hundred years? You think we're the only ones that didn't know about him being a traitor and all?"

She nodded.

"It's not as hard as you might think," she answered. "First few years after the War, nobody wanted to talk about it, nobody really cared about the truth. They're just trying to keep their farms from the Carpet Baggers. A generation later, no one wants to know because they have reasons to keep things as they were. Next generation after that cares even less. Tell a lie often enough and it becomes the truth. Tell the truth only rarely, people think it's a lie."

"What lie?" Ben asks.

"Let me show you something," she said, ignoring his question.

She stood slowly, struggled against her stiff joints. We followed her into her kitchen. Cats lounged about on the counter. She took us down a short, bare hallway and stopped before a closed door.

"You must never speak of what I am about to show you," she said. She stood looking at us, waiting for us to respond.

Ben and I nodded our consent. I shuddered to think what could be behind the door. Maybe it was something of the magic folks say she possessed. Maybe the dried bodies of her relatives. You could bet I would never tell. You could bet more I did not really want to even know.

She opened the door and we entered. The room was dark until she pulled a chain. Light from a single bulb flooded the room. All about us were piles of papers and books, many of which were obviously of great age. At first they appeared randomly scattered. On closer inspection, they were organized by age, type, and some sort of system recorded on cardboard markers. On the wall hung swords and medals, pictures of men in uniform, and women in antebellum dresses.

"Got more history in this room than the Daughters of the American Revolution ever knew existed," she said proudly. "That courthouse is a comic store book compared to what you're looking at."

Ben walked to a stack of papers and started to pick one up. The Cat Hag grabbed his arm.

"Don't touch anything," she said. "I'll find what you want."

She smoothed the paper Ben had touched, stroked it like she would one of her cats.

"What should we be looking for?" I asked.

"What do you need to know?" she asked.

"We want to know how Ebenezer Wiley died," I asked.

"Afraid how he really died isn't history, son," she said. "That's a murder mystery that's been hidden so long history does not record it. But I suspect you know someone who can answer that question for you."

"Who might that be?" I asked.

"Duncan's Estelle knows more than she's letting on," she responded. "Ask me something that could possibly have been recorded. That's history."

"How did Stenton Kresse die," Ben asked.

"Ah, now that's a question you should have asked long ago," she said. "Let me see."

The Cat Hag bent over a stack of papers, obviously some sort of hand written catalog. She shuffled the papers about, then went to a far corner where she dug some more. A minute later she stood up with a paper in hand. She handed it to Ben who read it out loud.

Stenton Augustus Kresse is found guilty of treason against the Confederate States of America and will be hanged until dead before midnight, December 2, 1862.

He handed the document back to the Cat Hag who carefully replaced it.

"It's an order from the Confederate Army," Ben said.

He turned back to the Cat Hag.

"Another report with the same date said Ebenezer was hanged. Why would the people of Toccoa think Ebenezer was hanged as a traitor when in fact it was Stenton Kresse who was hanged?" he asked.

"Straight to the point," she responded. "Ask me history, boy. Don't ask me to interpret it. People have to do that for themselves. You included."

"What do you mean?" I asked.

She shook her head and retreated to a dark corner of the room.

"What do you mean?" Ben asked as well.

"I will find almost anything in the history of this part of the country, but I will not answer questions about what it means," she said. "Ask me of history. That I'll give you. What it means, you'll have to find for yourselves. If you weren't Duncan's kin, I wouldn't even do that."

Ben thought for a minute.

"Do you have any documents that show why Ebenezer was blamed for Stenton's crimes," Ben asked.

"That's history," the Cat Hag said.

She moved back to her archive, searched through a few more stacks of papers, then handed a folder to Ben. Ben glanced through it, came to a relevant part, and then began to read aloud.

"In order to provide a believable cover story that may flush out more spy activities and traitors to the Confederacy, a Yankee spy shall be executed in full view of select witnesses including the media. The media and witnesses shall be told, however, that it is Sgt. Ebenezer Wiley who is executed. I expect this to provide extraordinary hardship to Sgt. Wiley and his family. I personally shall contact Mrs. Wiley to explain the extreme need for secrecy and prudence of this action."

"It's signed General Beaufort Clemson," he said.

Ben lowered the paper and looked at the Cat Hag.

"So they hanged Stenton Kresse for a traitor but told people it was Ebenezer Wiley?" I asked.

"That's what is says," the Cat Hag answered.

"The ultimate cover story," Ben stated. "That explains a lot. Why Jane Wiley wouldn't tell anybody about Ebenezer fathering her last child, how folks in Toccoa thought Ebenezer the traitor and all."

Ben stared at the document and read a little more which only confirmed what we had just learned.

"How on earth did you come by these documents?" he asked.

The Cat Hag backed against the wall as if the question insulted her.

"Got them here and there, some from my parents, some from aunts long dead," she said.

"You've got a whole museum worth of stuff here," Ben said. "You should show these to someone, maybe a history professor in Athens."

"No!" she shouted, snatching the document from Ben's hands.

"These are mine to keep, mine to show as I please," she said.

She now had a wild look about her, more the Cat Hag I had expected. She carefully replaced the document into its pile, returned the archive sheet to its place and pointed to the door.

"I'd like you to leave now," she said.

"But what about Papa?" I asked. "We still don't know where he is."

She pointed to the door.

"You got more than you know how to handle," she said, still pointing at the door.

Ben and I walked down the hallway. It had grown lighter as the day progressed. Hotter too. The air was muggy, still, and acrid from the dozens of cats which scurried across the floor.

"What about our grandfather?" Ben asked when we reached the door.

The Cat Hag pointed to the door. I got nervous, not knowing if we should risk her wrath by pushing her for more information. We started to open the door, but Ben wheeled around, pointed his finger at the old lady's chest.

"Do you know anything about our grandfather or not?" he shouted.

For a moment I thought he might strike her. The Cat Hag stood motionless, seemingly unperturbed by Ben's boldness.

"Do you have reason to think Duncan Davis wants to be found?" she said quietly.

Again the coolness and hint of education in her voice struck me as out of place. A gray cat wrapped itself around her ankle and purred loudly. Other cats peered from the darkness. They seemed to be watching us closely.

"Just tell us if you know anything," I pleaded, pulling Ben a step away from the motionless figure. She stood staring at us, like she was trying to measure our salt. The kindness had left her eyes. She took a deep breath and her face softened a bit.

"I know much you would not wish to know, much you would die to know, young ones," she said. "Your grandfather was on the Curahee last night. He was seen. I don't think he wants you to find him just yet."

"Did he tell you so?" I asked.

"Didn't have to," she said. "You had better stay away from the Curahee. It holds many secrets of its own. Perhaps Duncan Davis has gone to steal one of them for himself, use it in his fight against the Kresse family."

"We don't want to fight anyone," I said. "But someone killed our Daddy last week. Shot him dead in his own store. Papa thinks it's the Kresses or someone they put up to it. Now he's gone, you won't tell us where he is, and I don't know what to do."

I was on the verge of tears. When you're going on six feet six inches tall, there is no graceful way to cry.

"I heard of your father's death," the Cat Hag said softly. "He was a good and kind man. Good to animals and people alike. I watched him every Christmas sneak up the hill to give extra feed to the cows and your old roan horse. It speaks well of a man that he's kind to animals when he thinks no one is watching. He gave them Christmas. A man you should imitate, your Daddy."

"We need to find Papa," I said. "If he gets killed, don't know how the family'll stay together."

"Your Papa can take better care of himself than you know," the Cat Hag said. She reached up, almost had to stretch on her toes, and put a withered hand on my shoulder.

"Your Papa will find you when it's time," she said. "No harm has come to him, none will. I shall see to it."

"So you're not going to help us find him," Ben said.

The Cat Hag shook her head. The stringy hair swayed back and forth, again hiding her features.

"You have a more important job than bothering your Papa," she said. "Lanona Kresse has something you must find and take to your grandmother."

Ben looked at me and raised an eyebrow as if to discount the Cat Hag's words.

"Besides the land her ancestors stole, what on earth could Lanona have that Nana needs?" Ben asked

"Lanona holds a piece of history," the Cat Hag continued. "History that belongs to me. Truth that belongs to Estelle Davis, your grandmother."

"Would you speak plainly for us?" I asked.

"Somewhere in that cold house of hers, Lanona Kresse has hidden away a leather pouch with the seal of the State of Georgia. It is an old pouch, made and used during the Great War. In it is the final key you need to bring justice for Ebenezer Wiley and your grandfather out of hiding."

"And just how are we supposed to find and get this pouch?" Ben asked, again he raised his brow. The Cat Hag, if she noticed the gesture, ignored it.

"Yeah," I said. "Besides, how do you know she has this thing?"

The Cat Hag stepped back, turned away from us for a moment as if considering how much she should tell us.

"The pouch belongs to me," she said, turning back and raising her withered face to the light from the door.

"My family..." she trailed off as if thinking of family gone, normalcy lost. "My family keeps things. Even before America was America, even back in the old country, we kept things. I don't know why. It was like we were bred to it. We kept things of history, records of all kinds. All the children were trained to consider themselves the keepers of truth, hidden, useless truth as often as not. But truth just the same. They died away, one by one, leaving all this for me to manage. If I told you how long I have been keeping these things, you would think me more mad than you do now. But I have them. You've seen some of what I have. I have things about governors, senators, even a president or two, all cataloged here and other places around this county in places no one will ever find. The history and my cats are the only true friends I have. Lanona Kresse's grandmother took something that should have stayed in my keep. She and her cronies harassed and degraded my mother while I was still in her womb. But we never forgot. Never. You boys get that pouch and all will be set right. But you must promise me one thing."

She looked at us, waiting for agreement. Ben and I nodded as if we could possibly say, no.

"The pouch belongs to me and no other," she said. "After you have found it, show it to Estelle, and then return it to me. Agreed?"

Ben and I nodded again, not at all certain what we had just agreed to.

"Now go away from here," she said. Her voice held no hostility, just a simple command she expected to be obeyed. We did.

Chapter Twenty-Five

Ben and I all but ran down the steps. I turned to look back but the door was already shut. We ran back to the car, back to air without the smell of cats, a sky that was blue, not yellow. When I jumped into the car it was as if a demon left my shoulders. Ben started the car and spun the tires turning around. He was almost to the main road by the time either of us could speak. Our encounter with the Cat Hag seemed like a shared nightmare neither of us wanted to admit we had seen.

"How are we supposed to find an old pouch belonging to Lanona Kresse?" I asked when we were a mile or so away.

"It doesn't belong to her," Ben said. "It was stolen. You heard her."

"Stolen or not," I said. "Even if she still has it, even if she hasn't burned or buried it, even if it's in her house right now, how in the world are we supposed to get it?"

"Don't know," Ben responded. "But the Cat Hag knows plenty, that's for sure. If she says Papa and Nana need it, if it brings the people who killed Daddy what they deserve, then we'll find it."

I sat back in the seat. A steel spring poked through the upholstery into the base of my spine. I ignored it, as if the discomfort would ease my frustration. Daddy killed, Papa vanished into the forest, a crazy old hag giving us instructions to steal from the very people likely responsible for all our troubles. I did not think it could get any worse. I was wrong.

Ben drove the back roads, down to Highway 123, coming into Toccoa from the northeast. The road cut through Toccoa, crossed Big A Road, and headed directly toward the Curahee. At first I thought Ben intended to go back to the mountain to look for Papa. He had a determined look on his face I did not like. We would be out all night searching, I judged by the look. It did not matter that Papa was hiding and may not want us to find him. It did not matter that we had no chance of finding him anyway. Ben's look says we were going to try something until it works.

Ben surprised me when he turned left at the Clover Farm Store and onto Big A Road headed toward the Office.

"Where're we going?" I asked.

"Got to find the pouch," he said.

"You mean we're going to the Kresse's house?" I asked, hoping he would say no.

"That's where it is, that's where we're going," he answered. The look hardened.

I was temporarily relieved when Ben drove past the Kresse house. Lanona sat out front, did not appear to notice us. I thought it was a foolish risk, driving right by their house, and I told Ben.

"Sheriff's got no call to be after us," Ben said. "He'd be after Papa. Nana maybe. Not us."

I was not reassured. From what I had seen, he would as soon shoot us for spite. At the least he would try to hold us to get to Papa.

"Got to get that pouch," Ben repeated.

He was pale, sweating. He did not look at me when he spoke. Foolish as it sounds, I worried that the Cat Hag had put a hex on him and made him hers. I thought it best to go along.

We pulled up to the Office. The yellow police tape still circled the building. We parked out behind the number two chicken house where no one could see, then walked back to the Office. Ben went inside by a back window whose lock had long since rusted away, then let me in the side door. A few rats scurried across the floor. Ben found a flashlight and a bolt cutter.

"We may need these things," he explained. "We'll wait until dark, then you and I have to get the pouch."

We were about to go back up the hill when two cars pulled up. We crawled out the window, only to see our escape route cut off by two approaching figures. They had not seen us, so we slipped into the crawl space under the office. We heard voices above, one clearly the sheriff, one maybe the deputy. We could not tell what they said, though it was clear they thought we had been in the building. Soon they started calling our names. They called Papa's name too. We felt better knowing they had not captured him.

As my eyes adjusted to the light, I looked across the dirt floor. Ben and I had played there as children, often killing rats for Papa's five-cent bounty. The entire floor was peppered with rat holes. In my childhood I had always thought it looked the way I pictured a prairie dog town. From each hole the black furry face of a wharf rat protruded, slowly at first, then sensing no danger they came all the way out. Within a couple of minutes the floor seemed to undulate with dozens if not hundreds of them. I thought Papa had better raise his rat bounty.

Several rats ran across my boots. I kicked at them only to have Ben poke me in the ribs and signal me to be quiet. The people above us broke in the side door and entered the office. Lights flicked on and filtered through the floor boards. It only made our situation worse as the rats were now in full view. They took little notice of us, content to fight for seeds and flakes of feed that fell through the cracks. One particularly large rat sat up on its hind legs beside my left knee and sniffed the air, trying to figure out what we were. I raised my hand preparing to strike it if it decided to taste my leg but it turned and ran away. The others hesitated briefly, looked at me, and then went on about their business.

After a few minutes the lights went off and we heard the people leave. The cars pulled out of the drive, scattering pebbles behind them. Ben and I crawled from under the building and started to walk away.

Something happened just then that took me back to a memory at Big A Elementary School. In the sixth grade, Marsha Ripley was a big, somewhat brutal girl. She was stronger, faster, and more ruthless than any of her male counterparts, including me. One afternoon in late May, we were playing a rowdy game of touch football. The sun beat down, the red clay dust rolled off the ground in clouds and settled on us like pastel paint, streaked by drops of sweat. Marsha ran, blocked, and tackled, in rare form. Girls did not wear pants in those days, so Marsha's legs were skinned and scraped from her many falls. The boys' jeans offered adequate protection. She was on her way to her third touchdown, with me and the Hadderel brothers in hot pursuit, when she suddenly slowed to a walk then stopped. Her eyes rolled back in her head and she fell to the ground. I'll never forget the sound she made as her head jerked back and forth in the dirt and spit foamed up out of her mouth. Marsha's fit revealed her to be the only epileptic I'd ever known. We found out later her father had lost his job with the Forest Service and she had not had any medicine to take for a couple of weeks. I flashed back to that school yard and Marsha as I watched Ben that night behind the Office.

We were only a few feet away from the building when Ben dropped the bolt cutter and flashlight. Suddenly he started making the same sounds that Marsha had made on the playground four years ago. I thought how I should have known if my own brother was epileptic and cussed our family's love of secrets. Only thing was, Ben stayed on his feet, kept making the sound.

I thought surely he would fall any time and start foaming at the mouth. I kept scooting around behind him to catch him. Out teacher had said the stress of the game and heat set off Marsha. I kept thinking how much stress Ben and I were under, wondered if maybe it'd make him have a fit too. Ben then let out a wail and started cussing. By now the light had mostly gone and it was hard to see what he was doing. He appeared to be jumping up on alternate feet and grabbing his left thigh. Certainly, he was not having a fit and I thought maybe he'd been shot again. Seemed odd I had not heard the gun, though.

I grabbed his shoulders and tried to calm him, but he shook me off. He was attempting to say something, but the whispers sounded more like wheezes, the kind a sow makes when she gives birth, no longer like Marsha at all.

"What's wrong?" I whispered.

I tried again to steady him but he just kept jumping, grabbing his thigh, and wheezing. Finally I understood what he was trying to say.

"Rat!" he wheezed.

Ben stopped jumping, but in his tight fist through the fabric of his jeans he held a lump within inches of his crotch. With his free hand he unbuttoned his pants, pulled down the zipper and climbed out. This is not the first rodent to join a Davis in his pants. We regularly held rat killings in the chicken houses. The preferred technique is to pull the tractor next to a hole, put a stove pipe from the tractor exhaust to the hole, and choke the engine. I have always found it great sport to pop the carbon monoxide intoxicated rats with bricks, sticks, or lead pipes as they clambered from the smoky holes. Standing too close to the hole sometimes resulted in the confused rat entering the dark opening made by your pants leg. It always seemed prudent to grasp the creature while he was still in the leg portion of your pants. Despite having not worked the farm in several years, Ben's reflexes were intact and he caught the rat just before it became too intimate with his anatomy. Obviously, the surprise visit from the rat brought on his imitation of Marsha's seizure.

He stepped from his jeans, then let go with his fist. His tight grip had squeezed the rat to death and he had to shake it from his pants. He stood there in his boxer shorts for a minute, trying to regain his breath and composure. He kicked the rat toward a ditch, and then sat on the ground to put his pants back on.

Chapter Twenty-Six

When Ben was fully clothed again, we headed up the hill. On and off I fell into fits of laughter, cut short by a hard punch to the shoulder or stomach. I told him how closely he resembled an epileptic girl, bringing more punches as the light began to fade.

The homes of the Kresse sisters was at least two miles away. Ben and I crossed Big A Road, turned up a dusty dirt trail which wound around a junk yard toward the Brown family's house, a couple of hundred yards up a low hill. Darkness fell fast while we walked. We turned north just short of our burned home and crossed a series of corn patches and small pastures, and climbed one barbed wire fence after another. Dogs barked when we came too close to their houses. I stepped in a pile of cow manure that I hoped would come off in the grass while we walked.

No wind stirred the evening air. Lightning bugs flickered across the fields by the hundreds. Low clouds hid the moon and stars, reflecting lights from downtown Toccoa, six miles north. Lanona Kresse's house would be the first we came to as we approached from a small wooded area. We slowed as the forest thinned near her house. To our left, an old smoke house, not used in my lifetime, sat with its side opened by a long gone windstorm. Formosa trees lined the edge of her yard. Fortunately, Lanona had no dogs. She did, however, have a cantankerous flock of guinea fowl that could alert you to the presence of strangers more effectively than any hound. We stopped at the edge of the woods to look for the fowl. Thinking they would likely roost behind the smokehouse, Ben and I stepped cautiously into the yard. We stopped behind a giant oak to listen for activities.

I did not know the time but thought it was likely around nine o'clock. The Kresses, like most Georgians over the age of forty, would likely be in bed by now. Ben had not spoken much since his encounter with the rat. I still was not sure what he intended to do, but I knew I would not like it. I kept having visions of the Cat Hag and Ben acting like she had hexed him. But I had no choice but to go along. Ben intended to find that pouch or die trying and he would have no problem having me die with him or maybe even for him.

We eased slowly around the back of the house, all the while looking for roosting guinea that would give us away. We heard a short "put-put" sound behind the smoke house, the kind of sound roosting turkeys or guinea fowl make, and were relieved that they were not near the house. Ben flattened himself against the brick wall while I hid behind a flowering bush. We listened but heard no other sounds. Even the insects and tree frogs seemed muted. The clouds thickened, stifling what little light we had. We could barely see the outline of the white back porch and had to feel our way along its side. When we stepped on the porch steps, the old boards creaked. We both stopped for a minute listening for sounds from inside. Nothing, no light, no sound. Ben leaned the bolt cutter against the wall and eased forward. I never did know what he had intended to cut with them.

The porch floor was a cement slab which made no sound as we crept to the back entrance. The smell of cantaloupe, beans, and drying peppers filled the air. Suddenly I was quite hungry. The Cat Hag, the rat infested crawl space, and the circuitous walk here had taken all day. Mrs. Cobb's breakfast had long since been used and I was starving. As if on cue, my stomach began to rumble. Ben looked back at me, put his fingers to his lips as if I could hush my stomach. It churned and reminded me of my hunger. I tried not to think of it and hoped my guts would quiet down. I needed to pee.

The screened door was not latched and we slipped onto the porch. Ben tried the back door. It was locked. We then tried the windows one at a time. A window over the washing machine was unlatched so we quietly raised it and crawled inside to Lanona's kitchen.

I have stepped on rattle snakes that tried to bite through my leggings, I have slipped on rocks at the edge of hundred foot waterfalls, faced rabid dogs, and seemingly rabid football players. Later in life, I was shot during a botched robbery, shot again during a failed military mission. I felt fear all those times. However, at no time in my life then or since have I felt terror as I did at that moment. Toccoa has a few mystical figures in its complex social order. The Cat Hag was by far the oddest and most feared. The Lanona sisters came a close second, due mainly to their aloofness, old family history, and the economic power they wielded over so much of the town. Here we were, at the urging of the Cat Hag, breaking into the home of Lanona Kresse to find some Civil War relic. If the demons did not get me, Lanona would call the Sheriff to shoot us. Or if the mood struck her right, she would just shoot us herself. I was scared, almost to paralysis. If my legs had not been so stiff from terror, they would have shaken loud enough to wake the dead. My heart thumped in my chest and I had to remind myself to breathe. Every shadow seemed menacing. Every breath I took sounded loud and alarming.

I began to imagine I could hear whispers echoing through the old house. Ghosts of the Kresse sister's husbands come to complain to the living. Ghosts of Stenton Kresse come to protect his name. Ghosts of Ebenezer Wiley to restore his. Terror came to me that night as I had never known and would never know again. Ben pulled at my arm and forced me to take a step. My head was swimming. What little vision I had in the dark, closed in around me. Only good thing that happened was that as Ben pulled me along I was so afraid, my stomach twisted in knots and stopped rumbling. I just hoped I did not vomit.

We passed through the kitchen into the dining room. As my eyes adjusted further, I saw an old, oak table set with silver candlesticks. I brushed my head against a chandelier and it made a slight tinkling sound. We stood frozen until it stopped and listened for signs that Lanona had awakened. Nothing.

We stepped into a long hallway. A grandfather clock ticked loudly at the end toward the front door. A polished banister led upstairs where we believed Lanona would be sleeping-- at that moment I thought, possibly in a casket surrounded by dirt from the Motherland.

I stopped. Ben continued a couple of more steps then turned to look at me. In the darkness, hoping he could see, I raised my hands and shrugged as if to ask, "where now?" Ben shrugged in response. In another time or place I would have punched him. He signaled me to follow. I stood my ground, knowing full well that this was a bad time to back out. He waved me to follow again. This time I came after him. The brief rebellion calmed me slightly and I no longer feared my heart would explode. But I had a terrible urge to empty my bladder.

Ben stepped around a wide doorway into what was probably the formal sitting room. He looked around, pulled the flashlight out and clicked it on. The beam instantly focused our attention and seemed to make the surrounding darkness even darker. He shined the light on an old piano with its lid closed. We saw a table covered with a white, knit doily; mantle with pictures, and a sofa. In a corner by the front window was a rocking chair. He shined the light toward it.

In the rocking chair, still as death, sat Lanona Kresse. Ben flicked the light off and we both stood quiet, expecting her to shoot us, scream at us, maybe turn us into lizards. I was so frightened I do not think my feet were in but the lightest contact with the floor so a puff of air could have floated me out the door. Lanona had us. We were dead, doomed to have her drag us to hell.

I turned, prepared to run, when Ben grabbed my arm. As my eyes adjusted to the darkness again, I saw him put a finger to his lips and signal for silence. I wanted to scream, run, give Lanona Kresse a new front doorway.

Ben gently turned me around, pointed to Lanona. He brought his mouth to my ear and whispered as gently as the beat of a moth's wing.

"She's asleep," Ben said.

I do not know what was worse. Wondering if Lanona had laid in wait for us, or wondering if she would wake up and kill us. We listened a minute. In the darkness we heard her breathing. It was shallow, labored breathing. Something people do when they're dying. But she was definitely asleep and did not know we were in the house. In the distance a car horn beeped and someone spun their tires, probably teenagers showing off. I wished I was with them. Lanona's breathing changed, became softer for a few breaths. She stirred slightly, then started again with the labored sound. She sat there in the dark, thinking she was alone, sleeping secure in her place in the world.

Ben signaled for me to follow him. Back in the hallway I pointed to the door. Ben shook his head. He was not leaving without the damned pouch. He started sneaking up the stairs. Each step made a creak, each step I knew would wake Lanona. But Ben kept stepping, me after him. If she stirred, we did not see her. If she heard us, we had no sign. We kept walking, creaking up the stairs. At that moment I hoped Lanona was deaf as a river rock.

We made it to the second floor without getting shot, to that date the greatest miracle of my young life. We stopped and listened for Lanona. At first we heard nothing. Then we barely discerned the faint sound of her breathing. Ben went into the first room. I stood at the top of the stairs, told myself I was watching for Lanona when in reality I did not want to see in any of those rooms. I kept having visions of every cheap horror movie I ever saw with ghosts living in mirrors and closets. I heard Ben shuffle around in the room for nearly ten minutes. His flashlight bounced off the wood paneling of the hallway onto the dozen or so paintings. The paintings were all of women and carried some vague resemblance to Lanona, all ugly and cruel. All watching me. I remembered a movie where a ghost lived in a painting and could reach out and pull you in to it, drag you to eternal damnation. Thinking of it made the paintings look more real, seem almost to breath. Somewhere I remember that the ghost in the paintings could drag you to hell if you looked in their eyes so I didn't.

Ben came out, shook his head at me, then went to the next room. Another fifteen minutes, another shake of the head. The third room took nearly half an hour, or so I judged by the number of times the grandfather clock downstairs chimed. The clock struck a single chord on the quarter-hour. I do not know why anyone would want to listen all day to such a thing.

The last room looked out over the front yard. Its door seemed larger, darker than the others. I assumed it was Lanona's room. Ben went inside. The door creaked slightly when he opened it. I watched for Lanona.

Downstairs a light flicked on. I could not tell what room it was but I suspected it was the sitting room. Lanona was awake. I was going to die.

I floated, or so it seemed, to the bedroom and blew through my teeth twice. Ben appeared before me with his flashlight between us. It made shadows on his face that looked monstrous.

"I think she's coming!" I whispered.

Chapter Twenty-Seven

Ben grabbed my arm, pulled me into the bedroom. Just as we reached the door, a light over the stairwell clicked on. We saw Lanona's shadow on the wall as she walked up the stairs. I thought I saw the top of her head as Ben eased the door closed. If she heard us, she had certainly armed herself.

We slumped to the floor against the door, listening to the sound of Lanona's hard shoes. We heard her reach the top of the steps, pause, then turn toward us, or so I imagined it. We braced ourselves against the door. She walked past us to the last bedroom Ben had searched. This was not her room, though it seemed it should have been. I do not think I breathed until I heard her close the door to the other bedroom.

We sat there a while, listening to the sounds of Lanona prepare for bed. We heard her talking to herself, using different voices as if to have a conversation. A couple of minutes later the talking stopped. We waited a few more minutes in the dark. Our breathing sounded as loud as a train horn, but we heard nothing from Lanona's room. A few agonizing minutes later we heard a light snort which turned into a regular snoring sound. Finally, Lanona slept.

Ben turned on the flashlight, held his hands over the lens to make the beam softer and not so bright. We looked around the room. It was obviously a girl's bedroom. The furniture and decorations reminded me of Nana's room, mostly pictures, old furniture, and doilies. He looked in the closet and found nothing but old clothes and a disassembled sewing machine. He looked under the bed and through the dresser, nothing. At the foot of the bed sat an old pineboard chest.

Ben got on his knees next to the chest and eased it opened. On top was an old dress, something Scarlet O'Hara should have worn. Ben set it aside. Beneath it was a coat from an obviously old Confederate uniform, covered with medals and pins. Ben gave me the light and held up the coat. It seemed in perfect shape. He laid it carefully, almost reverently, on the bed.

Ben took out a box or two, inspected their contents of mostly old money and pictures, then set them one by one on the bed beside the uniform. He then reached deep in the chest, rummaged for a moment, and pulled out a tattered, leather bag the size of a brief case.

Neither of us could believe our luck. He had found the Cat Hag's pouch. We knew it without even looking inside. In gold leaf letters on the front was the words "State of Georgia" surrounded by gold leaf branches.

Ben clutched the pouch to him, seemed at first to say something, and then started for the door. He stopped and went back to the bed. He carefully repacked the chest the way it had been before we opened it, minus the pouch, then he slowly closed the lid. We went to the door, paused for a minute. Hearing no sound he opened the door and we crept downstairs. I was floating again, not really sure my feet touched the ground. Still the floor creaked, threatened to wake Lanona. I turned silently toward the kitchen, all the time fighting the urge to run. I thought Ben was behind me, but when I turned he was not there. I backtracked and then heard him in the sitting room. I looked in to see him standing in front of the rocker in which Lanona had been sleeping. The pouch was tucked under his left arm and his hands were in front of him. Just then I heard the sound of water dripping. Ben turned around and zipped up his pants.

I floated faster than ever to the kitchen, out the window, then across into the woods. I did not care if Ben came or not, I was getting out of that house. We had guaranteed Lanona would know someone was there, guaranteed that if she looked hard she would know the pouch was stolen. I wanted to relocate somewhere west of the Mississippi River, maybe west of California. I grabbed the unused bolt cutter and Ben followed me. He seemed to float as well, seemed happy, bouncy as we ran to the woods. He grabbed the bolt cutter from me and waved it over his head like a flag.

We were ten feet from the relative safety of the dark woods when the world exploded. All about us vague shapes crash to the ground and through the brush, the sound of bodies moving so fast they made wind sounds. In the briefest of instances a mind can register, I thought I had been blown up by a land mine, engulfed and sent to hell by demons, attacked by the Sheriff's henchmen, or sucked up into the ionosphere by a tornado. An instant later I realized we had stumbled upon the roosting guinea fowl. They scattered in all directions, making clacking sounds as they flew. We left them behind and ran even faster. How we negotiated the trees in darkness and at full throttle, I could never explain. I ignored branches that pounded me in the face and tore at my clothes. I ran, dodged the larger branches, and flew into the deep woods away from Lanona, away from the demons.

Once we were out of earshot of the house I stopped and wrestled Ben to the forest floor. He had always been stronger than me, but this time he let me take him down and sit on his chest, the pouch between us.

"Why did you pee of Lanona Kresse's chair?" I asked.

Even as I said it I had to suppress a belly laugh.

"Just wanted her to know what it's like to get pissed on," Ben said. He laughed out loud. In the darkness, it could have been Papa's laugh.

"I can't believe you did that," I said. "She'll know it was us. She'll get even, you know. Mark my word."

"How's she going to do that?" Ben asked.

He wiggled out from under me and sat with his back against a pine tree. We both knew we would likely get chiggers sitting here this time of the year, but we did not care. We had just robbed and defamed Lanona Kresse. We took her past and her pride all in one night. I began to feel glad Ben had peed on her chair, wished I had done so myself.

"This thing's so old, she might not know the significance of it, or even notice it's missing. If she does, she can't tell anybody we took it," Ben continued. "You heard the Cat Hag. The Kresses stole it themselves. Likely she doesn't want anybody to know what's in here. She'll never tell."

"She'll tell the Sheriff," I said. "Whatever's going on, he's already in it."

"So what," Ben said. "The Sheriff's already after us. How many times can he shoot us?"

I leaned against the tree next to Ben, feeling very much the outlaw, more strangely, I found myself starting to like it, now that we were safely away.

"Let's see what's in there," I said.

"Let's wait 'till we get where there's some light," Ben said. "Can't see enough here to read anything. Besides, I'd hate to lose something important out here in the dark."

I reached over to an arrow weed, pulled off a cluster of the spears and chucked them at Ben's leg. A couple of them stuck. He flicked them away.

No history worth remembering, no blood worth saving.

Lanona's words seemed foolish tonight. We had created history, risked our own blood. If nothing else happened from all this, we had made our own history, Ben and me. We would never fear the Kresses again. We sat for a moment, felt the chiggers wind their way to our private parts, caught our breath, and reveled in the glory of what we had just done. We had won against Lanona Kresse. We left her an unmistakable sign of our contempt, taken what she should never have had, and gotten away with it. I put my arm around my brother Ben there in those dark woods and grinned like a possum.

For a minute, I forgot that Daddy was killed, Papa was missing, and we would likely run from Lanona's wrath for the rest of our natural lives. We were victors, heroes, my brother and me. I wanted to remember that moment forever, remember the feeling, that even then I knew would fade. Like many memories of glory, this one would grow fainter and come to me only when summoned, and then only appear as a shadow of what we felt that night. Ben and I wallowed in it for a few minutes that seemed like forever.

Chapter Twenty-Eight

When we were breathing normally again, we got up and made the trek back to the Office. Only an occasional distant car or dog broke through the silence. The air was thick and wet, filled with the scent of farms and rotting plants. It sat heavy in my lungs. I saw Ben well enough to tell he was sweating heavily as he walked along, clutching the prized pouch. Once in a while he stretched the shoulder where the bullet had grazed him.

By the time we got back to the office, both of us were so tired we had to drag ourselves over the last fence. We watched from behind some pokeberry bushes for a few minutes to make sure no one was waiting for us, and then we crossed the road to find the car. Minutes later we headed back down the road toward the interstate. Ben said he wanted to get to Atlanta with the pouch, give it to Nana, and see how they might find Papa.

I looked at the pouch on the seat between us. It lay there, a black hole in the darkness, but the brightest trophy I ever saw. We drove through the tiny town of Martin, and crossed the tracks. No one followed us. We caught the interstate just short of Lavonia and headed south. Atlanta was two hours away. Ben was not sure he could find Aunt Fanny's house, just knew she lived in Alpharetta, a suburb on the northern edge of the growing metropolis. She had just moved there and we'd visited only a couple of times. We hoped he would recognize the correct turns when we got there. When we were miles south of any of the Toccoa exits I opened the glove box so its light would turn on. I opened the pouch. Inside were a couple of medals, letters, and a stack of papers, some bearing official appearing wax seals. Ben kept glancing at me, prodding me to be careful as if the contents were fragile or dangerous.

I could not read the papers so I put them back. Whatever was important in the pouch would take some study in good light to find. I fingered the medals a minute, and then put them back too.

Ben pulled us over outside of Athens to a truck stop beneath a giant University of Georgia Bulldog billboard. We filled the car with gas and went inside. Ben carried the pouch. The lady at the counter brought us flapjacks, thick bacon, and black coffee of the type truck drivers too long on the road use to stay out of the ditches. We gobbled the food, looked at the pouch and wondered what was so important about it. The Cat Hag had said Nana needed something inside it. She would know what to do. Nana or Papa always know what to do. We did not look inside again that night. We felt we had no right, heroes or not.

It was well past two in the morning when we finally found Aunt Fanny's house. She lived at the bottom of a long hill only a couple of miles off the interstate. Even in the dark, Ben found it easier than he had expected. We pulled into the driveway before a darkened house. A couple of beagles began barking. A minute later a light went on in one end of the house, then the porch light came on. I saw a face peek out from the window. I opened the door so the inside car light would show them who we were.

"Stay where you are, keep your hands in sight, and identify yourselves," a voice from behind me bellowed. I turned around, almost expecting to see Sheriff Bowers. In the darkness I saw a large black man in a State Patrolman's uniform. He had his hand on his holstered gun.

"We're Ben and Roy Davis," I said. "This is my aunt's house."

The patrolman stood his ground.

Aunt Fanny stepped onto the porch, saw us, then waved the patrolman off. He backed away in the dark but kept eyeing us like we were dangerous. Aunt Fanny held the door open and we went inside.

"You boys ok?" Aunt Fanny asked. Her real name was Frances. We began to call her Aunt Fanny years ago as a joke, but the name stuck. She probably hated it but was much too good natured to complain.

We told her we were fine but we had lost Papa. She insisted we start at the beginning. We filled her in on what had transpired since the house fire. Half way through the story, Nana came in and we started over. It took us nearly an hour to bring them up to date. We left out the part about pissing on Lanona's chair. When we finished, we handed the pouch to Nana.

She took it in her withered hands and felt the leather, rubbed her fingers over the gold seal.

"What's in it?" I asked.

"The Cat Hag told you to get it?" she asked.

I nodded.

"Nana," I persisted. "What's in this thing? We risked our lives to get it to you. The least you can do is tell us what it is."

She kept fingering the pouch. Finally she opened the flap and pulled out the contents. She carefully laid out the medals and pictures. Then she took a few of the documents and stacked them together. Finally she pulled out a folder containing the official appearing papers we had already seen.

"This is it," Nana said. She whispered the words almost as if to say them loudly would break a spell.

"This is what, Nana?" I asked.

"This is the proof we needed to clear Ebenezer's name, restore our family honor and lands," she said. "As a child the Cat Hag told me this thing existed. Now you've brought it to me."

"How do you know the Cat Hag?" I asked.

"Oh, we've known her and her sister, and her family, from as far back as I can remember," she said.

She saw the puzzled look on my face when she mentioned the Cat Hag's sister.

"Most people don't know about her twin," Nana said. "Their names, by the way, are Meriweather and Grace. Grace likes to live in the fields and woods. She only comes inside during the coldest weather. She's the one most people see roving around. She collects things, mostly documents and newspapers. Meriweather lives at the old family home. She's the one you met. That family knows more secrets than you can imagine. They horde historical documents, newspaper clippings, everything you can legally get hold of. Some odd family inclination that goes back generations, even before they immigrated to America. Her mother used to speak of her family recording the deeds of kings and princes. Their own family legend is that they are of a line of people bred and trained to keep the history of feudal tribes, then monarchs. Meriweather told me once her family lived in stone huts on the coast of Ireland. Claimed they kept records for Saint Patrick, himself. I don't know about any of that. I really think they're just a little odd. Course, the only people that aren't just a little bit crazy are people we don't know very well."

That explains how the Cat Hag could be at the Curahee one day and her house the next without driving, I thought. We tracked Grace at Hershel's place and met Meriweather at the house. When I thought of our encounter with her, I did recall she never actually claimed to have seen Papa on the Curahee.

"What's in the pouch, Nana?" Ben asked.

We were tired and not in the mood to hear Nana ramble. When we were better rested such things might be interesting, but not now.

"Let's see," she said.

She took the first paper from the stack she had made and began to read.

Be it known that Sergeant Ebenezer Wiley, in recognition of his valiant and heroic behavior behind enemy lines, and despite hardships placed on himself, the men in his command, and especially his family; Sergeant Wiley is hereby awarded the Distinguished Service Medal of the Confederate States of America. Be it also known that all records of his alleged illegal activities during this campaign were necessary fabrications by our government directed at hiding and protecting Sergeant Wiley in the commission of his duties.

Nana seemed to swell, grow proud and strong as she read. The hunch in her back straightened slightly and her voice stopped quaking. For a few seconds she was young and proud again. The spark Papa had longed for showed itself for a few brief moments.

In recognition of his distinguished and courageous service, The State of Georgia and the Confederate States of America wish to grant to Sergeant Wiley and his immediate family, possession of the government lands known as the Oggs Creek Hollow, transferring immediately and irrevocably all rights and possession of such lands. The land grant hereby described is detailed more precisely in the accompanying map bearing the Seal of the Confederate States of America and the State of Georgia. In addition, the lands previously seized under the false, but necessary pretenses created by Sergeant Wiley's heroic undercover services are hereby returned to the Wiley family with our deepest apology and gratitude for a job well done. Such lands are also detailed more precisely in the accompanying map.

Nana stopped, steadied herself against the chair.

"The rest is just government gobbledygook," she said. "Old Ebenezer was a hero. We always thought so. Sounds like you fellows already found that out at the Courthouse."

Ben and I nodded.

"Sounds like we've got some land to claim," she added.

Ben and I listened as Nana and Aunt Fanny made plans. First they needed a lawyer, no several lawyers. They talked about the one Papa had already met with, the one who handled the case about the Indian land. I told them we had to find Papa. Nana seemed to imply she knew where he might be. She ordered us to stay out of Toccoa for now, away from Sheriff Bowers and Franklin Pearce. The State Patrol are still around, maybe the G.B.I.

Nana and Aunt Fanny talked on and on, so fast I could hardly catch most of their words. What will Bowers and the Kresses do when Nana announced her ownership of almost all of the business district of Toccoa? That meant we owned the Ice Company, the Tire Store, Belk Gallant. We actually own Lanona's house. On and on they went. I looked over and saw Ben asleep on the couch. I went into a spare bedroom and within minutes fell asleep too. Meanwhile my stooped over grandmother plotted how to take possession of the town of Toccoa.

Chapter Twenty-Nine

Ben and I slept until after noon. It felt good to finally be in a normal house without someone shooting at us. Aunt Fanny put great piles of fried okra and big beans on paper plates for us. We chased it with cornbread and washed it down with iced tea.

Nana had gone into Atlanta, Aunt Fanny told us, she thinks to see some lawyers. They had not heard from Papa. Through the front window I could see a patrol car across the street.

"Any more sign of Pearce or his boys?" Ben asked between mouthfuls.

"Just that first day," Aunt Fanny replied. "I don't think they'll mess with us again. Sorry about your house."

"It's ok," I said. "I wasn't much of a house anyway."

Ben kicked at me beneath the table just as Momma stepped into the room. I am sure she heard me. We rose and hugged her. She cried, hugged us, cried some more.

"You boys ok?" she asked.

Of course we knew Aunt Fanny and Nana would already have told her we were.

"Still don't know where Papa went off to," she said. "That old cuss. I never could keep up with him."

Aunt Fanny grunted her agreement as she shoveled some more okra and slabs of corn bread onto our plates. Aunt Fanny never ate at a table except at the most formal family affairs. One could wonder how she maintained her significant girth until you watched her in the kitchen. Every time she stirred, ladled, or spooned a dish, she took a swallow. I never saw a circle of cornbread come from her kitchen without a bite or wedge removed. Aunt Fanny had inherited Papa's good nature and zest. That and her great cooking skills made her almost everyone's favorite. Her husband of nearly forty years died last spring from a stroke. She talked constantly of moving back to Toccoa but never got to it.

"Did Nana take the pouch to the lawyers?" I asked.

"I think so," Aunt Fanny replied. She stood over me with her mouth was full of cornbread. "I know it's not here."

"Don't you think we should look for Papa?" I asked.

"Sure," Ben replied. "Any suggestions where to start or how to keep the Sheriff from blowing our heads off while we look?"

I did not answer.

"You boys need not fret about your Papa," Aunt Fanny said. "We'll find him. In the meantime, he can take care of himself just fine."

The girls came in from playing with the neighbor children. They covered Ben and me with hugs and kisses, then started kidding us about smelling bad, having stubby beards.

"Where's Katrina?" I asked.

"She's over at Uncle Peter's house," Momma said. "Frances was running short of room so we stayed with them last night."

We talked some more about the Cat Hag and the Kresse sisters. We again told the story of taking the pouch from Lanona's house but still left out the part where Ben peed on her rocking chair. Momma and Aunt Fanny both chided us for taking such risks. In the light of day, I did not think so much of what we had done either. But Nana had the pouch, seemed to think it would make some difference. I still wondered if we would ever get around to looking for Daddy's killers.

We sat around, played cards, and talked like it could be a holiday or something. Aunt Fanny bubbled, kept saying how much she missed us, and how she still planned to move back to Toccoa someday. I think she really missed her husband. I saw her a few times glance at his favorite chair like she expected him to be there and then drop her eyes to the floor when he was not.

It was midafternoon when Nana came back. She looked pleased with herself.

"Lawyers tell us we have a legitimate claim to almost half of Toccoa," she said. "They say the standard set by several claims made by Indian tribes in South Carolina and Florida give us what they call "clear and overriding precedent" to claim the land immediately. He's started the paperwork. Says by next week, they'll deliver eviction notices to the merchants, even to the Kresse sisters themselves. They say there's bound to be a law suit after that. Whole thing could take months or even years."

"You won't really evict all those store owners, will you?" Momma asked.

"Of course not," Nana answered. "But it'll tell them right off who that land lease money goes to. The Kresses, however, are a different matter."

"'Vengeance is mine ', saith the Lord," Aunt Fanny said.

"'Eye for an eye, tooth for a tooth,'" Nana responded. "I'll do what's right, best I can figure. But the Kresses done had my boy killed, these here boys nearly killed. Their house burned down. I'd say we got ample cause to ask them politely to leave my land."

The older women kept talking about the land, money, lawyers. Nana seemed to avoid talking about Papa. Ben went back to the bedroom to sleep some more. I went outside to play with the girls. We built a fort of fence posts, caught a few spring lizards, threw maypops at one another, and gathered some muscadines. It felt good to act normal, to play with the girls, and to touch the land. I forgot about Papa, even Daddy, for a while. I lay back in the grass with the girls on either side of me trying to blow dandelion puffs into my hair. Trees as old as Ebenezer's grave covered the sun and made shadows that moved slowly across the yard. I wanted to be normal again. I wanted to worry about jumping higher, finding a girlfriend, learning to dance. I was tired of being afraid, looking for secrets, letting dead people direct my life. I did not want to inherit anything and have people think I got anywhere because of an accident of birth. I wanted Daddy's killer found, tried and hanged in public, even if they did not do such things anymore. I wanted his blood to mean something, to cost somebody. I did not want him forgotten and covered up by Nana's land.

No history worth remembering, no blood worth saving.

I could not let Nana's war with the Kresses swallow Daddy up like he'd never existed. I knew it could. You think you will remember people and events, but things swallow up memory, drown it out. I would not let that happen, I told myself. Better the Kresses keep the land than Daddy's memory disappear. It would be like killing him again.

But events had gone past the point where anything could ever return to normal. We were just along for the ride, the kids and me. I had no idea where they would take us. I wondered if we would ever again cut watermelons with Papa, spend all night catching chickens, bushhog the fields, or watch a football game. At the time it seemed these things were gone from my life, driven out by ghosts and dark secrets.

No history worth remembering, no blood worth saving.

People have a way of trying to hurt you, take your pride, make you feel like nothing. The Kresses had taken the soul of the Wiley family many years ago. Marriage bound the Wileys and the Davises which made it Papa's problem too. It was not enough for Lanona to have the land. She wanted our souls. Her hate and greed affected everyone she contacted, infected the entire town of Toccoa.

"You boys' family might be the only ones in these parts who didn't know about Stenton Kresse," I had heard the Cat Hag say.

People lived and worked on the land that the Wileys should have owned. They took advantage of Ebenezer being falsely accused. I was not sure I could stomach living in Toccoa again anyway, knowing how all those families took from us, let us feel like nothing. I wondered how many of them really knew the truth. Mostly, I bet, they just settled into what felt like the truth because it fit them. The truth being that the Kresses let them use the land for lease money which was less than a bank mortgage. Would the older people have told their children about Stenton? The Cat Hag suggests they did. I doubted it. It would serve no purpose. Whatever happened, whoever knew the truth chose to hide it, take advantage of it. A public secret, a private lie. Makes little difference now.

We spent the evening in Aunt Fanny's den watching the news, playing gin, and eating. Ben said something about going back to Carnesville or losing his job. He seemed content to lose the job. Katrina came over, sat for a while, looked anxious and beautiful, like a caged lynx. Still we heard nothing from Papa. Nana was to meet again with the attorneys the next morning. Seems they were going to pull half a law firm off other cases to handle this one. Land in Toccoa's not like land in Atlanta. But even in a small town, claiming the land on which such a large number of buildings and businesses sat was a deal no lawyer could resist. "Case of a lifetime" the lawyers had told Nana.

Nana sat in the corner, slowly lapsing back into her practiced state of mourning. She looked over the contents of the pouch we had brought her, sorted them over and over again. She had Ben bring a large trunk from her car. Inside were more old documents and photographs. She matched some of them with those from the pouch.

Uncle Peter came in later. He had been to the Atlanta branch of the Daughters of the Confederacy with the reference numbers we had gotten at the Toccoa Courthouse. He had copies of Ebenezer Wiley's service record in the Tennessee Reconnaissance Battalion, records of his covert actions, even a copy of the commendation letter from General Lee. All this matched the original documents from the pouch. We stayed up late into the night discussing the findings, what they meant, who was involved. It was clear that the Kresse family could not have pulled off this deception alone. At least a few of the local merchants had to participate, both in Ebenezer's time and recent years. It also seemed that Ebenezer and Jane themselves had to have gone along, at least in part.

Ebenezer had to have stayed in hiding from the time he returned from the war until when he was killed or else the ruse of his death would have been known. Why would he do such a thing? The greatest mystery to me was, who killed Ebenezer? A single shot through the skull, that's what Papa had said. Someone had to kill him, then buried him in a marked grave where he would not be found for a long time. It made no sense. If you wanted someone dead and hidden you would dispose of the body, not mark the grave. If someone else killed him and Jane Wiley buried him, why did she not seek justice? No one could answer these questions. It seemed that I was the only one particularly troubled by them. Everybody else talked about the land and lawyers.

The next morning Nana left for the lawyers. Ben and I decided we should go to the Georgia Bureau of Investigation to tell them of our problems with Sheriff Bowers and Franklin Pearce. We drove past the beltway, to a section of Atlanta near the Georgia Tech campus. We found the five-story glass building with a cement sign out front. Ben's friend had found out who we should talk to. He was on the third floor.

We ascended the elevator, one of those kind with an outside glass wall. As we went up we could see the Georgia Dome where the Yellow Jackets played basketball. We had gone there once to watch the Stephens County Indians play in the state championship tournament. We only lasted one round that year before losing to a team from Vidalia. I hoped to return with our team some day, though that was a little more normal than I thought our lives could ever be again.

We found the office of Captain Jerry Steele, a friend of Ben's friend's father. He greeted us, had us sit while he settled behind a gray steel desk. On the wall hung pictures of Captain Steele receiving awards, holding fish, and wearing a uniform. At the moment, he wore a gray suit, black tie, white shirt. He looked very serious, though amicable, his hair cropped tight, dark eyes intent on us as we spoke.

We told him the whole story, except the part about breaking into Lanona Kresse's house. Told him about Franklin Pearce setting fire to our house, him riding in the sheriff's car after the funeral, being seen outside Aunt Fanny's house a couple of days ago. I told him how the Sheriff roughed me up, threatened me, lied to us about having the G.B.I. help investigate Daddy's killing.

Captain Steele listened, asked a few direct questions.

"Where is your grandfather now?"

We did not know.

He went on to ask about Daddy's friends, business acquaintances, things like that. We told him the same thing we had told the sheriff. We could think of no real reason, other than the land dispute with the Kresses, for anyone to want to hurt him. He was not prone to getting into scraps, or even arguments.

Captain Steele then asked about Papa's friends and business. We told him much the same. I started getting mad, him asking about us when he needed to be asking about the Kresses and the sheriff. He went on, asked about Momma's family, Ben's work, Katrina. He asked about everything you could think to know about one family.

We told him what we had learned about Ebenezer and Jane Wiley, what we had learned about Stenton Kresse. Ben told him he could get copies of the documents from Nana's lawyer. He seemed interested enough, but he kept coming back to our personal affairs. I did not like it. I had nothing to hide. I just would have felt better about it had he asked why we were not surprised the sheriff could be involved with Daddy's murder, why Franklin Pearce was feared around town, thought a bully. Things like that. Instead, he seemed to be looking for reasons to suspect us. He finally found one.

"Have any of you ever been arrested?" he asked. He looked down at a printed paper as he asked.

I said, no. Ben hesitated. I looked at him, he looked down.

"I was arrested last year for possession of marijuana," he said.

"Convicted?" Captain Steele asked. He continued to look at the paper. I got the impression he already knew the answer.

"Pled guilty," Ben answered. "What's this got to do with Daddy's killing and all?"

"I hope nothing," he answered. "But we don't take lightly charges that a local sheriff is crooked. We've got to investigate every possibility."

"Including the possibility that we're lying and the sheriff's got something legitimate on me?" Ben asked.

"Don't take it personally, kid," the captain answered. "If I go to my boss and say I've got to go up to Toccoa to arrest a sheriff for murder and extortion, and the only evidence I've got is the word of someone convicted of drug possession, he'd laugh me off the force. Better we get all this stuff in the open."

"So tell us what you're going to do," I said.

"I'm going to find out what's going on up there," he said. I believed him. "If you boys are clean, you've got nothing to worry about. If you're not, you'd better tell me now."

"We're clean," Ben said.

I nodded.

"That's quite a story you've just given me," he said. "I've already checked with the Gainesville office. Sheriff Bowers never asked for the lab people, so that part of your story checks out. I've got a feeling the rest of it will too. You boys go back to your aunt's house and sit tight. We'll do the rest. Whatever you do, do not go back into Stephens County. If you do before we can formally charge the Sheriff with anything, you're in his jurisdiction. We couldn't stop him from arresting you. I don't think you'd like to be in his jail right now."

We agreed.

We left the building feeling good about our chances against Bowers and Franklin. They had been seen at the house fire, Bowers had lied about contacting the state lab, Franklin was seen outside Aunt Fanny's house. They would have a hard time lying about this many things. All we had to do was sit back, catch a few Braves games, and let them do their job. I only hoped things would be cleared up before school started. If I missed too many classes, I would not be eligible to play ball that year. Ben started talking about school again, going back to his job. I think he wanted to stay in Toccoa. I just wanted to be normal again, play ball, get a girl. With Daddy gone, the house burned, Sheriff Bowers now a proven criminal and us the ones who proved it, things would never go back to normal. People would notice us, we'd stop being invisible. I was not sure I liked the thought of being noticed, particularly for that sort of thing.

We started back to Aunt Fanny's house with Ben driving.

"What's this about you and drugs?" I asked as we left the parking lot.

"None of your business," he answered.

"I'm going to find out sooner or later, Ben," I said. "I'd just as soon have your version. Did Momma and Daddy know?"

"They know," he said.

"What happened?"

"I'd just as soon not go into it," he said. "But I'll tell you this once then you drop it. Last year a few of us were driving back from a concert in Athens. We stopped to pick up a hitchhiker. This guy was loaded with joints. We were a little pumped from the concert, a little drunk already. When he started passing them out to pay us back for picking him up, I took one and smoked it. The cops stopped us in Ila, smelled the smoke and busted us. Daddy bailed me out, hired a lawyer, got me my license back. When it was over, he never even spoke to me about it. I'd never done any drugs before or since. Satisfied?"

"I won't let on I know about it," I said.

Ben grunted, I think it was a thanks.

We pulled off a four-lane highway to a side road which would lead us back to I-85. Ben turned on the radio, rolled down the windows, and started singing with the Altman Brothers. We stopped at a light, pulled back onto the interstate and headed north. Within a few minutes we expected to be back at Aunt Fanny's house. Unlike most days, Ben went the speed limit. Cars passed us, looked at us like we were holding up traffic, going too slow. In Atlanta, only old ladies stayed under the speed limit.

A blue sedan pulled up beside us in the passing lane. It matched our speed. We looked across to see a familiar figure sitting by the window in the back seat. It was Katrina.

Chapter Thirty

Someone had their arm around her neck and she looked scared. Ben started to slow down, the car slowed with us. A few cars pulled behind us, began to flash their lights. We were going forty-five in a sixty-five road.

In the front passenger side sat Franklin Pearce. He rolled his window down, spat on the road, looked like he wanted to say something. We slowed some more. Cars started honking their horns at us.

"You want to see your sister again, you meet us at top of the Curahee," he shouted. We could barely make out his words over the road and wind noise. "Tell anyone and she dies."

The car sped away. Ben started to speed up, follow it, but they were much too fast.

"What're we going to do?" I asked.

"What else can we do?" Ben said. "We've got to go to the Curahee."

"Should we stop by Aunt Fanny's?" I asked.

Ben shook his head.

"They've been following us," he said. "How else could they have found us? Likely as not, another car's following us now. We'd better go straight there."

Ben drove past the exit to Aunt Fanny's house and continued north.

"Do we still have the shotguns?" he asked.

"In the back."

"We need them up front," Ben said.

"We're going to need gas soon," I said. "Pull up to a pump where I can't be seen and I'll get'em."

We drove north until we came to one of those truck stops with dozens of gas pumps spaced far enough apart to allow large trucks to maneuver easily. Ben pulled to a fairly remote one, went in to pay for the gas so they'd turn on the pump. I took an old jacket from the back and covered the shotguns so nobody'd see me with them. Truck stop owners get real nervous around guns. I took a couple of boxes of shells too. Unfortunately, they were mostly bird shot and a few number fours we used for rabbits. Up close they'd kill you. At more than a couple of dozen yards, they only sting a bit. Hopefully, if we needed the guns at all it would be just for show.

Back on the road, I told Ben about the guns and shells.

"Better'n nothing," he said.

We decided to take an early exit near Athens. It would lead us as straight as any road to Toccoa, but had the advantage of being rarely traveled. If anybody was following us, we'd see. We made the turn then went slowly down a winding, country road. Behind us, a light blue sedan exited the interstate and followed. Ben made a couple of more turns that would get you to Toccoa, but would not be normally used. The sedan made the turns as well.

"They're definitely following us," Ben said. "I wonder if we should turn back and get Officer Steele?"

I knew he did not mean it. He probably said it so I'd feel better thinking it. I did not even reply.

He sped up slightly and the sedan stayed barely in sight. He slowed slightly and they matched our speed. If they did not intend to be seen, they were not very good at it.

An hour later, the stone face of the Curahee came into view around a bend in the road. The sedan still followed.

We turned onto the last paved road running on the mountain's northwest side. It ran past several ponds and pastures, turning steep at the mountain's base. A textile plant, abandoned all of my life, sat where we made the turn into national forest property. We slowed, watched for the sedan, which was no longer visible. We turned into the dirt road and immediately started the sharp ascent. This would be my third trip up the mountain in the past week—once to find Katrina the night they killed Daddy, once to find Papa, and now looking for Katrina again.

Had it rained within a couple of days, we would not have been able to make the drive in a car moving as fast as Ben drove as the road was hard packed red clay. Dry as it was, the surface was smooth and stable. The only danger was taking turns too fast on the down slope and having the gravel roll under your tires to send you into a tree or off the embankment.

We went over two rises, past a forester's house, and started the final ascent. I had made the drive dozens of times, maybe hundreds. It was a beautiful road, trees hanging over, always a deer or two on the side. We took some horses up the mountain by this road a couple of times. It was one of my favorite places. It always reminded me of the town's name, Toccoa. If we tried we could see the four or five miles to the waterfalls on the campus of a small Bible college. As the Cherokee name stated, it was indeed beautiful. Today we would not notice.

Ben and I talked on the way up and tried to plan what we would do. It was not likely Pearce just wanted to talk. He wanted the pouch or the diary. We had neither. We did not think it likely we could get out of there with Katrina and without a fight. Our only hope was to negotiate for something they wanted. The fact was, I do not really think either of us thought we would leave the Curahee alive. Surely Franklin and Bowers knew we'd talked to the G.B.I. Surely they know would be top on the list of suspects if we got killed. What possible reason could they have for kidnapping Katrina and us? And why the Curahee? Maybe they had caught Papa or trapped him here. We had no choice. Neither of us even considered leaving, going for help, and leaving Katrina in Pearce's slimy hands. The thought of her even near him made my skin crawl. If he'd touched her, hurt her in any way, I'd make it my life's passion to make him pay.

The road got steeper and the car slid a little. Ben was experienced driving roads like this and compensated expertly. As we neared the top we saw a car pulled off to the first stone overlook. I could not tell if it was the car we'd seen holding Katrina. Ben stopped beside it and looked across the stone escarpment, but saw no one. We continued around the road which made a half circle to the very top. A chain link fence over ten feet tall surrounded the base of a radio tower. The road ended in front of the fence. A trail skirted the fence to the right, leading to the top of the bare stone face of the Curahee. We saw no other cars. Ben pulled up to the fence and stopped. He left the motor running while we looked around but saw no one.

We called Katrina's name. No answer. We called Franklin Pearce's name and heard nothing.

Ben turned the motor off and we sat in the car. We listened to the insect noises, the sounds of birds, and a few wild dogs in the distance. No sign, other than the empty car, that anyone else was around. We waited for a few minutes.

Ben got out of the car and called for Katrina. Still no answer. We were talking about leaving when we heard someone coming up the trail behind us. A black man stepped out. He was big with heavy wrinkles down the back of his neck. He showed no emotion and seemed like he had never had any. He raised an arm, thick as my leg, and waved us to come after him. I reached into the back seat and pulled out a shotgun. I was about to hand it to Ben, when I felt something press into the side of my neck. I froze and turned just my eyes to look at Ben on the other side of the car. He stood still and shook his head at me as if signaling for me to be still. I slowly turned my head. The black man had a hawk-bill knife pressed against the side of my neck where the large blood vessels ran. He had moved fast and quiet. I never heard or saw him coming.

"Won't need those," he said.

I put the gun down and backed slowly away from the car. He maneuvered himself between me and the guns, then pulled the knife away. As he moved the knife, he nicked me with its tip. I flinched. He laughed, pushed me toward the trail, and waved Ben to follow me. When we were away from the car, he took the lead but kept looking back at us. He grinned a few times, like he knew we were in for something bad, like he wanted to hurt us.

We followed him around the fenced area beneath the radio tower. He took us across the road to a trail I did not know existed. The trail dropped off a rocky bank, turned back parallel to the road, then around below the stone face. The ground was steep and rocky. We slid down stone streaked with water from hidden streams, trudged across fallen logs, and around rough chunks of granite which protruded randomly from the forest floor. The woods were old, virgin oak, too steep to log. Little underbrush blocked our way. By the time we made it to the ledge at the base of the stone face, we were sweating profusely.

The black man stopped at a twenty-foot wide ledge looking out over a series of farms. In the distance, a few house lights blinked on as the light failed. The shadow of the Curahee began to creep across the lowlands to the southeast, a distinct entity that seemed to engulf the pastures and lakes below. Already to the east the first stars had come out, bright against sea of dark blue. To our left the sky was red and featureless. A couple of buzzards circled overhead as they prepared to roost on the radio tower. Squirrels barked from the old oak trees, finding each other for night. Six hundred feet below us and half a mile south, I saw the single light from Hershel's tractor bouncing across a dark pasture, squeezing just a few more minutes from the workday.

From around an upright granite slab at the far end of the cliff, Franklin Pearce stepped into view, Katrina's arm clutched in his left hand. Her hair swung into her face and sweat stained her blouse, otherwise she seemed fine. We started for her when Franklin spoke.

"You boys stay right there," he said.

We stopped and looked at the black man beside us. We both knew he would not likely have much problem tossing both of us off this cliff. He had his hand in his pocket, probably around his knife.

"What do you want from us?" Ben asked.

"Same thing I told you the day after your Daddy was killed," Sheriff Bowers said, stepping from behind a bolder uphill from us. We swung around to look at him, a dark figure against the red sky. "We want you to come clean, tell us everything your Daddy and Granddaddy have been up to. Give us everything you've found."

"Like what?" I asked.

I had no idea how much they knew, or why they'd care, unless Lanona Kresse had bought them off. I did not want to be the one who told them anything.

"Like the papers your Granddaddy dug up from Ebenezer Wiley's grave," the Sheriff said.

"How'd you know about the grave?" I asked.

"We know, that's all that matters," he answered.

Franklin pulled Katrina to him, put his arm around her waist like they were girlfriend and boyfriend. I started to go for him but Ben stopped me. The Sheriff pulled his gun.

"No need for things to get ugly, boys," the Sheriff said. "We know you found some stuff that'll get your grandmamma all stirred up, thinking a crazy family legend about Ebenezer being a hero is true. We all know it's not. All this is old stuff, happened before any of us were born. Not worth getting hurt for. Now tell us what we need to know."

"Where's Papa?" I asked.

Pearce and Bowers looked at one another. The Sheriff pointed with his gun out over the cliff.

"He's out there, somewhere," he said. "We know he's somewhere among these rocks. Could be a thousand places. It'd take an army of people weeks to find him."

I was again relieved that they did not have him.

"He's got what you're looking for," I said.

Ben gave me a dirty look. Katrina too.

I did not care. If Papa had what they needed and giving it up would save our sister and maybe us too, I did not give squat about Ebenezer's name, the land, or family honor. I wanted off this mountain with my sister, brother, and grandfather alive. Nothing else mattered. I would give them anything they wanted.

"That so?" the Sheriff said. "Then you boys'll just have to help us get him out."

Franklin pulled at Katrina again and put his ugly face in her hair. Katrina twisted around, smacked him against his left ear and brought her knee up into his groin. He let out a squeal that echoed off the mountain. Katrina pushed him hard, and then ran toward us. Franklin teetered at the edge of the cliff, all doubled over, still squealing. He pulled his hand away from his head. Blood trickled out his ear. He tried to stand straight, but the air was gone from him. He stumbled forward against a cragged pine, growled like a dog, and came lurching toward us.

When the black man grabbed my shoulder I thought he might crush it. I froze. Katrina reached Ben who swung her behind him. Franklin limped forward, growling, cursing our mother and all that's holy, swearing he'd kill Katrina. Ben stood before him. No way would he touch our sister again, Ben would see to it. Katrina backed up against the rock ledge.

Franklin tried to push Ben away as if he was nothing, like he would be afraid to fight. Ben staggered back, then again placed himself between Franklin and Katrina. Franklin then swung at him, landed a hard blow to Ben's stomach which sent him to the ground. Franklin cursed some more, tried to kick Ben in the head. Ben rolled over, barely avoiding Franklin's boot. I tried to reach him, but the man grabbed my other shoulder and held me tight. I felt foolish and weak, watching my brother defend my sister alone.

Ben rose to his feet, dodged another swing by Franklin, and landed a solid punch to his flabby jaw. Franklin's head bounced back slightly. The blow did not seem to hurt him at all. Ben hit him two more times before Franklin even raised his hand. Neither blow slowed him down. Franklin finally landed another blow, this one broke Ben's nose. Blood poured down his upper lip, dripped down his chin. He ignored it, continued to rain punches on Franklin. I was so intent on watching Franklin I forgot about the Sheriff.

Ben seemed about to gain the upper hand, broken nose and all, when the Sheriff snuck up behind him and popped him on the head with a long, black flashlight. The light broke. Ben dropped to the ground and did not move. The black man released me and I ran to him. Katrina and I squatted beside him, and rolled him over. He was breathing but did not answer us. Blood ran from his nose and scalp.

"Better get him to a hospital, Roy," the Sheriff said. He stood over us with his gun drawn. "Better help us quick or he just might die up here on this mountain. There's no need for it. No need for anyone else to get hurt. Just help us."

Katrina hurled some curse at him. Franklin started for her until Bowers stopped him with a hateful gaze.

"I told you already," I said. "Papa's got the papers from Ebenezer's grave. We've got nothing you want."

Katrina stood up and screamed more curses at the Sheriff. He drew his arm up to back hand her and she stepped away. She knelt over Ben.

"We need you to call your Granddaddy out of these rocks," he continued.

Franklin stood beside him, eyed Katrina. His left ear was swelling quickly.

"Tell me what you want," I said. "I'll do it."

"Just what I said," the sheriff answered. "Call him. On a still night like this, sound travels for miles up here. You call him, he'll hear."

"Even if he is here, what makes you think he'll come out for you?" I asked.

"Well, maybe we just need to give him a little incentive," Franklin said.

He grabbed at Katrina again. She was too fast for him. She ducked behind me and cursed him some more. I had heard her swear a few times in the past, but the sounds that came from her pretty lips that night had no business in a civilized woman's vocabulary. She flung words at him and bobbed around my back. She grabbed a couple of rough stones and pelted him with them. One caught him in the cheek and made a deep gouge. He swore some more and started after her again.

"Leave her alone," Bowers said. He looked bored with the contest.

Franklin ignored him and grabbed again for Katrina.

The Sheriff swung his nightstick and struck Franklin in the lower back. I think the layer of fat that rolled about on his back saved him from any real damage. It did, however, succeed in making him stop grabbing for Katrina. He stood upright, rubbed his back, tossed some curses of his own toward Katrina, and backed off.

"Now, if we could get on with this," the Sheriff said. "Call your Granddaddy."

"You mean just yell out into the woods and you think he'll hear us?" I asked.

"He's around here somewhere," Bowers said. "Yell loud enough, he'd hear you all the way to Hershel's place."

Chapter Thirty-One

Maybe it was coincidence, but his reference to Hershel made me wonder if he'd known where we were all along. I also began to wonder about the Cat Hag. Maybe she had followed Papa to be around in case Bowers and Lanona came for him. I looked at Ben. He laid on the ground motionless and with his eyes closed. Katrina held his head in her lap and brushed blood-soaked hair from his face. She kept eyeing Franklin.

"Call him," the Sheriff said. "Call him now or we'll let Franklin there have his way with you and your sister."

Franklin grinned at me. The large black man stood silent.

"Papa," I called as loud as I can. "It's me, Roy. Can you hear me?"

I waited until the echo died away, then repeated my call. We waited a couple of minutes.

"Let's get his attention," Bowers said. He drew his gun. I thought he was about to shoot one of us. Instead he fired two shots into the air.

"Call him again," he said.

"Papa. If you're out there, I need you to answer me."

"I'm here, Roy," Papa shouted. He was far away. The echoes made it impossible to tell how far or even from which direction.

"They've got us, Papa," I said. "Sheriff Bowers, Franklin Pearce, and another man. They've hurt Ben, maybe bad. They've got me and Katrina up here. Say they need something from you."

He did not answer.

"Better listen to me, old man," Bowers shouted. "You know what we want. Lead us to you and we'll let 'em go. Play with us and they'd better learn to fly. You know I'm not bluffing."

"You ok, Roy?" Papa asked.

"I'm ok, so's Katrina," I said. "But I think we'd better get Ben to a hospital real soon."

"Let the children go," Papa said. "I'll give you what you want."

"That's real good, Duncan," Bowers said. "You know we'll want the diary and whatever you've found out there before we let anyone go. Call us in. Let's settle this face to face. No need for the children to get hurt. You can stop it. Call us in."

"Follow a trail to the left," Papa said. "You'll find three boulders together against a fallen oak. Turn back to the right then follow the cliff. I'll call you in from there."

"Let's go," Bowers said.

The black man pushed me toward the trail. I stopped to face them.

"I'm not leaving Ben up here by himself," I said.

"You'll go where we say, boy," the Sheriff said. "Now go."

I stayed put, figured I'd just as soon die right there as have them drag me down the mountain to die in front of Papa. If Ben died up here on the top of this cold rock, so would I.

"You move now or we kill you where you stand," Bowers said. "I'll take my chances that the old man will barter for the girl alone. May even make him more cooperative, knowing we'd killed so quick. Now move."

"You hurt him, and before I'd go with any of you, I'll die here too," Katrina said. "Then my Papa'll hunt you down, kill you all. You got no chance of finding him in these woods. But he'd find you, alright. You know he can, too."

Bowers stood still, thought for a minute. Likely he thought Katrina was right. Papa would kill them if they hurt us but did not get to him too. He would find a way. It gave me no comfort.

"Can't leave you here, boy," he said. "Guess I'll just kill the girl."

"I can't leave Ben alone," I said. "Leave Katrina with him."

"I don't think so," he replied. "Now move or I'll have to do something you won't like."

I stayed put.

"Let her stay," Franklin said. "I'll stay with her."

He eyed Katrina in a way I did not like.

"You let him near my sister and we'll both die rather than do anything you say," I said. "We mean it, Sheriff."

"Ok," Bowers said. "Franklin, go on down the trail like Duncan said. You, little girl, come here."

He pulled Katrina to a small cottonwood near Ben, took out his cuffs, and locked them around Katrina's wrist and the sapling.

"That'll keep you," he said. "Satisfied, Roy?"

I looked at Katrina. She could not reach Ben, but she was close enough to call for help if anyone came near. It would have to do.

Bowers pushed me ahead of him. I looked back at Katrina. She tried again to reach Ben who still did not move. The three of us found the trail and followed Papa's directions. Ten minutes later we were at the base of one rung of the cliff, sixty or so feet below Katrina and Ben. I called again to Papa. We waited a few minutes.

"Come toward my voice," Papa shouted in the distance. He was down hill and slightly to our right. The mountain was so steep we had to hold small trees to keep from sliding. A couple of hundred yards further we stopped and listened.

"Face the mountain, turn right," Papa shouted.

We did as he said and found an old trail leading along a row of white pines. It may have been a well-traveled road at one time. The row of trees seemed a little too straight, the trail, a little too level to have formed naturally. But it only lasted about fifty yards more before ending in a jumble of boulders and rhododendrons.

We waited for Papa to give us more directions.

"Stop right there," Papa called from above us. He was somewhere in the boulders, not more than fifty or sixty yards away at best, though the echo from the mountain made it hard to judge.

"Send Roy over here alone," he said.

"Nothing doing, Duncan," Bowers shouted. "You show us the cave, we'll give you the boy. The other one and the girl are still up top. You can have them too. Now don't play games with me."

"Kill 'em if you must," Papa shouted. "You'll never find it without me and I ain't showing you nothing until they're safe. Likely as not, I'll get you first."

I wondered what cave they meant. The mountain was dotted with them. We'd found dozens ourselves, some with Indian artifacts on the floor and odd paintings on the walls. I had no idea why Bowers and Franklin would care if Papa had found another one.

"I just might kill this one, use the other ones to change your mind later," Bowers said.

"If you'd kill one, you'd kill us all if you got the chance," Papa shouted back. "I want him with me, then I'll tell you how to find the cave. It's close. Closer than you'd ever imagine. But a hundred years of hunters and climbers didn't find it. I suspect you won't either. Make your choice. Let him go and get the cave, or kill them and get nothing. You'll never find me, you know that."

Franklin said something to Bowers I could not hear. Bowers nodded. Franklin and the black man crouched slightly then began working their way slowly up the side of the crop of boulders.

"Franklin's trying to get around you, Papa," I shouted, just before Bowers clubbed me with his pistol. I fell to the ground, fighting to stay conscious.

"Make another sound and I'll break your neck, quiet like so the old man can't hear it," Bowers said bending over me.

"Sneaking around like that won't do no good," Papa said. "I can see 'em from here. I'll shoot him, the other man too, if they go any further. You touch my grandson again, I'll shoot you too."

Franklin stopped and stood his ground, looked back at Bowers.

"Ok, Duncan," Bowers shouted. "The boy's yours."

He pulled me to my feet and shoved me toward Papa's voice. The ground kept coming up at me and the world tilted. Blood trickled down my face and got in my eyes.

"I'm coming," I shouted.

"Walk, don't run," Papa shouted. "Come in through the boulders. You scum stay back. When you're close enough, Roy, I'll come to you. Just keep walking directly away from them and keep the mountain to your left."

I wove my way through the jagged rocks and over a few logs. Within minutes I lost sight of Bowers and Franklin. I went on, kept the cold, dark presence of the mountain to my left as Papa had instructed. Somewhere up there my sister sat chained to a tree, possibly watching my brother die. I hoped Papa had figured out some way to give these men what they wanted and get us all back home safe. I somehow doubted he could do it. A hundred yards further, the boulders gave way to thick underbrush. A single outcrop of granite leaned against the cliff to my left. I heard a gentle whistle to my right from somewhere in the bushes.

"Come here, Roy," Papa whispered.

I ran toward him, stumbled in the darkness.

"I told you to walk," Papa said sternly. "You ok?"

"Bowers pistol whipped me," I said. "I'm a little dizzy, but I can move just fine."

"Good," Papa said. "Come with me."

I followed Papa through the dense brush and around the outcrop. We climbed up to a ledge some twenty feet from the forest floor. Barely, through a few gaps in the trees, I could see a little movement.

"I lied about seeing Franklin," Papa said. "Can barely see any of them from here. All I can do is tell if they're still where they started."

Against the open rocks I could see Papa a little better. His beard was longer, more scraggy. His clothes sat stiff on him, like he'd sweated and dried in them a few times. He also seemed to have lost a little weight. His shotgun lay in the crook of his arm, extra shells in every pocket.

"What cave do they want?" I asked.

Papa put his finger to his lips for quiet.

"You've got the boy, Duncan," Bowers shouted. "Tell us how to find the cave."

Papa turned his face to the cliff and shouted into the stone. The sound of his voice spread, seemed to come from everywhere. It was a nice trick I had used myself while playing hide and seek.

"Go the way Roy went," he shouted. "When you get to the other end of all those boulders, go downhill for a hundred yards until you find an old logging road. Turn east until you get to a dry creek bed. Follow the creek bed uphill. You'll find the cave at the end. Look where is seems the water comes from when that creek is wet. I'm setting the boy free then I'll meet you there."

"You double cross me, I'll kill you and your family," Bowers shouted.

"I know that, Sheriff," Papa said. "I just assume you're going to get what you want from the cave and disappear. That right?"

"You got that right," Bowers shouted back. "If you're telling me the truth, you'll never set eyes on me again, Lanona be damned. Lie to me and you're dead."

Papa pulled me back from the ledge.

"That should keep 'em busy for about half an hour," Papa said. "We'd better hurry. There ain't no dry creek bed down there."

Chapter Thirty-Two

We ran back along the cliff for about ten minutes until Papa found a trail up. It looked familiar. I thought it ran from Hershel's to the top, a route I'd taken with friends past. Papa began climbing as fast as he could. I took the gun from him so he could go easier. We climbed for about twenty minutes almost straight up until we reached the rounded forest edge of the top. We then ran as fast as the terrain let us toward the stone face. I guessed we were about at the same level as Ben and Katrina. I guessed right.

Ben had wakened and was trying to break the sapling holding Katrina. Her wrist bled from pulling with him against the handcuffs. Ben stopped when he saw us. He looked pale, not really alert. I guessed I looked about the same to him.

"The tree's green," he said. "I can't break it."

All three of us pushed, then I stood on the tree. It bent double and its bark cracked, but it stayed together. Ben and I jumped up and down on the bent tree. Its bough stayed intact and bent with us. We moved up the trunk to the first large limb and tried to break it there. It bent and broke on one side, leaving green stick and bark holding on the other. We bent it in the other direction and it came loose. Katrina slipped the handcuff off the tree and threw herself into Papa's arms.

"Enough of that," Papa said. "We'd better get off this mountain before the Sheriff realizes I sent him on a wild goose chase."

We turned to run up to the road but stopped in our tracks. Standing above us in our way were the Sheriff, Franklin, and the silent black man.

"Think I'm a fool?" Bowers said. He had his pistol drawn and aimed at us. "Put down the gun."

Papa eased his shotgun to the ground.

"I ought to kill the young ones where they stand and beat what I want out of you," Bowers said.

"You hurt them, you'll get nothing out of me. Wouldn't matter what you did to me," Papa said.

Katrina held tight to him. Ben swayed slightly, looked confused like he had to fight to stay awake.

"You're just ornery enough to mean it," Bowers said. "We'll all go to the cave. Let us have what we want and you'll all go free. Buck us and I'll take my chances that Franklin and ol' Drake here'll be able to persuade you to help us. Got that?"

Papa nodded.

"Now, let's go," Bowers said.

We headed back down the trail with Papa in the lead. Twenty minutes later we found ourselves again at the base of the stone face. Clouds moved in and the light failed. We could barely see one another. Bowers kept waving his gun so we could see it. Franklin and Drake stayed behind us, making it impossible to run. Several times, Ben stumbled and seemed even more disoriented. Katrina and I held him between us as best we could.

Papa led us through a maze of boulders and tree debris that had fallen from further up the mountain. We squeezed through a gap between two giant slabs of granite and down over a slight rise. He stopped beside another slab which leaned against a rounded stone outcrop. An opening barely three feet high and two feet wide sat between the two stones, partially covered by a laurel bush and a double tree trunk.

"That's it," Papa said. "The cave's in there."

Bowers stuck his head in the opening for a second.

"Maybe you'd better go first," he said to Papa. "Don't suppose you've got a light on you, do you?"

Papa ignored him and squeezed through the opening, disappearing into the dark. Bowers took out a cigarette lighter, flicked it a couple of times until the flame stayed on, and went after him. He too disappeared except for a faint glow from the lighter.

"Bring the others," Bowers said from within.

Franklin and Drake pushed us toward the stones. I went first, leading Ben by the hand. Katrina came after us, stumbling for being pushed from behind.

The passage narrowed to barely the width of a man's shoulder. I did not think Drake could make it. Ten feet further it widened, rose a few feet, then dipped sharply to a wide oval floor maybe thirty feet across. Bowers lit an old kerosene lantern, probably left there by Papa. Papa stood against one stone wall watching Bowers. Katrina and Ben stumbled into the cave.

"Drake can't get through," Franklin shouted.

"Tell him to wait outside," Bowers shouted.

I heard Franklin mumble something to Drake, then saw him push his way into the cave and stand beside Bowers.

"Where's the gold?" Bowers asked Papa.

"Back there," Papa said, pointing to a dark recess to his right.

Bowers held the lantern up and looked where Papa had pointed. He let out a loud yell which reverberated in our ears.

"Franklin, my flabby friend," Bowers said. "We are rich."

Franklin leaned down, then crawled back into the recess. I noticed food wrappers and juice bottles on the floor where Papa had been eating. Franklin backed out on his hands and knees, carrying something in his left hand. He held it to the lantern in Bowers' hand and rubbed at it. As he did, it seemed to glow and sparkle in the lamplight. It appeared to be a chunk of gold the size of a brick.

"Got to be twenty or thirty of 'em back there," he said to Bowers. "Lots of other stuff too. Books, papers wrapped in oilcloth, couple of muskets. This is the place."

"Forget the other stuff," Bowers said. "Drag out the gold."

Franklin crawled back into the recess. We listened to him puffing and grunting. One by one, he pushed blocks of gold out in the open. We heard him toss other metal objects out of his way. He stopped a couple of times and caught his breath. In half an hour, he'd moved out a couple of dozen chunks of gold the size of bricks. Bowers' eyes glowed with a madness. For a minute he seemed to have forgotten us as he stood there fondled the gold mumbling to himself. I thought about jumping him and moved closer. He saw me eying him and waved me back with his gun.

"No use hurrying up what's going to happen anyway, boy," he said.

Papa stood still and watched them gloat over the treasure.

"No need to hurt anyone," Papa said. "You can't stay here in Toccoa anyway. Folks would know how you came on all this wealth. Why not just take off tonight, leave us be? You hurt us, you've added murder to the list of why the law'd be after you."

"Murder's one thing, already on the list," Franklin said.

Bowers' look told him to shut up.

"Don't make no difference anyhow," Franklin said. "We're going to kill 'em anyway, right?"

"The law does tend to go after murderers harder than thieves," Bowers said.

"How's anybody going to find out?" Franklin said. "Nobody's found this cave in a hundred years. Won't matter if they find it in another hundred with a few skeletons in it."

"Franklin's got a point," Bowers said. He pointed the gun at Papa. "Can't think of any real reason to let you go."

"You don't need to do this, Bowers," Papa said.

Papa eased between Katrina and me. He seemed to be thinking hard of something to say. Bowers smiled, his face lit from the lamp making it look evil, not human at all. I kept thinking of what Pearce said, "murder's one thing, already on the list." Sounded to me like a confession, or else him saying Bowers killed Daddy. No matter which one, they're all in it. Now they were going to kill all four of us, leave us in the cave to rot.

"Drake out there won't let you live, anyhow," Bowers said. "No matter what I do, he'll kill you tonight, right here on this mountain."

"Why would he have anything against us?" Papa asked.

"You got his brother killed," Bowers said. "That night when the boy's house burnt down, that was Drake's brother was shot."

"Wasn't me or either of the boys shot him," Papa said.

"He won't see it like that," Bowers responded. "You walk out of here and he'll take that knife of his and open you like a box of peaches. Told us so."

"Leave us here," Papa said. "He can't get to us."

"I don't think so, Duncan," Bowers said. "Sorry, old man. But, I do appreciate you finding the cave for us."

He cocked the gun, aimed at Papa's chest. Just then we heard a noise outside. Drake shouted something. We heard a sharp thumping sound, then silence.

"Drake," Franklin shouted.

Bowers kept the gun on Papa. No answer.

"Drake, if you're still out there you'd better speak up," Franklin shouted again.

No answer still.

"Go check on him," Bowers said. "Take the old man's gun."

Franklin picked up Papa's shotgun which Bowers had been straddling and eased slowly through the cave's entrance. He shouted for Drake a couple of more times.

"What's going on out there?" Bowers shouted.

We heard Franklin say something, but the mountain swallowed the sound. Then another thump, and silence.

Bowers shouted for Franklin, but got no answer in return. He waited a couple of minutes and then stuck his head into the cave's entrance and shouted again. No answer.

"You got people out there, you'd better tell 'em to back off," he said to Papa.

Bowers grabbed Katrina, pulled her against his chest. She struggled against him, but he was too strong.

"You tell 'em to back off now or she's the first one to die," he said, pushing the gun against her temple.

Katrina squirmed a bit more, then stood still. She winced as Bowers gripped her even tighter.

"I don't know who's out there," Papa said. "You know I haven't had a chance to call anybody. No need to put that gun on the girl."

"I'll put my gun anywhere I please," Bowers said. He shouted Franklin's name again. He called for Drake. No answer.

"You two just ease outside, one at a time," Bowers said. "Keep where I can see you. You try anything and the girl here dies. Got that?"

We nodded. In the dim light, Bowers looked deranged and evil. His shadow rose to the ceiling and danced with the flicker of the lantern's flames. He sweated great drops that fell on Katrina's head. I wanted to charge him and drag my sister away from his dirty hands, but it would get her killed and me along with her.

Chapter Thirty-Three

Ben left the cave slowly, feeling his way forward in the darkness. He was a little more alert now, though he still did not speak. I went next, keeping a hand on Ben's back. I heard Papa's breathing with a slight wheeze behind me. It reminded me of his age and how the last few days had to have been hard on him.

We stepped out into starlight filtering down through the trees. Franklin and Drake were nowhere to be seen. Bowers stepped out with one hand around Katrina's neck and the other gripping the gun pressed to her temple. Katrina carried the lantern. He again called for Franklin and Drake, but again they did not answer.

"I don't know what's going on here," Bowers said. "But if someone's out there, you'd better show yourselves or I'm going to start shooting."

No answer. Crickets, tree frogs, and distant dogs made the only sounds we heard.

"Franklin," he shouted again. "If you're out there, answer me."

Nothing. Bowers kept tugging at Katrina's neck, holding her close against whatever he feared was out there.

"You got about ten seconds to show yourself," he shouted. "Then I'll kill one of these people at a time until they're gone. Then it'll be just you and me."

Nothing. Bowers waited half a minute or so, then pointed the gun toward me and pulled back the hammer.

"Last chance," he shouted.

In the dark, I could barely make out his details. I saw enough to know he was about to shoot me. I saw Katrina struggle and Bowers hold her. To my right, I saw movement. It blended in the darkness of the rocks. At first I was not sure what it was, whether I saw something real or just a trick of the night. Then I saw it again. Definitely something or someone had circled Bowers and was coming up behind him. Katrina twisted in his grip. I saw her legs flailing, trying to escape. She dropped the lantern. Its glass shattered and burning kerosene splashed up on her and Bowers. Bowers pushed her away, bent over and rubbed dirt onto his pants to put out the flames. I grabbed Katrina and pulled her away. I pushed her to the ground and patted out the small area of fire on her jeans. It all took only a second or two. Bowers kept his gun aimed at us as well as the faint light allowed. The kerosene that splashed on the ground flared, then began to fade. As the fire died, the darkness closed in on us. I heard movement and the rustle of leaves.

The dark shape flew at Bowers. It moved faster than a person should, more like an animal, a cougar or dog. Katrina screamed at Bowers, a shot pierced the night as the dark figure converged on him. Katrina and I ran toward Papa with her still screaming. Bowers and whatever the dark figure was rolled on the ground, entwined in battle.

"Get out of here, now," Papa shouted.

Ben grabbed Katrina's arm, she grabbed mine, and we followed Papa up the mountain. Behind us in the dark, we heard the sheriff fighting with whatever had attacked him and saved us. The sound followed us. He shouted and cursed. We rounded the first turn up the trail, headed back across the top of the stone face. Still the sounds of the fight echoed around us. We heard Bowers shout, scream, seem to growl himself. Ten minutes or so after we'd left him the sounds of fighting stopped. Papa stopped to listen. He tried to hear if Bowers had won and was following us. We heard nothing. We followed the trail to the top and got in our car. Ben had left the keys in the ignition. Ben and Katrina got in the back. I got in up front with Papa behind the wheel. Papa drove like a madman off the mountain and did not stop until we were in town.

"Anybody hurt?" Papa asked.

Ben did not answer so I answered for him. His head bobbed back and forth at an unnatural angle. I was not sure he was conscious all the time. Katrina seemed fine. She kept hold of Ben's head so his neck would not turn too much.

"I think we'd better get him to a hospital," I said.

Papa nodded, and then turned north toward the county's only emergency room.

"What was that thing that attacked Sheriff Bowers?" I asked Papa as we drove.

"Don't think it was a thing," he said. "More of a who."

"Ok," I said. "Who was that?"

"That, my boy, was Grace Turner," he said. "You know her as the Cat Hag."

"I don't think so," I said. "That thing moved too quick. Fought the sheriff like an animal. I saw the Cat Hag up close. That old woman couldn't stop Nana."

"I thought maybe Nana told you," he said. "You saw her sister, Meriweather. Grace lives in the woods, never goes inside. She's about as tough as they get. Likely she took out the other two as well. Snuck on 'em, bopped 'em on the head or dropped a noose on 'em."

"You can't be serious," I said. "Franklin and that other big goon took out by an old woman?"

"Old don't mean helpless, boy," Papa said. "And you'll talk about Grace with respect or I'll show you what an old man can do."

"Have you been up here with her the whole time?" I asked.

Papa laughed.

"Not with her," he said. "She kept her distance and watched me. I knew she was there. I heard her carrying on the night I left you boys with Hershel. She just watched from a distance. I can't say exactly why. She never showed herself until just now when Bowers threatened to kill us. She and Meriweather never liked Bowers, Lanona either."

We got off the mountain onto a paved road. We drove through the north edge of town fast, hoping the deputy did not see us. Papa ignored all the traffic signs, even ran the one light we passed. It made me worry more about Ben, Papa driving like he thought Ben was in danger. The asphalt road merged with an old one of cement slabs. The road made a rhythmic thumping sound under us. Ben lay in Katrina's lap without moving.

Papa turned hard by the hospital sign. We drove into the emergency room drop off area and parked. We did not see any other patients. A nurse met us at the door, looked us over quickly, then seemed to decide Ben was the patient. Ben swayed and fought to keep his eyes open. She pulled out a stretcher. We laid him on it and she rolled him away, leaving us in the reception area with a secretary. Papa gave the lady our names, some insurance information about Ben, which I think he just made up, and the nature of his injury.

"Got bopped on the head by Sheriff Bowers," Papa said, loudly, as if he was proud of it.

"Why did the Sheriff hit him?" she asked, looking over her black-rimmed glasses at him.

"Sheriff tried to steal from us, kidnapped my granddaughter there," he said, pointing to us. "Ben tried to stop him, got bopped for it."

"I see," the secretary said curtly. She picked up the phone and asked for security. A minute later a man who seemed older than Papa came to the room. He wore a wrinkled uniform, carried a gun and a radio, and a huge ring of keys. He glanced at Papa, spoke to the secretary, and then walked to us.

"Evening, Duncan," the guard said, extending his hand.

"Thomas," Papa replied. They shook hands, seemed to be old friends.

"Sheriff really hit Ben?" he asked.

Papa nodded.

"Really assaulted this girl?"

"Him and that rogue, Franklin," Papa answered. "One other man too. A big black man they called Drake. Came after us on the Curahee. Somebody came to help us or else we'd be stashed away in the rocks, dead as dead can be."

"Who helped you?" Thomas asked.

"Can't say," Papa replied.

"Can't or won't?" Thomas asked.

"No need to make trouble where it don't belong," Papa said. "How about you call the G.B.I. for us, Thomas. Tell him who to ask for, Roy."

I handed him the card Captain Steele had given us.

"Will the Sheriff come looking for you, Duncan?" Thomas asked.

"Not likely, but can't say for sure," Papa said.

"Come with me," Thomas said.

"I'd like to find out how Ben's doing first," Papa said. Katrina nodded our agreement.

"The doctor's with him right now," he said. "Probably going to do some x-rays. You come with me. They'll let you know the minute there's anything to know."

We followed him down a long hallway to his office. We sat in a room surrounded by black and white monitors showing different parts of the hospital. Thomas and Papa talked for a while. Turns out Thomas and Papa were old friends from the Post Office. Papa told him about the grave, the diary, even the part about Ebenezer being a hero and Stenton Kresse being a traitor. It surprised me to hear him talk so openly. The only thing he left out was the cave and the gold. Katrina and I exchanged glances, wondered why Papa'd suddenly become so talkative.

While they talked, I began to watch the monitors. I saw a lady bring an old man to the emergency room. He seemed to be having trouble walking, one side did not move well, maybe a stroke. Most places, they'd have come by ambulance. In Toccoa, no one wants to call attention to their own illnesses, so they come by car. One screen showed the front door, which was closed. A few people walked up, tried the door, read the sign, and left. A few tried a side door as well.

Katrina and I talked for a while. She told me how Franklin and Drake grabbed her from Uncle Peter's walkway, forced her into a car and followed us. Franklin threatened her, told her how he would kill her if she fought him or made noise. She cried a couple of times while she talked. I do not think they really hurt her. Mostly, she seemed mad. If Franklin Pearce was alive, Katrina would find a way to get him. I only hoped she would not expect me to do it for her.

I looked up on the screen and saw someone else enter the emergency room. At first, I could not believe it. I stood to get a closer look. Papa and Thomas stopped talking and looked at the screen with me. Sheriff Bowers stood at the entrance, talking to the secretary. His clothes were torn and his hat missing. A couple of scratches trailed blood down one side of his face. Thomas picked up the phone, dialed the operator and talked for a while. When he hung up, he pulled out his gun and checked the chamber.

"You stay here," Thomas said. "G.B.I.'s on the way."

He left us in the room watching the monitor. A minute later, we saw Thomas appear on the screen and walk up to Bowers. They spoke for a moment. The Sheriff appeared dazed, kept rubbing the cuts and bruises on his face and neck. His shirt was torn on one shoulder.

Bowers began to act agitated, seemed to shout at Thomas but the monitors did not give us sound. The secretary reached for the phone. Bowers knocked it from her hand. Thomas grabbed his arm. Bowers pushed him to the floor. Thomas reached for his gun and struggled to draw it from the holster. Bowers was faster. We heard the gunshot echo down the hallway. On the monitor we saw Thomas shiver on the floor, then lay still. The secretary stood with her hands over her mouth. Bowers shot her in the face.

Chapter Thirty-Four

"We'd better get out of here," Papa said.

We ran out the door and down the hallway away from the emergency room.

"What about Ben?" Katrina asked as we ran.

"Can't help him now," Papa said. "Keep running."

We got to an intersection in the hallway. Not knowing which way to turn, Papa took us to the right. We heard a sound behind us like someone kicking in a door. Bowers was after us.

Papa came into a small lobby, the kind you wait in to get blood drawn or x-rays taken. Papa started for another door. Katrina pulled him to stop. We could hear Bowers running in the hallway behind us.

"Follow me," Katrina said.

The door she tried was locked, so she climbed over a counter into the receptionist's area. We followed her, knocking over phones and appointment books. She then lead us down another hallway, past some rooms containing x-ray units and other gadgets.

"There's a side door down here," she said. "Only employees can use it. I use it sometimes when I'm late."

It being late, we were not surprised that we had not seen anyone else in the hallways. Behind us we heard someone shout, then quiet. We kept running, turning down different halls. Then we heard the crash of another door being kicked in. I guessed Bowers saw the mess we'd made of the receptionist's desk and followed us.

Katrina finally stopped us at a locked doorway. A sign indicated the door was locked after six o'clock but would open automatically in case of fire. Katrina began pressing buttons on a keypad on the wall.

"Better hurry, Honey," Papa said. "Sheriff's right behind us."

She kept pressing keys. Her hands shook so badly, I could not see how she hit the numbers she aimed for. She cursed, took a deep breath and punched more numbers.

"They change the code every month or so," she said. "I don't think the one I know works anymore."

"Any other way out of this hallway?" Papa asked.

Katrina shook her head. We were dead.

I began looking for a way out, the sounds of Bowers' footsteps pounding in my ears. I happened upon a fire alarm. I flipped up the plastic cover and pulled the alarm.

Immediately, lights on the walls began to flash and a bell rang. Katrina pushed the door and it gave way. We ran out the door into a parking lot on the opposite side of the hospital from the emergency room. Bells rang all over the hospital and people peeked out windows and doors. Katrina led us to a cluster of bushes where we crouched in the dark.

Sheriff Bowers burst from the door, pistol in hand. He looked around, started to run to the left, and then stopped. He looked toward the brush in which we were hiding for a long while. Then he started running around the building toward the emergency room.

"We'd better clear out of here," Papa said. "He'll find our car and when we're not in it, he'll come back looking for us."

We moved back into a wooded area behind the hospital and down the hill. We walked, stopped to listen a few times, then walked some more.

"Think he'll kill Ben?" I asked Papa.

"Ben'll have people with him, looking after his head," Papa said. "Not likely Bowers'll try anything with too many people around. Ben's ok for now."

Fire trucks, sirens blaring, rushed down the road toward the hospital. We walked through some woods, crossed a creek and headed up a steep hill. Papa took us toward nearby Toccoa Falls Bible College. Papa said he knew a man who took care of the college landscaping and lived just off campus. He headed down a long bank toward a small house.

We walked across the front of the dark campus, feeling dangerously exposed. A car passed, headed up the mountain. A few minutes later, a State Patrol car with its blue light flashing pulled into the hospital. We kept walking, hoping Bowers would not see us.

"Maybe we should flag down one of the State Patrol cars," Katrina said.

"For all we know, Bowers' has them out looking for us, callin' us killers," Papa said. "I'll feel better if we get out of this county."

We circled back toward the road and kept in the edge of the woods, until we came to a small wood frame house. A small johnboat and trailer sat to the side under a wood basketball backboard with no net. Junk bicycles and car body parts ringed the back yard.

It must have been two o'clock in the morning by now. Papa had us wait in the yard while he went up the front porch. He knocked on the door a couple of times.

A light went on in the back of the house. Then the porch light lit up. Someone pulled apart the curtains over a small window in the door and looked outside. To whoever was inside Papa must have looked a sight with his scraggly beard, torn clothes, and wild hair. We were not much better.

"That you, Duncan?" the man inside called out.

"Yeah, it is, Grady," Papa answered. "Sorry to bother you this late, but we've got troubles and could sure use some help. The tree's a falling."

Papa used the old password for the only civic organization he'd ever joined, Woodsmen of the World. The "Tree's a falling" statement is used to alert other Woodsmen of the World lodge members that a fellow Woodsman is in trouble. The phrase is supposed to be a great secret, shared only among the Woodsmen themselves. Unfortunately, the lodge, which has not been open since I was born, seemed to attract men who could not keep such things to themselves. As a result, almost everyone in Toccoa knew the secret phrase. I knew it because Papa told me, repeatedly. Each time he spoke in a hushed voice and swore me to secrecy. Each time I vowed never to let on that I knew the Woodsmen's most prized secret. I never thought anyone would actually use the code words, until that night.

The door opened and Grady Henderson stepped out, wearing nothing but pajama bottoms. His round belly fell over the pajamas and jiggled as he spoke.

"Come on in, Duncan," he said. He glanced past Papa toward us. "Bring the youngsters too."

We hurried into Grady's living room. It was a mess. Grady's wife had died a few years earlier, leaving him with ineptitude at housekeeping perfected by forty years of practice. Beer cans piled against an old reclining chair. A television set sat on the floor next to a gas heater. Old newspapers and magazines covered the other two chairs.

"Sit," he said, pointing toward the chairs and sofa.

He did not seem in the least uncomfortable that we saw himself or his house in such disarray and him looking like a drunken hobo.

"What's going on?" he asked Papa.

"Sheriff Bowers tried to kill us," Papa said. "He hurt my grandson, Ben. We brought him to the hospital and Bowers followed us. He killed a guard. You know the man he killed. It's Thomas Sosebee. Came after us again. We ran away, ended up here."

"Bowers killed Thomas?" Grady said.

"Killed some lady who was working at the desk too," Papa said. "He'll kill you too, if he finds out you helped us."

"Why's the Sheriff after you?" Grady asked.

"He tried to steal something from us," Papa said. "Can't go into it right now. Just got to take my word for it. He wants something we have. He might be working for Lanona Kresse, or might be after it for himself. Makes no difference now. We just need to get away until the G.B.I. men can sort it out."

"What could you have that Bowers'd kill for?" Grady asked.

"We found the Pauper's Cave," Papa said.

Katrina and I sat up, listened. It was the first time Papa had mentioned the cave, first time we had heard the name.

"I never thought it really existed," Grady said. "Just the kind of thing old women talk about when they run out of gossip or want to put children to sleep."

"It's real, ok," Papa said. "Found it on the Curahee, just like folks said."

"People been looking for the Pauper's Cave for a hundred years," Grady said. "How'd you find it?"

"Found a diary," Papa said.

Katrina and I looked at one another. We could not believe Papa was telling this story to Grady, Woodsman of the World or not.

"Belonged to Estelle's grandfather," he continued. "It gave directions to the cave. I found it, found the gold and everything. Bowers found out about it, tried to steal it from us. Had Franklin Pearce with him."

Grady wrinkled his nose at the mention of Pearce's name.

"What gold?" I asked.

"Folks around here used to talk about a cave up on the Curahee," Grady said. "A Confederate deserter was supposed to have lived in it for a few years. Even had a rumor that he'd stolen a shipment of gold meant for the treasury up Richmond way and hid it in the cave. People said the man died without a penny to his name, only the hidden gold. That's why they called it the 'Pauper's cave.' Never gave it much stock myself. People looked but never found it."

"I found it, Roy," Papa said to us. "Ebenezer Wiley, Estelle's grandfather, used the cave to hide out after the war. Found papers, some more diary entries and letters. I've spent the past few days hiding up there, going through all the stuff. That's why I left you and Ben. I needed to find the cave and spend time in it. Figured if you didn't know where I was, you'd have an easier time of it if the Sheriff caught you. Hope you don't mind."

I was about to light into Papa for leaving us. We had spent a day looking for him, even went to the Cat Hag's house for him. I was just about to speak when Katrina interrupted me.

"Was Ebenezer the deserter they called the Pauper?" Katrina asked.

"Ebenezer was no deserter," Papa said. "Remember that. Some folks may have called him one. But he wasn't. I think the legend of the cave may have started with Ebenezer, though."

"And the gold?" I asked.

"Not Confederate gold," Papa said. "Yankee gold. Ebenezer got it off a train they sabotaged, brought it here toward the end of the war. Some letters he wrote, other stuff still in the cave talk about it. The war ended just as he got back to Toccoa and he didn't know what to do with it. Been up there all these years."

"Why couldn't you tell us?" I asked. "We might have gotten ourselves killed just looking for you."

"Sorry about that," he said. "Didn't think you boys'd care to go looking for the cave. Ya'll gave me the idea you both wanted out of all this. I figured you'd just pack up and go to Frances' house."

"We looked for you most of the night and part of the next day," I said. "We were afraid the Cat Hag'd gotten you. Some campers told us they'd heard her the night you left us. Hershel found her tracks following you."

Papa laughed.

"She must have thought she was protecting me," Papa said.

"What're you going to do about Bowers?" Grady asked.

"Nothing, right now," Papa said. "We got away from him tonight. Don't want to chance running into him again until the G.B.I. people get him. Can you help us get to Atlanta?"

"Sure," Grady answered. "Want me to take you tonight?"

"Don't want you to take us at all," Papa said. "Just lend me your car."

Grady thought a minute. You could tell he did not relish the idea of someone else driving his car. People in small towns tend to protect their sisters, dogs, and cars, in that order.

"I'll give you my keys," Papa said. "My car's in the hospital parking lot. If you need it, take it."

"Yeah," Grady said. "I drive your car and Sheriff Bowers shoots me for helping you. No thanks. You shouldn't drive to Atlanta by yourselves, anyway. I'll drive you in the morning."

"I don't think that's such a good idea," Papa said.

"Won't hear of anything else," Grady said. "Been meaning to go to Atlanta, anyway. I'd like to see the Braves play again, maybe grab some onion rings and a dog at the Varsity."

"I don't' think you'd better get any closer to us than you have to," Papa said.

"Enough talk," Grady said. "You three look hungry. Let me fix you something."

I glanced through the small dining room and into the kitchen. Dishes, crusted with old food debris, sat in piles on the counter.

"I'm not really hungry," I said. I nudged Katrina, motioned for her to look at the kitchen.

"I'm not hungry either," she said.

"Well, you two sack out in here," Grady said. "I'll put out a bedroll for the floor and a quilt for the sofa."

"Listen, Grady," Papa said. "We'd better get going tonight. Right now. Bowers'll be looking for us, maybe with help. If you'd allow it, I'd really rather drive your car by myself. You'd better stay here."

Chapter Thirty-Five

Papa and Grady talked on for a while. I lost interest. I leaned back in the sofa and fell asleep. When I woke up, the sun was streaming in the side window. Katrina's head lay against my shoulder. I could not see Papa or Grady. I slowly eased forward and settled Katrina's head on the cushion. She stirred briefly, then went back to sleep.

No one was in the kitchen or dining room. I looked outside to an empty driveway. The bedrooms were empty. Papa and Grady were gone.

Katrina finally stirred, looked around as if trying to remember where she was.

"Where's Papa?" she asked.

"Gone somewhere with Grady, I suspect," I answered. I hoped Papa did not go off without us again. It'd be just like him. If he had, I swore, I would never get in another car with him again. I would find a job like Ben had. I would never work for him again. Papa had better start talking to us about what's going on and never go off without telling us what he is doing again or I would be through with him. Daddy killed. The Sheriff after us. Katrina kidnapped. Ben shot, then his head nearly caved in, and Papa's gone off again. The more I thought about it, the more worked up I got.

"I'm hungry," she said. She looked inside the kitchen again. "But not that hungry."

We settled back on the sofa, dozed on and off, and talked about last night. Maybe the sheriff had gone back, gotten the gold, and disappeared. Neither of us thought he had. He'd murdered two innocent people, rampaged around a hospital as if he did not care who saw him. The Sheriff was out for us, would kill anyone who stood in his way. We hoped the G.B.I. would come and arrest him.

Katrina could not believe it was the Cat Hag who attacked Bowers on the Curahee either. It looked like her, she thought. But whatever it was moved too fast. Papa had to be mistaken. We owed whoever it was. We talked of how we hoped they were fine and Bowers had not killed them. We were dozing again when Papa and Grady came back.

"You children ready to go to Atlanta?" he said.

"Can we stop and get something to eat on the way?" Katrina asked. "I haven't eaten since yesterday morning and I'm starving." She glanced at Grady when she realized she'd insulted him by not taking him up on his cooking.

Grady looked down and acted hurt, seemed to know we did not think much of his kitchen.

"Let's get on the way," Papa said.

We climbed in Grady's white Chevy Impala, Papa and Grady up front, Katrina and me in the back. The car stalled on the way out of his driveway. Grady started it again, acted as though that was normal. He headed north into the mountains, the old route to Atlanta. We rolled the windows down. The morning air felt like the Appalachians, cool, wet, fresh. Kudzu covered patches of the roadside, sometimes acres at a time. Otherwise deep forest peppered with homesteads and small pastures surrounded us. Rain had been scarce the last few weeks and some of the corn and grass had a slight brown edge to it.

We went up toward Tallulah Gorge, wound around a few roads which bypassed Toccoa, then turned south toward Gainesville. Grady wanted out of Stephens County as fast as possible, away from Sheriff Bowers' jurisdiction.

"Where were you two?" I asked once we were underway.

"We went back up the Curahee to see if Grace was hurt," Papa said.

"Took a helluva chance, didn't you?" Katrina said.

"Grace took the chance, going after those three men," he responded. "Didn't seem right leaving, not knowing if she's hurt or dead."

"Did you find her?" I asked.

"Not a sign," he said. "No sign of Franklin or that other man either."

"Think she's ok?" I asked.

"Likely she kept Bowers busy 'till she was sure we'd gotten away," he said. "That woman could blend into the woods quicker than Bowers could draw a gun. Ben's fine too. They moved him to Emory in case he needs a neurosurgeon. Say he's fine and he'll likely be out in a couple of days."

The convoluted way Grady went took us almost five hours to get to Aunt Fanny's house. We drove up, were confronted by a State Patrolman again, and then went inside. Captain Steele was already there, sitting at the kitchen table talking to Nana. Katrina hugged everybody, reassured them she was fine, then went with Aunt Fanny to the bedroom. Nana and Papa kissed briefly.

"We know what happened at the hospital, "Captain Steele said. "The whole thing was caught on surveillance tape. We've issued a warrant for Sheriff Bowers' arrest. Sorry I didn't take you boys more seriously."

"What about Lanona Kresse?" Papa said.

"I know you think she put him up to all this," he replied. "But we don't have direct evidence to link her to your son's murder or your attack. Just your suspicions. I'm afraid there's nothing we can do."

"Meanwhile, she can go out and hire somebody else to kill the rest of us," Papa said.

"Listen, Mr. Davis," he said, rising from the table. "I'll do what I can, short of breaking the law. We'll protect you and investigate any hard evidence you can provide us. But don't expect us to arrest people on your suspicion alone."

Nana slipped her arm around Papa's, seemed to be trying to calm him. He took a deep breath.

"We appreciate your help," he said. "Did Estelle fill you in about the grave, the land and all?"

"She did," Captain Steele said. "Sounds like the town of Toccoa's about to change hands. I'd love to be your real estate dealer."

Papa looked at Nana who smiled and nodded.

"Lawyer says we can claim the land and it'll stand up in any court in the country," Nana said. "Say's we can expect a long legal battle, but when it's all said and done, we'll end up with a clear title to all of Ebenezer Wiley's original land and likely a little more from the grant the State meant to give him. Lanona's house is on our land. Most of the rest of Big A Road too."

"That's good news," Papa said. The tone of his voice said something else.

"What's wrong, Duncan," Nana said. Papa at first did not look as if he wanted to respond.

"I found the cave," Papa said. "Sure as hell, that's where Ebenezer hid out."

"Tell her about the gold," I said.

Papa shot me a look. I shut up. But I was glad I said it. I was tired of secrets, especially those we held from each other. I wanted Papa to know he could not expect me to keep any of them for him, ever again.

"Gold?" Nana asked. "What's he talking about?"

"Nothing," Papa said.

Captain Steele raised an eyebrow. He was not a man who liked for people to keep secrets around him, especially when it related to a case.

"Something else you need to tell me?" he asked Papa.

Papa frowned at me again.

"I found a cave where Ebenezer Wiley lived for the first few months after the Civil War," he said. "Cave's dry as a bone. Probably had not been water in there for a million years. Everything was in good shape, letters, journals, even a few books. Kept in boxes. Rats got into a few. Ebenezer had a stash of gold bars up there. The Sheriff seemed to know about it. He forced me to show it to him and tried to kill us when we did."

He then went on to tell Captain Steele all about the last two nights. Told him about how he found directions to the cave in Ebenezer's diary, how people around Toccoa always kept a tale about some old cave where a Confederate treasure was stashed.

"This gold," Captain Steele asked. "Who owns it?"

"I assume I do," Papa said. "I found it."

"Not necessarily," Steele said. "It was on federal land. Unless you've got some more legitimate claim to it than just that you found it, I likely belongs to the U.S. government."

"Ok," Papa said. "You just tell them to find it like I did."

"We don't need the gold," Nana said. "We've got the land, more money than we could ever use."

"I'll not tell them how to find it," Papa said stubbornly. "Let'em take another hundred years looking."

"Duncan," Nana said softly. "What's wrong? You're not telling us something. I know it's not the gold. What is it?"

Papa crossed his arms, looked out the kitchen window. He set his jaw, seemed like he was considering whether or not to answer. It could have been Daddy when Momma tried to tell him something he did not want to hear. He stared out the window and watched the girls play. Nana touched his arm and you could see him soften.

"I'll show them where to find the cave," I said. Katrina nodded and took my arm.

Papa shot us a hard look, then looked at Nana. She nodded.

"Tell us, Duncan," she said.

"Ebenezer left some papers," he said. "Things about the war, things about his wife, Jane."

"What kind of things?" Nana asked.

"Things I'm not about to get into in front of all these people," Papa said.

He rose and went out the back door. We watched him settle into the swing on the back porch.

"I'll talk to him later," Nana said. "Your people looking for Bowers and Franklin?"

"We'll find him," Steele said. "We already discovered some irregularities in the report he filed on your son's murder. Our lab people went over the store where he was killed. We found the slug that killed him still embedded in a wall. It matched the caliber and type of weapon Sheriff Bowers carries. Not enough to convict him, but enough to justify opening an investigation. If we can get his gun it'll be different. Ballistic tests will tell us if it's the murder weapon or not. Even if it's not, we've got witnesses to the two murders at the hospital. I've got a feeling those slugs will match the one that killed your son. If so, we'll get him and he'll pay for it."

"Thank you, Captain Steele," Nana said. "What can we do?"

"Not much, ma'am," Steele said. "We'll take it from here. You'd be most helpful staying safe and away from Toccoa and anyone connected with the case. But if your husband has information about this case, including the location of whatever cave he was talking about, he'd better come forth with it now. It could help us find your son's killer and keep him out of trouble. It's a felony to conceal evidence of any kind. Tell him that. Tell him I'll have a team of searchers with dogs all over that mountain if I have to. Whatever cave he's talking about, we'll find it ourselves sooner or later. It would be better for everyone if he cooperated."

"I'll tell him," Nana said.

Steele rose and went to the door, Nana behind him. They spoke again at the door for a minute before he left.

"What's this about a cave?" Aunt Fanny asked me.

"Papa's been hiding out in a cave up on the Curahee," I said. "Some old stuff up there. Gold too. Somehow, Bowers knew about it and used Katrina, me and Ben to flush him out."

"It's the Pauper's cave," Grady said. He had been sitting across the living room listening to the conversation.

"What on earth is the Pauper's Cave?" Aunt Fanny asked.

"In the old days, before anyone discovered the high mountains and lakes were good for tourists, people used to talk about a cave hidden somewhere on the Curahee. Said the Indians used it first. Later, a deserter from the Confederate Army lived out the war in it. Before the war, only a few people knew how to find it and they didn't speak of it. After the war, weren't nobody left who knew how to find it. That places is a maze of rocks and ravines."

"What's that got to do with Ebenezer Wiley?" I asked.

"Not sure," Grady said. "Could be Wiley was the deserter."

"But he was not a deserter," I said. "You heard Papa. We've already proved he was no deserter."

"Don't matter what you've proved, son," Grady said. "People back then say he was a deserter, they'd have hanged him. He'd likely choose a cave over a rope any day."

"Don't make sense," I said. "He could clear his name. He had the documents to do it. He could take back the land they gave to the Kresse family. Why would he hide in a cave? The gravestone says he died about a year after the war ended. He'd have to live there all that time, waiting for something. What?"

Nana came back, heard part of the conversation.

"No sense in speculating on such things when we've got more than enough hard facts to keep us busy," she said.

She looked out the window at Papa, still rocking back and forth in the porch swing. The girls occasionally pelted him with sweet gum balls. He ducked with great drama, acted hurt. You could tell, though, he wished they would leave him alone.

"I better go find out what's eating your Papa," she said.

I watched her go out and settle in next to Papa. She waved off the girls. They spoke for a while. She settled her hand on his arm, rocked with him. I do not think they talked much about Ebenezer Wiley. I think they were just glad to be together again.

Later, Papa and Nana came back in and joined us for lunch. Aunt Fanny did herself proud with every kind of vegetable I ever heard of that was grown in these parts. We ate until we were stuffed. Then we took a bite from fried fatback and slugged down some tea. As expected, the fatback and tea rekindled our appetites and we went at it again.

The phone rang as we finished. A nurse from the hospital told Aunt Fanny that Ben was doing well and they would not have to do any surgery. He could likely go home tomorrow.

Home to where, I wondered? He had likely lost his job in Carnesville, spending all this time away without an explanation. Our house was burned down. Daddy killed. All we had was the promise of land and wealth now held by the Kresse sisters. It did not feel right. I could not feel the roots underneath me. I had lost my bearing on the Center of the World as I knew it.

No history worth remembering, no blood worth saving.

I kept thinking of Lanona Kresse's hateful words to Papa. The past and the present seemed so jumbled, I kept thinking of Ebenezer and Jane Wiley as though they were people I had met, people as real as my dead father. The Kresses had spilled Daddy's blood, used it like it was worth nothing. Tried to wipe out the history of Ebenezer Wiley. Left to them, we'd all disappear like we had never existed at all. We would become as unreal as Ebenezer, gone, forgotten, defined in terms of the victor's choosing.

Later that day, Nana asked us some questions about the night on the Curahee. She did not seem at all surprised that Papa thought the Cat Hag had saved us. I still could not believe an old woman could take out Franklin, Drake, and tangle with the Sheriff like what we saw.

"No matter if you believe it or not," she said. "That woman's got power you'd never think possible. She's lived in the woods and fields all her life so she's tough and stronger than anyone would expect from an old woman. In the dark woods, I don't think she'd have much trouble taking out any man alive."

I still was not convinced. Neither was Katrina. We both wondered if Nana referred to physical power or something else, but were afraid to ask. Like most of the older people of the Georgia mountains, Nana was a bit superstitious. She even did a few things like burying frogs at full moon to keep away flu. Once, she took me to a man who claimed to be able to talk away the warts on my hand. I really did not want to hear that Nana thought the Cat Hag capable of her own magic. I could much sooner believe that an old crazy woman could sneak up on a man at night and club him unconscious.

"What's the lawyer going to do next?" I asked, changing the subject.

"He's already filed some papers with the state," Nana said. "We'll have some kind of preliminary hearing in a month. He's also had a judge put some restraining orders on the Kresse's. They cannot build on the land until we settle with them. All the lease money they collect from here out goes into what they call an 'escrow account.' That means if we win the suit, we get the money. It also means Lanona's got no more steady income. That should get her attention."

Papa had come in from the swing but sat silently in the corner listening. You could tell he had something on his mind, something we all needed to hear. But he just sat there, watched us talk. What I found most troublesome was, he did not laugh at all.

"What're you going to do when you've got all that money?" Aunt Fanny asked Nana.

Nana wrinkled her already considerably wrinkled brow as if the question was somewhat tasteless. But we all turned to her and waited for an answer.

"Haven't given it much thought," she said. "Likely I'd pay off all my notes, send in my tithe, and take a trip to Colorado. How about you, Duncan?"

Papa finally chuckled.

"I've always wanted to see the Rockies," he said.

"What about you, Roy," Nana said. "You and your Momma are likely to move into one of the Kresse's houses. Maybe you'd like to live in Lanona's house."

I remembered Lanona's house in the dark, the guinea fowl, the rocker stained with Ben's pee, the feel of holiness and evil mixed together. There was no way in hell I would sleep in that house.

"That'd be just fine," I lied.

Chapter Thirty-Six

"When do you think it'd be safe for us to go home, Duncan?" Nana asked.

"Seems it'd be ok, now," Papa said. "Lanona's henchmen are gone, the Sheriff's on the run from the G.B.I. We got nobody to fear back home."

"You heard Captain Steele," I said. "He thinks we'd better stay clear of Toccoa until they get hold of the Sheriff."

We talked about it for a little while. Everyone finally decided we'd wait a couple of days, and then check in with Captain Steele. If they had not caught up with Sheriff Bowers by then it was likely he had fled the state.

We spent the next two days being real Atlanta tourists. We visited Grants Park. Momma got into a staring contest with Willy Bee, the aged gorilla. Willy won. We visited Six Flags Over Georgia, rode the rides, ate hot dogs and candied apples. Uncle Peter even got us all tickets to watch the Braves play. I almost caught a foul ball. It was the best time with family I had experienced in years. I kept thinking of how we never did such things when Daddy was alive, at least not with the whole extended family. I kept expecting to see him at the table or walking slightly ahead of Momma in the park. Sometimes I would see Papa or Ben and, for a flash, think it was him.

The stress of Daddy's killing and all the threats to us brought us together as nothing ever had. It made me feel more at home, more rooted than I had just a couple of days earlier. I guess we really root ourselves in people, not places and things. A burned down house for some people can build a home better than any amount of money. I thought I could see the Center of the World again, distant and faint, but there all the same. It was family, my family. It did not matter if we lost the lawsuit, lost the land. We had found family again. Too bad Daddy could not see it. In my mind I could see the proud look he would cast across the gathering of Davises. Maybe, I thought, he had that look right now in some other place.

Couple of days later, Papa called Captain Steele. Sheriff Bowers had fled the area. He still advised us to stay away, but we all decided to go home.

Aunt Fanny gave a plea for everyone to stay, maybe for the rest of the summer. But I told her I had better get back to working out and playing ball regular like the coach told me. Nana's garden needed tending. The backside of Papa's land still needed fencing. We packed a few things, gathered the little one's from Uncle Peter's house and loaded Papa's and Ben's car.

We drove back on the interstate, Papa in his car up front, Momma driving Ben's car behind. I kept looking back, still expecting the Sheriff to come for us. We turned down highway seventeen and headed for Toccoa. We passed the turn toward Gumlog. I thought I could feel the presence of the Cat Hag watching, maybe even smiling for us. Every car we passed seemed to slow down a little, watch us. We passed the burned out shell of our house and Momma started crying. We passed the office, still wrapped in yellow police tape, and Katrina started crying too.

By now, word of the lawsuit to reclaim Nana's land had hit the papers. Everyone in Toccoa knew about it. It would be the only topic discussed at the barber shop and sandwich shops around town. People would wonder what it meant for Toccoa, how things would change.

People watched us. A couple of cars pulled off the road like we were a funeral procession or something. Every time we topped a hill, rounded a bend, or slowed down for a car, it seemed people turned to stare.

No history worth remembering, no blood worth saving.

The Davises were no longer invisible.

Chapter Thirty-Seven

We moved in with Nana and Papa for the year. Momma went to work for the new K-mart that opened just outside of town. Katrina returned to the hospital for a few more weeks, then left to go to nursing school in Greenville. Ben recovered from his head injury just fine and took over the Office. He immediately started selling an expanded line of garden chemicals and tools. Come spring, he got married to a girl he had dated in high school. His wife, Christine, looked like a young Momma. When I saw him with her in the store, I felt I had stepped back in time and could watch my parents struggling with a new business, Daddy out front advising customers on the right kind of fertilizer or insecticide while Momma sat at the register or worked on the checkbook. Under Ben's management the store stayed busy.

Months before Daddy's death, Papa had ordered a load of chicks, intending to raise them to pullets and sell to another egg farm. They came in two weeks after school started. The whole family gathered to help get the incubators ready, attach the water hoses, and prepare the feed bins.

The chick came in cardboard boxes, fifteen thousand chicks in all. Papa hired the sorting crew. They all came in a van and sat across from one another at a big wooden table. Every man on the crew was Chinese. Papa said the Chinese could tell the hens from the roosters better than any white man. I watched them and asked questions, just as I had done the many other times they had come to our farm.

"It's a secret," Papa said, when I asked him how they told the sexes apart. If the crew spoke English, they never let on. They just ignored my questions and kept sorting chicks.

Later in life, the roosters grew larger crowns than the hens so anyone could tell them apart. The fuzzy yellow things that came in the carts from the brood farms all looked the same. Papa could not tell them apart either. The Chinese men could. They would pick up the chicks, turn them upside down and separate the feathers between their legs and look closely. I watched over one of their shoulders but could not see anything. The hens, he put in another cardboard crate for us to release in the small pens we had made inside the chicken houses. The roosters he would toss into a barrel to die.

White Leghorns were bred to be nothing but egg factories. They produced little meat but big eggs. Broilers were the opposite. They would make two or three times the meat per pound of feed than the best cattle did. But their eggs were small and fragile. White Leghorn roosters were useless, not worth the feed it took to raise them to maturity.

In years past, Ben and I would gather a couple of dozen of the condemned roosters and take them to some locals to sell.

"What kind of chicks are these?" they would all ask.

"White Leghorns," Ben would say proudly.

"Those White Leghorns are good layers aren't they?" they ask.

"The best," Ben would say. "It's all we'll raise."

We would sell the chicks for a quarter apiece, a steal for healthy hen chicks. We would sometimes meet one of our customers months later and hear the inevitable statement.

"Know those chicks you sold me?" they'd ask.

Ben would nod, act like he hoped they were satisfied.

"Every one of 'em turned out to be roosters," they'd say. "Can't get a single egg from any of 'em. They're so scrawny I can't even get a good dinner from one."

"Not a single hen? Well, what are the odds of that happening?" Ben would say like he was amazed. "Tell you what. We've got another shipment due next month. I'll put you on the list for a couple dozen at a real good price."

We sold four generations of chicks to the same farmer before he found out what we were doing. Daddy made us work for him for a month to pay him back. He nearly killed us bailing hay and cleaning out two barns.

This time, we let the rooster chicks die. With Daddy gone, Ben and Papa had to tend the chicks alone. Keeping varmints and rouge cats away was the hardest job. One morning Papa found five or six chicks had been chewed up by rats. We had rat killings two Saturdays in a row. We must have killed a hundred rats each day. None made it into our pants.

Each of these things was part of the rhythm of our family, events we marked in our childhood memories. Each of them reminded me that Daddy was dead and his killer still not brought to justice. But they also moved me back a little closer to feeling normal again.

I started for the varsity basketball team that year. We lost only one game during the regular season, even got ranked in the top ten in the state for a month or two. Next to the last game of the season, our top scoring forward got in a fight and broke his hand punching a hatchet player from Gainesville. We won the last game of the season at home without him, but none of us thought we could get very far in the tournament. We were right.

Since we had won the regular season title, we got a bye for the first round. We watched the other teams in our region play the first round in Elberton. Hartwell County had the best team by far, lead by a set of twin black players who had just moved down from Detroit. I studied them as best I could and planned how to defend against them.

The next night they beat us by a dozen points. I played poorly, felt I had let the whole town down. No Davis had ever done anything worth remembering and neither had I. It did not matter that we had the best overall season in Stephens County High School basketball history. We ended with a loss and that is about all anyone remembers. Coach McGee sat us down after the game, gave us a talk.

"Only one team in the state gets to end their season with a win." It was the only thing I remember him saying. Lanona's words seemed louder. While he gave us his end-of-season speech, I thought of Daddy, Ebenezer, and Jane Wiley. It seemed to me that the most important thing is how you finish your season or your life. People forget what came before. Mostly, they remember the end.

We did not hear from the Kresse sisters much that fall. They would send messages back and forth by their lawyers. Nana's lawyers worked on retainer, something I learned later meant they would get paid only if we won money. But Lanona and her sisters had to pay for theirs from their own bank accounts. It must have cost them a fortune. But it was a fortune they were trying to preserve.

I started dating that year, even tried to dance. When you're six foot six, you do not blend into a dance floor very well. I did my best, ignored the stares and occasional snickers. The rest of my team, which were most of my friends, floated around me like I was the punch bowl. I wiggled in time, tried to act as though I'd danced all my life, tried to act like I did not care if I looked silly. I got turned down for quite a few dates. I finally fell for a girl named Wendy Crawford. She wore hot pants and felt jackets and looked like someone off American Bandstand. She hardly spoke, which suited me just fine. I never learned to talk to girls, never knew what to say to them. Wendy did not mind. We held hands, sat close at the Wigwam, and she taught me to kiss properly. I was proud of her and even thought about marrying her.

When the basketball season ended, Wendy dumped me for a football player. She announced our breakup in front of all my friends during lunch one day. I acted like I did not care. In reality, I did not really care about Wendy as much as I wondered if I would look like discarded goods to the rest of the girls. The fact that I had once had a steady girl, however, apparently made me more desirable to the rest. A few even consented to go out with me the first time I asked.

Only a few people talked to me about Nana's lawsuit and attempt to own the town of Toccoa. A few children of merchants whose businesses sat on the contested land made snide comments which I mostly ignored. Nana had her battles and I had mine. I wanted to keep it that way.

We still had heard no word on the whereabouts of Bowers or Franklin. I would not feel real secure until they were dead or behind bars. After much grumbling, Papa lead the G.B.I. to the Pauper's cave, turned the gold over to the state, just as Nana asked him to. They found some signs of a struggle near the cave, but no bodies. They even found part of Franklin Pearce's shirt and one of Drake's shoes, but no bodies.

Nana went to visit the Cat Hag at Gumlog. She did not tell us much, just that Nana had asked to be allowed to keep the pouch until the suit ended, it being evidence and all. The Cat Hag must have allowed it because the lawyers showed it to the judge during the trial.

Local paper carried parts of the story in almost every issue. They interviewed Nana, Papa, Ben, me, Katrina, and even Aunt Fanny. People noticed us when we walked in town or ate hamburgers. Nana ignored them, seemed content to act like they did not exist. Papa carried on like he enjoyed all the attention. He laughed at every corny joke from every fawning businessman whose store sat on Nana's land. Katrina stayed away. She hated being interviewed, hated having her picture taken. For the first few months of nursing school, she came home every weekend. As the people got more intrusive, more curious about our lives, she came home less. Later in the year she stayed away altogether. I found out she was dating a banker's boy from Furman University who was trying to get into medical school. Months into the romance, she still had not introduced us to the boy. Momma took it badly, thought she was ashamed of us. I thought so too.

Nana sued to get possession of her land, just like the lawyers advised. The case came to court on a cold Tuesday in late March. Since we did not make the state tournament, I missed school to attend. We sat in a courthouse in Gainesville while the lawyers sparred over words, historical documents, and stuff like statutes and precedence. I slept on and off,. Ben punched me so often in my ribs it hurt to breath. I did my best to pay attention when I could stay awake. I did not know about legal stuff, just what I had seen on television, but it seemed Nana's side was winning big time.

Chapter Thirty-Eight

The courtroom held about fifty people. The bailiff saved a couple of rows for us. He ushered us in like it was a wedding and put us up front close to where Nana and Papa sat with their lawyers. We rose and sat every time the judge came in, just like on the movies. He was the fattest man I had ever seen. The black robe splayed out on either side of him for almost as far as the desk was wide. Circles of fat came out the top of the robe, hiding a neck somewhere within great, flabby folds. Even his eyelids looked fat. When he spoke, which was not often, he took at least two or three breaths with every sentence. I feared he would not live long enough to finish the trial. I think he was bald, but I could not tell for the way he swept the hair from one ear across the top of his head to the other side.

Lanona hired a hotshot lawyer out of Washington. He spoke in a Yankee accent, wore three piece suits, and looked down at the witnesses like they were trash. He took deep, dramatic breaths before every question and put on a terrible act of surprise every time someone said something he did not like. His hair did the strangest thing. It was wavy on top, then changed to straight and slightly grayer just above his ears. Ben said it was a toupee. I had never seen one, or did not think so, but this looked awfully silly. I did not like him at all. From the looks the jurors cast toward him, I would say they did not like him much either. He was Lanona's worst mistake.

Lanona's lawyers called Papa to the stand on the fourth day of testimony. He came up, dressed in a brown suit and the ugliest green and brown tie I had ever seen. I thought he looked as somber as the day Daddy had died.

"Do you have any proof the diary you have provided the court was really that of Ebenezer Wiley?" the lawyer asked.

"Had his name on it. Found it in a grave with his name on it. What more proof do you want?" Papa replied.

"Is it possible for you to have fabricated the journal?" the lawyer asked.

"You mean make it up? Write all those things myself?" Papa asked.

"Exactly," the lawyer responded.

Papa laughed, but it was a tense sound, not like him.

"No," he replied.

"What would keep you from getting some old journal, writing some things in it, burying it in the ground somewhere, and claiming it was Ebenezer Wiley's diary?" he asked.

"I might have some bit of trouble getting somebody to volunteer to get buried with it," Papa replied. "There was a body in there, you know."

The audience laughed. The judge tapped his gavel and everyone quieted. The lawyer kept at him, tried to get Papa to agree he could easily have lied about the diary and made it up himself. Papa fielded the questions with common humor and refused to let the man rile him. He went on asking questions, I think to get Papa to say something wrong. He started asking about the Office, finances, debts and the like. Papa answered when he knew how, laughed it off when he did not.

"Tell us about the cave you found," the lawyer asked.

"The diary had directions to a cave on the Curahee," Papa said. "I found it. It had some gold, a few letters and papers."

"Do you know the origin of the gold?" he asked.

Papa hesitated, looked at Nana. The lawyer sensed he had struck upon something.

"Whose gold was it?" he asked again loudly.

Papa sat still as death, looked around the courtroom.

"You will answer," the judge said.

"It was taken from a Union supply train in Ohio," Papa answered.

"By whom?" the lawyer asked.

"By some men under Ebenezer Wiley's command," Papa answered.

"And how did this gold end up in the cave?"

"Ebenezer took it there toward the end of the war," Papa answered. "He could see the South was losing, he wanted to secure a future for his family."

"So he stole the gold?" the lawyer asked.

"The Confederacy was dead," Papa said. "There was no government left to give it to. Maybe he wanted to use it for his family's future. Maybe he didn't want to give it to the government that had just pillaged his homeland.

He was in a war. Wouldn't be right to call it stealing. He never spent any of it anyway."

"If it was for his family, why did he keep it in the cave?" the lawyer asked. "Why not bring it out and buy some land, something for his family? I understand from earlier testimony the Wiley family at the time was living in relative poverty."

Papa sat still. He looked at his hands, then smoothed his shirt collar a little.

"Mr. Davis," the judge said. "You must answer the questions put to you. Do you understand?"

Papa nodded, still looking at his hands.

"Do you know why Mr. Wiley kept the gold?" the lawyer pressed him, leaned over the wood rail toward him.

"Objection, Your Honor," Nana's lawyer said. "For Mr. Davis to answer that question, he would have to speculate as to Mr. Wiley's motives a hundred years ago."

"Sustained," the judge said.

"Do you know why Mr. Wiley stayed in the cave instead of going home?" the lawyer asked.

Papa sat quietly.

"Objection," Nana's lawyer said.

"I'd like to hear the answer to that question," the judge said, waving Nana's lawyer to sit.

"But Your Honor," Nana's lawyer said. "Again, it requires Mr. Davis to speculate as to Mr. Wiley's motives."

"I simply want to know if the witness knows why Mr. Wiley stayed in the cave and away from his family," the Yankee lawyer said. "If he does not know, he need not speculate."

"It's a fair question," the judge said. "Please sit down. Mr. Davis, you will answer the question."

"I repeat," the Yankee lawyer said. "Do you know why Mr. Wiley chose to hide out in a cave rather than rejoin his family?"

Papa clenched his teeth, fiddled with the lapel on his suit.

"Mr. Davis," the judge said. "I will not waste more time admonishing you. You will answer the questions put to you."

"Why did he stay in the cave?" the Yankee lawyer asked. He leaned into Papa, inches from his face. Papa ignored him, then looked up and coughed. The Yankee straightened himself quickly and stepped back. Papa chuckled to himself, must have thought it funny how easy it was to get the Yankee to back away. Just cough at him, make him think you're giving him some disease. After all, we were Southerners. Aliens, to someone like him. Who knows what mysterious disease we carried?

"Please, Mr. Davis," the judge said softly. I think he felt bad for the way the Yankee lawyer spoke to Papa. "Can we get on with this?"

"He learned some things about his wife," Papa said.

The courtroom fell silent. Only the sound of the gas heater popping and sizzling penetrated the silence. Papa looked at Nana. She looked away. Whatever he was going to say, she had heard it already.

"What did he learn?" the lawyer asked.

"I don't see how this has anything to do with them stealing Ebenezer's land," Papa said to the judge.

"I'll decide what is and what is not relevant here, Mr. Davis," the judge replied. "You will answer the question."

Papa looked out at the crowd, like someone there could say or do something to let him keep just one more secret. He looked at Nana, but she still did not look at him. He glanced at me and Ben, then Momma. We could not help him. He shook his head.

"He found out his wife was unfaithful," Papa said.

Nana leaned her head on the table. Momma gasped.

"With whom was she unfaithful?" the lawyer asked.

"Can't say for sure," Papa said.

"You have no indication at all who Mrs. Wiley's secret lover was, Mr. Davis?" the lawyer asked.

"Not for sure," Papa replied.

"Mr. Davis," the lawyer went on. "We have had the documents you provided this court gone over by experts in history and law from all over the country. We know what Mr. Wiley's personal papers say on this subject. Would you like to answer the question truthfully, or would you like us to answer it for you?"

Papa looked trapped. I did not know what was coming but it could not be good.

"Ebenezer thought Jane was unfaithful with Stenton Kresse," Papa said.

The people in the courtroom began to mumble among themselves. It ran across the room like a wave. You would think they were talking about the local minister rather than someone who died a hundred years ago. The judge tapped his gavel a couple of times and silence returned. Lanona sat at her table and smiled to herself.

"Why did Mr. Wiley think such a thing?" the lawyer asked.

"Because Jane Wiley told him," he said.

"This is in the diary?"

"No, sir," Papa replied. "It's in some letters I found in the cave."

"What else do the letters say," the lawyer asked.

Papa hesitated again.

"Mr. Davis?" the judge asked.

"Jane told him Stenton Kresse was Celia Wiley's father," Papa said.

"For the record, Mr. Davis," the lawyer said wheeling about to face the jury. "Who is Celia Wiley?"

"Celia Wiley was Jane Wiley's youngest daughter," Papa said. "She was my wife Estelle's mother."

"You have contended in public, and some of the documents you have supposedly found suggest that Stenton Kresse was executed by hanging in December of 1862, is that not right?" the Yankee lawyer asked.

"That's right," Papa said.

"If that is so," he continued. "How could Stenton Kresse be the father of a child born nearly four years later?"

"He wasn't hanged on that date," Papa said. "They hanged another traitor, claimed it was Ebenezer Wiley."

"Can you explain?" the lawyer asked.

"It seems Stenton Kresse had been assigned to some pretty important missions, early in the war," Papa said. "Missions for the Union Army not the Confederacy. They caught him and planned to hang him. But someone got involved and made a plea for his release, or at least that they not hang him. The Confederate Army agreed. No explanation, nothing. They just let him go. Problem was that the deal was struck after the story of his being killed as a hero in battle had been released. The stories people read in the paper made Ebenezer a traitor and Stenton a hero. No one could set the record straight because Ebenezer was still fighting in secret up north. Stenton was free, but he had to hide himself."

"Do you have idea who stood up for Mr. Kresse?" the lawyer asked.

Papa looked down. Everyone in the courtroom leaned a bit forward.

Papa did not at first answer.

"Mr. Davis," the lawyer said, more loudly this time. "Who talked the Confederates out of hanging Stenton Kresse?"

Papa looked at the judge as if asking for permission to stay silent. The judge nodded slightly to Papa. He would have to answer.

"Jane Wiley," Papa said.

People leaned back and looked at one another.

"And why would she do such a thing?"

Papa hesitated, looked again at Nana. She did not return his gaze.

"Jane Wiley took up with Stenton Kresse," Papa said. "Went on all during the war."

"'Took up'" the lawyer repeated. I hated the man for making Papa say such things in public. "Do you mean he had an affair with Mrs. Wiley?"

Papa nodded.

"Could you speak up?" the lawyer asked.

"Yes, she did," Papa said.

She kept her head down as though she was still ashamed of something this old and this many generations removed from her.

Lanona smiled. I hated her too.

Mumbles and whispers spread across the room again. They died when Papa began to speak.

"That's why Ebenezer shot himself," Papa said.

More whispers. Nana moaned.

"Tell us the whole truth, Mr. Davis," the lawyer said.

Papa looked at Nana. She kept her head down, cried quietly.

"It would better if you just told us what you know, Mr. Davis," the judge said gently. He looked embarrassed for Papa.

"Ebenezer had nothing to come back to," Papa said. "By the time the war ended, Jane was pregnant with Stenton's daughter, his family's land was confiscated, his name and reputation besmirched. I think he would have fought for the land, fought for his name back. He wrote of his great love for Jane, even after she'd betrayed him. But he would not fight her for her affections. That he wanted given to him.

"The thought of her carrying Stenton Kresse's child was too much for him. After Jane told him about the baby, told him who'd fathered it, Ebenezer decided to take his own life. Before he did it, he wrote to Jane, asked her to bury him in a secluded part of the land where no one would find him. He thought he'd die quietly, let people think he'd been hanged instead of Stenton. She found him dead on the Curahee, just like his letter had said she would. Jane never told anyone about the cave. Never told anyone about her being with Stenton Kresse. She buried Ebenezer in a secluded area where no one would find him for a very long time. But I think she wanted someone to know what happened. In the end, she wrote of her love for him too. She regretted taking up with Stenton Kresse. Regretted betraying her husband. Spent the rest of her days mourning Ebenezer in secret. That's why she buried Ebenezer's diary and a few papers with him. Wrapped them in wax cloth and sealed them up for us to find. I think she'll rest better now that it's out and Ebenezer's name has been cleared. She wanted us to find that grave. No other reason for it being where it was."

More whispers. The judge tapped the gavel again, called for order. Nana raised her head and looked toward Papa. Nana took all this in like it was the first time she had heard it. I think it was the just first time she believed it.

"So, Mr. Davis," the lawyer continued. "If Stenton Kresse was Celia Wiley's father, that would make Lanona Kresse and your wife first cousins, isn't that true?"

"It don't make that witch nothing to us," Papa responded.

"Is Lanona Kresse your wife's cousin or not?" the lawyer asked.

I heard Lanona's words come from the lawyer's mouth, her contempt, her spitefulness. Nothing useful could come of making Papa say these words yet the lawyer pushed him.

"Not in my eyes," Papa said. "Not in Estelle's either. She's a hateful old crone, it don't matter what Stenton Kresse and Jane Wiley did a hundred years ago."

"You cannot admit that your wife is related to the Kresses, can you, Mr. Davis?" he continued.

"Enough, Mr. Sattler," the judge said. "I think you've made your point. Do you have any other line of questioning to pursue with this witness?"

They went back and forth for over an hour. Papa told of how Stenton Kresse had changed his name and moved on to Arkansas. They never heard from him again. Papa expressed contempt for the lawyer and anything associated with the Kresses at every opportunity. Nana's lawyers sat there, and looked confident of the end results. The Yankee lawyer had the same look. Nana's lawyers were right. Like I said from the start, Nana owned most of Toccoa.

Chapter Thirty-Nine

The jury found that Nana had a legal right to all the Kresse family land holdings. Lanona fainted in the courtroom when they read the verdict. Her sisters clustered around her, held her head and fanned her. Nana sat cold stone still. Papa sat with her. He did not seem as happy as I had expected.

We waited in a small office off the main courthouse lobby until most of the people cleared. Nana did not want to speak to anyone. Some newspaper reporters found us and pushed their way in. Papa cursed them and shoved them outside. A few minutes later, Nana's lawyer found us.

"They want to negotiate a settlement," he told Nana. "They say they'll appeal and it'll stay tied up in court for years if you don't go along."

"I've gone this long without our land," Nana said. "I can wait."

Papa nodded his agreement.

"I think you should hear what they want before you decide," the lawyer continued. "All they want is for Lanona to keep her house."

Papa laughed. Nana smiled to herself. I sat on a creaky, high-backed wood chair and tried not to move. I feared they would make me leave if they noticed me.

"Ebenezer Wiley himself built that house," Nana said. "Tell them they can keep one of the other houses."

The lawyer nodded, and then asked a few more questions and then slipped out the door.

"Should we wait for him?" Papa asked.

Nana shook her head as she opened the door.

"They know where to find us," she said.

Later, when everyone had left, the lawyers from both sides sat down to work out the details of how the land would be transferred and what to do with the stuff on it. I found out later it was a bit more complicated than we ever thought. Nana's lawyers agreed with Lanona's that an appeals court would likely modify the verdict, let the Kresse family have at least one house.

Nana agreed to let the Kresse's keep a house, but not the main one. Lanona at first vowed to fight on with her last penny, all the way to the Supreme Court. Her lawyers advised her against it and she eventually conceded. Nana let the Kresse sisters keep the house most distant from the main one, one that before now had belonged to the youngest of the sisters. They would have to share the home and live out their days on their combined savings.

The negotiations went on for weeks. Eventually, Lanona moved out of her house and in with her sisters. I frequently passed their house on the way to town. Winter took the leaves off the trees and gave it a bleak and dead look. I never saw them outside like we did before. Never saw smoke from the fireplace or even cars in the driveway. For all we could tell, the sisters closed the doors and died inside or left in the night for parts unknown.

Nana stayed away from the Lanona's house until a few months after she obtained the deed. Papa looked in on the barn and a few of the animals Lanona had left to starve.

On a fine spring Saturday afternoon, I drove Nana to Lanona's former house. She strolled around the yard, now overgrown from a month of neglect. She unlocked the door and went inside. Lanona had left most of her furnishings, not having any place to put them. The old grandfather clock sat in the hallway, quiet now since no one had wound it. I saw the urine stained rocker, still exactly where we saw Lanona asleep. Lanona never brought up the incident. She had taken all the paintings, probably thinking Nana would burn them. She was right.

"Think your Momma'd like this place?" she asked.

"I think she'd like it just fine," I said.

I did not tell Nana I would not move in this house with Momma.

"I don't need a house," she said. "Your Papa and I are just fine where we are. Maybe I'll rent the other ones, give them to Katrina or you when you get married."

She walked around the house, ran her hands along the walls. The floor creaked as we walked. Otherwise there was no sound. The house felt dead. We went upstairs. Lanona's bedroom was completely empty, but the furniture in the other ones was still there. I showed her the chest where Ben and I found the pouch.

Nana opened the chest and took out the Confederate uniform. She laid it on the bed and straightened out some of the wrinkles. As she did, she felt something in the inside pocket. She reached inside and pulled out a watch and chain. She tried to open the watch, but time had fused the hinges. She handed it to me. I spit on the hinges, and then took out a pocketknife and carefully pried open the face. Inside was a picture of a man and a woman standing side by side. From the other pictures I had seen, I could tell it was Ebenezer and Jane Wiley. I showed it to Nana. She read an inscription on the inside cover.

To my dearest husband on the day of our wedding, June 12, 1853

She closed the watch and handed it to me.

"You should have this," she said.

I put the watch in my shirt pocket.

Daddy would have liked to see this watch, I thought. He liked old things and stuff about the family history.

"Look in here," Nana said.

She held open the lapel of the uniform. The initials "E.E.W." were sewn inside.

"Only way Lanona could have had Ebenezer's uniform was to get it from her father who would have stolen it from Jane's house," Nana said. "They kept it all these years and passed the secret down for three generations till you boys found it. She knew my grandmother was Stenton's daughter, knew Stenton was a traitor all along. She left these things here so we'd know she knew."

I did not say a word, just kept thinking about what Lanona had said to me last time she saw us in her yard.

No history worth remembering, no blood worth saving.

What the Kresses did to Nana's family came back to their own. Papa would say it was the way of things, like we lived in a big circle. Men at the church would say it was just sin. I think that anybody would have a hard time resisting the power and wealth that events thrust upon the Kresse family. While I like to think the Davis' would have acted more nobly, I cannot say for certain we would.

We walked back toward the smokehouse. The guinea fowl clucked at us, scattered as we walked toward them, then continued pecking bugs and seeds off the ground. We walked back to her empty pasture and past an overgrown apple orchard. I picked a couple of green ones. The air was fresh and clean like is only found in the Appalachians in spring. Not too much water in it, not too much smell. Just clean air washing down off the mountains. Back here the place did not have the bad feel to it like the house. Felt normal, like anybody could have owned it, worked it. I had a hard time imagining that it was Nana's, had been all along. You could not hear the sale barn from here.

You would hear the racetrack, I imagined. If the night was still enough you could hear it on the other side of town.

We walked through the woods and stopped by a creek lined with maypop vines and honeysuckle. A black snake raced into the brush as we walked. Seeing the snake did not bother Nana in the least. We circled back down the hill, headed back to the house. When we came to a hedge at the end of the pasture, Lanona Kresse stepped out in front of us.

Chapter Forty

"Evening, Estelle," Lanona said. Wrinkles covered most of her eyes making them appear as evil slits in her face.

"You're on my land," Nana responded. "Got business here, or should I get Roy here to throw you off?"

She laughed at Nana. I could not see myself even touching Lanona, much less throwing her anywhere.

"I bet you found Ebenezer's coat, didn't you?" Lanona asked.

"I found what your family stole," Nana said.

"Now, that's no way to speak to your long lost cousin, is it?" Lanona said.

"Wouldn't claim you for kin, no matter we came from the same womb," Nana said. "Got no call to be here, Lanona. You can say all the hateful things you like. Won't change what's been, won't get you back in that house."

"Oh, I'll be in that house soon enough, but I won't stay," Lanona said. "I think you're about to find out why."

Something struck me in the back of the head and drove me to the ground. I could still see, but just barely. I heard Nana scream and reach for me. Someone held her back. Then everything got fuzzy and seemed to spin around. I saw Sheriff Bowers lean over me and kicked me hard in the ribs. Nana clawed at his face. He backhanded her and sent her sprawling into the weeds. Bowers popped me in the face with something, I think a gun. Blood poured from over my right eye clouded my vision further.

"Get up!" he shouted at me.

I tried to stand, but got dizzy and fell over. Bowers kicked me again. I struggled to my feet and called for Nana. She answered me. I could barely see for the blood and swelling over my eyes.

"Take 'em back to the house," Lanona said.

Bowers stood behind me and poked me in the back with what felt like a gun. I stumbled toward the house with Nana beside me. I tried to check on her, see if she was hurt, but I could only make out her outline. She seemed to be walking just fine. We walked around back where Lanona used her own key to open the back door. Bowers popped me in the back of the head again and then pushed us into the kitchen.

"Can't stand people getting what's theirs, can you?" Nana said to Lanona.

"Shut up," Bowers said.

He pushed her into the kitchen.

"Why would you kill for her?" Nana asked Bowers.

Lanona laughed.

"He does it for the money, you old fool," Lanona said. "Why else?"

"Hard to believe you have enough money to pay someone to murder," Nana said. "Good help is so hard to find, though. Even for honest work."

Lanona laughed again, a hateful laugh, full of venom.

I wiped some of the blood from my eyes and looked at Lanona as she laughed. Grey hair fell across her face, hiding her eyes, but the broad smile exposed the same snuff stained teeth. I do not think I've ever seen anything quite so ugly in my life. The Cat Hag was a beauty queen compared to Lanona at that moment.

"Don't have to pay him now," Lanona said. "We've kept us an insurance policy with the Bowers family for three generation."

Nana reached over, held my arm as if to keep me from falling.

"So you paid his Daddy too," Nana said. "Just means the whole lot of 'em are rotten."

"You don't have the slightest idea of what you've gotten into, have you?" Lanona asked. "My family purchased the services of the Bowers family just after they tried to execute Stenton Kresse."

"We know he was a traitor and thief," Nana said. "It's in the records you tried too long to hide. Ebenezer wrote of it."

"Ebenezer was a liar and a bandit," Lanona said. "A weak man. Couldn't even keep his own woman."

Nana lunged at Lanona, tried to scratch her face. Bowers grabbed her by the hair, flung her back toward me. I caught her as she fell backward.

"Since the Confederacy seemed intent of rewarding such a small, weak man for doing only that which was his duty," Lanona said. "My grandmother, God rest her soul, saw fit to ask Sheriff Bowers' grand patron for help. With the help of the Bowers family, the Kresses secured the cooperation of the entire town in getting Ebenezer's land granted to us."

"Why would the rest of the town go along with such a terrible thing?" Nana asked.

I propped her up, held her arm in case she tried to go after Lanona again. Bowers could kill my Nana with the back of his hand if he wanted.

"Why wouldn't they?" Lanona said. "My Grandmother offered them cheap leases on some prime land. Some of those land lease agreements are still in effect today. If they cooperated, Sheriff Bowers' family offered to stop hurting them. What else could they do?"

"You mean everybody in the town knew Ebenezer was innocent?" Nana asked.

"Everybody except poor Jane," Lanona said. "By the time she found out, she'd already cast her affections toward Stenton and carried his child. Ebenezer lost her, lost his land, lost his family, lost his name. You'd had been better off letting them stay lost."

"So what's that got to do with you now, Sheriff?" Nana asked. "You still strong arming people for her? Are you ready to die for her?"

"My father, his father's father all protected the Kresse family," he said. "My father told me all about it when I was nineteen. Said to keep the Kresses and they'd keep you. He's been right so far."

"What're you going to do with us?" Nana asked.

"You wanted my house," Lanona said. "You'll spend the rest of your life here. Course, that won't be a very long life."

Lanona reached over and opened a door. The passageway beyond was dark. We could only see the first two steps, enough to see they went down to the cellar.

"Get in there," she said.

We walked over and looked into the darkness.

"Get in," Bowers said.

He pushed me. I caught myself at the top step. Nana still stood in the doorway.

"They'll hang you for this," Nana said.

She slapped at Bowers. He punched her in the face and Nana dropped. I lunged at him and tried to grab his gun. Lanona got behind me with a cast iron skillet. I barely saw her swing before everything went black.

Next time I saw light, Nana and I were in a cement block room with a dirt floor. She held my head, kept asking me if I heard her. My head hurt. Everything was blurry, kept going in and out of focus. Minute later I saw

Nana clearly. She had been roughed up a little, had a cut over one eye, but otherwise seemed fine.

"What's going on?" I asked, sitting up.

"They left us," she said. "Locked us in the basement."

I tried to stand, but the floor seemed to move from under me. Everything went black again. I woke up with my head back in Nana's lap.

"I need you to wake up right now," Nana shouted at me. Her voice pierced my skull like an ice pick.

I stood up again, this time slowly and leaned against a metal pole. Tools and boxes lay scattered around the floor. Windows, much too small to climb through, let in some light.

"They're going to set fire to the house," Nana said. "Going to burn us up with it."

"How'd we get in here?" I asked.

Nana pointed to some wooden stairs. I went to the top and tried the lock. The door was bolted from the inside. I tried an outside cellar door too. It was chained from the other side. I lifted it a ways and looked through the crack outside. Sheriff Bowers stood thirty feet away, pointing a gun in my direction. I ducked back inside just as a bullet tore through the wooden door.

"They're going to watch us burn," I said to Nana.

Puffs of smoke squeezed through the floors over our heads, made a layer of white against the boards. I ran around, tried every window, but they were too small and too high. I tried the door to the house again, pounded against it with my shoulder. It did not give.

Nana found an ax laying in the dust. I took it and started pounding against the door. I cut a notch around the lock, kept on pounding until it gave way. I stepped into Lanona's kitchen. Smoke filled the room, made it hard to see which way we were going. Nana ran for the door, but I stopped her. Bowers could see the porch from where he had shot at me. I pulled her into the house, down the hallway, and into the dining room. Through the smoke I could see the outline of the paintings that Lanona had removed from the walls. I tried a window, but it was painted shut. I was afraid that if I broke it out, Bowers would hear. I tried another one, then the last. None of them budged. I had no choice but to risk Bowers hearing me break one.

"Stand back and be ready to run," I told Nana.

I took a chair, raised it over my head, and threw it against the window. It gave way in a crash of splinters and glass. I helped Nana through and she dropped six feet amid some bushes. I followed her. I held Nana's head down behind the bushes and looked around for Bowers. When I did not see him, I grabbed Nana's hand and started to run. Fortunately, our car was on the other side of the house from where I had seen Bowers. We ran through an overgrown garden toward the woods, me practically dragging Nana. I pulled so hard on her arm I was afraid it would break. A shot rang out behind us and clipped a feral sunflower plant to my right.

I shouted for Nana to run faster, but she moved no faster than what for me was a brisk walk. I knew Bowers would catch us in seconds. Another shot rippled the weeds in front of me. I fell to the ground and rolled to one side.

"Keep running, Nana," I said. "It's our only chance."

She hesitated, looked back toward the house, then ran toward the woods. A few seconds later, Bowers trotted up to me. I lay on my stomach, hoping he'd think he'd killed me. I heard the hammer of his pistol work, prayed he was releasing it, not cocking it to finish me. Bowers kicked me hard in the side, flipped me on my back. I kept still and held my breath. He leaned down and felt my neck for a pulse. I reached up, grabbed his head and pulled him on top of me. He reached to the ground to break his fall and dropped his gun. I rolled over on top of him and began punching his with everything I had. Bowers pushed me off him then rolled to one side looking for his gun. While he was feeling around in the grass, I got to my feet and kicked him in the ribs as hard as I could. He kept groping for his gun. I kicked him again in the ribs. I could not tell if it hurt him or not. I remembered his iron grip around my throat the day after Daddy died, and thought it would seem easy for him to break my neck. I did not think I would win this fight.

I kicked him again, this time in the head. Bowers rolled to one side then rose to face me. I did not know exactly what to do. I raised my fists like a boxer and tried to punch him. He moved quickly to one side, then hit me hard in the nose. I heard the bones crunch, felt blood gush down my upper lip. I swayed but somehow kept my feet under me.

I faced Bowers again, again he hit my face. I felt myself weaken and grow dizzy.

I am losing this fight and he's going to kill me, I thought. I wondered how far Nana had gotten. I faked like I was going to punch the sheriff, but instead broke out in a dead run back toward the house. I heard Bowers behind me, cussing, running to catch me. I ran into a clothesline I did not see and fell backwards. I rose with Bowers just a few steps from me. I ran around the front of the house. Windows were beginning to shatter and let smoke and flames pour out.

I ran toward the car, jumped inside, and locked the doors. Bowers ran up and started pounding, then kicking at the windows. I fumbled in my pocket for the keys. By the time I found them, Bowers had picked up a cinder block and caved in the side window. He grabbed at me through the jagged glass while I tried to start the car.

The engine finally caught but by then Bowers had managed to reach into the car. We grappled, but he finally managed to get both hands around my neck. The power of his grip stunned me. I could not break it. I pulled the gearshift in drive and stepped on the gas. The car lurched forward. For the third time that day I felt consciousness leaving me. I pushed hard on the gas. Somehow, Bowers managed to hold on to my neck. I aimed the car at an old oak on the edge of the driveway. Bowers did not see it coming in time. The car brushed against the tree and ripped Bowers from the car and me. I saw him rolling in the dirt, then lay still. I stopped to watch him for a moment, then I watched in horror as he turned his head and looked at me.

Without thinking, I put the car in reverse and floored it. I felt the car strike Bowers, then I heard him being dragged beneath the car for a second, then felt another bump as the front tires ran over him. I stopped again to watch him, this time not moving and with his head turned at an impossible angle.

I put the car in park and limped over to stand over him. Bowers was finally dead.

Nana came running up to me, hugged me briefly, then walked over to Bowers. She spit at him, then walked back to watch the house burn. The fire now reached the roof. Smoke poured up and out of sight. Within a few minutes, someone would notice and call the fire department. But it would be much too late. The house was gone. Lanona was nowhere to be found.

"Couldn't have thought of a better end to this place myself," Nana said.

We walked back to the road where an old man picked us up. We rode back to town and told about what happened to the new temporary sheriff. The deputy, same one that threatened to shoot me the day after Daddy died, sat at a desk and acted like he did not hear us.

The new sheriff let me go with him when he went to arrest Lanona. None of her sisters were at home. The sheriff tried the door. It was open. He called and no one answered. He stepped inside, called again.

We walked around back and found Lanona. She swung from the rafters of her sister's back porch, a fallen wood stool under her, a square knot around her neck. Even on television westerns, the sight of someone hanging was ugly. In person, it was worse. Lanona swung slowly and twisted around on the rope. Her mouth hung opened and exposed her snuff-stained teeth and gums. Her eyes bugged out of their sockets, frozen open in a terrible stare. Worst of all, she had scratched her neck around where the rope dug into the skin. The sheriff pointed to the scratches after he had cut her down.

"Happens all the time," he said. "She changed her mind. Tried to claw the rope off of her own neck."

I wished he had not told me that. For years afterwards, I saw the image of Lanona hanging from a rope, clawing at her neck to get free played again and again in my mind.

Chapter Forty-One

Two days later they buried Lanona at a site she had bought years earlier. Only her sisters and a few distant cousins showed up. None of them cried. Papa and I sat in his car at the top of the hill and watched them lower her into the earth.

"I sure miss Daddy," I said.

"I do too," Papa said.

We could see Daddy's grave from here. I was glad it was on the other side of the hill from Lanona's. Momma had just put fresh flowers on it. Yellow buttercups she likely found growing wild.

"Ever find out how Bowers learned about the diary?" I asked.

"What do you mean, son?" he asked.

The few people around Lanona's grave began to walk slowly back to their cars.

"We found Ebenezer's grave on Saturday, they shot Daddy Sunday evening, barely more than one whole day later," I said. "If Bowers killed him for it, how did they find out about it so soon? I did not tell anyone. I don't think Daddy did either."

We could see the Curahee from here, its stone face, marked with a pattern of moss and grass. The pattern made something new today. Maybe a face, or a map, or something. It should have been a pattern that made sense, should have told us something, that mountain. It had seen everything that happened in Toccoa.

"Good question, boy," Papa said. "What do you think?"

"I think you told him," I said after a minute or two. "I think you wanted them to know you'd found the grave and Ebenezer's diary. I think you wanted to rub their noses in it, make 'em afraid of what would happen."

"Sound reasoning," Papa said.

"You got Daddy killed," I said.

"That the way you see it?" Papa said.

His voice trembled ever so slightly, made me almost wish I had not said it. But I needed to. I needed to get that one thing out from between Papa and me, pain or no pain. I would never say it again, but just once I had to tell him I knew he had made a terrible mistake that cost us my Daddy's life. I would get past it, never poke him with it again, but only if he acted like he knew it too.

"It's the only way I can see it, Papa," I said. I tried to say it soft, like I did not hold it against him. But it did not matter. Papa knew I was right.

"Is that the way you see it?" I asked.

Papa waited a long minute, then spoke softly.

"Maybe," he said.

Looking back now, I should have let it go. But at the time, the pain of Daddy's death was too sharp.

"Was it worth it, Papa?" I asked. "Daddy killed. People hurt. All that trouble. Was it worth it?"

"Weren't nothing in the world worth getting your Daddy killed over," Papa said. "If I'd thought Lanona'd be capable of such a thing, I'd have tried to prevent it. I'd have tossed that diary in the river and plowed over Ebenezer's grave."

Papa laughed silently to himself, his chest moving a couple of times like he thought of something funny no one else knew. He glanced at me, then looked down like he realized I saw him acting like something was funny when nothing should be. I knew it was just his way of pushing pain down where it cannot be felt. He meant nothing by it and I took nothing from it. But I did not feel like letting up on him, not just yet. I needed to hear things. I needed to know if Daddy dying had brought anything good. I needed to know why people did not talk to us like we were one of the normal people any more. I wanted Papa to tell me why the money and land seemed so foul, so dirty, like Lanona had spit her snuff juice on it and cursed it from her grave.

"Was it worth it, Papa?" I asked again.

"Don't really matter now, does it?" he said. "Sometimes things, events, history, they take on a life of their own. We're just around for the ride. Not like we weigh the costs, decide if it's too high or too low. We just go along, try to swim across the current and land near where we aim. Don't matter if we think it's worth it or not. But, sometimes you're better to just let bad people win, let things be. Even when you win, you risk becoming like them. Best just to let them have their way and let God even things out in the end. I think this was one of those times."

All the people had left. The graveyard was empty. A few crows glided over and called to one another. The sky was cold blue, like I always thought the ocean would look. A few flowers, dots of color against a sea of grass, sat on new graves. Some sat on Lanona's grave, evidence that at least a few people would miss her and wanted her passing noticed. Or maybe they just felt obliged. I wondered if the other sisters really cared for Lanona or each other. I had never spoken to the other three sisters, only Lanona. She seemed so cold, so full of hate, looking at the rest of us like we were things to be used and discarded or just passed by. It was hard to imagine she ever loved, ever missed or was missed, even by sisters.

"How's Nana?" I asked.

Papa seemed puzzled at first. We had both just left her. Then he chuckled and looked up at the Curahee. The stone face looked back at us with the same countenance it had carried for ages uncounted. Somewhere up there, to the left of the face, sat a cave where Ebenezer once lived. An empty cave, empty as the promise Jane made on their wedding day, empty as she must have felt when Ebenezer and Stenton Kresse both left her in shame. I hoped no one ever went to it again, hoped it was forgotten again. In despair, Ebenezer shot himself in the cave. Jane found him there, hauled his body all the way back to River Road to bury him in a hidden cove. Sadness like that needs to be buried and forgotten, dug up only for the most desperate need.

Papa laughed again, settled back in his seat and stared at the Curahee as if it could answer the question for him. He looked years older than he had last spring. His oldest son killed, maybe his own fault. His life overshadowed by history circling back on him. His wife bound to mourn herself to the grave and take him with her. The only thing left was the money and the land. Papa cared little for either.

"The spark's not back in your Nana, if that's what you mean," he said. "It's gone for good. I know that now."

He sounded like Daddy, just home from a long haul, so much so my chest hurt from missing him.

"Then it wasn't worth it, was it?" I pushed one more time.

This time Papa answered me with what I needed to hear.

"Not even close, son," he said. "Not even close."

THE END

23080906R00133

Made in the USA
Middletown, DE
16 August 2015